The Diamonds

W9-BNR-353

The Diamonds

◆ TED MICHAEL ◆

DELACORTE PRESS

This is a work of fiction. Names, characters, places, and incidents either are the product of the author's imagination or are used fictitiously. Any resemblance to actual persons, living or dead, events, or locales is entirely coincidental.

Text copyright © 2009 by Ted Michael
Illustrations copyright © 2009 by Kate Berthold

All rights reserved. Published in the United States by Delacorte Press, an imprint of Random House Children's Books, a division of Random House, Inc., New York.

Delacorte Press is a registered trademark and the colophon is a trademark of Random House, Inc.

"Into Your Eyes" by Peter Lerman. Copyright © 2009 by Peter Lerman. All Rights Reserved. Used by Permission.

Visit us on the Web! www.randomhouse.com/teens
Educators and librarians, for a variety of teaching tools,
visit us at www.randomhouse.com/teachers

Library of Congress Cataloging-in-Publication Data
Malawer, Ted.
    The Diamonds / Ted Malawer. —1st ed.
        p. cm.
    Summary: When popular high school senior Marni is publicly dumped by her boyfriend, she and her best friends, collectively known as the Diamonds, take over the school's mock trial system and turn it into a form of peer mediation, until a rift between them turns the tables.
    ISBN 978-0-385-73579-7 (hc)—ISBN 978-0-385-90565-7 (glb)—ISBN 978-0-375-89201-1 (e-book)
    [1. Mock trials—Fiction. 2. Interpersonal relations—Fiction.
3. Cliques (Sociology)—Fiction. 4. High schools—Fiction.
5. Schools—Fiction. 6. Peer mediation—Fiction.]   I. Title.
    PZ7.M2896Did 2009   [Fic]—dc22   2008035685

The text of this book is set in 12-point Goudy.
Book design by Vikki Sheatsley
Printed in the United States of America
10 9 8 7 6 5 4 3 2 1
First Edition

Random House Children's Books supports the First Amendment and celebrates the right to read.

For my sister, Abby,
who sparkles more than any Diamond I know

PART ONE

Let us not be too particular; it is better to have secondhand diamonds than none at all.   —*Mark Twain*

◆ 1 ◆

Congress shall make no law respecting an establishment of religion, or prohibiting the
free exercise thereof; or abridging the freedom of speech, or of the press; or the right of
the people peaceably to assemble, and to pe-
tition the Government for a redress of grievances.   —*The First Amendment
                    to the United States Constitution*

I was in English when it happened.

AP Literature, to be specific. Next to me were Eric
Rogerman, who listened to his iPod during class and
was prematurely balding, and Mary Aberfeld, who
smelled alternately like cheese and pickles and was prematurely balding, too. Behind me sat Dara and Dana
Hoebermann, identical twins with lazy eyes and a pen-
chant for gossip. The rest of the class, more or less, was
filled with people I didn't particularly care about—not
in a rude way, don't get me wrong, but in the sense that
my life with or without them would be exactly the
same.

It was the third day of school. So far, we'd read

scenes from *Romeo and Juliet* (Shakespeare, 1597) out loud while Mrs. Bloom spoke the stage directions with an affected British accent.

Fact: Bloom is a complete nutjob.

It wouldn't surprise me to learn she was from another planet entirely, one where it was acceptable to leave your house in the morning with curlers nestled in your hair, wearing a necklace of baby spoons and forks strung on mint-flavored dental floss. (I won't even try to explain that one.)

Still, there's nothing better than performing Shakespeare—even if it's not onstage. I'd been stuck with the role of the Nurse; at first, this offended me beyond belief. The Nurse was old and probably fat. Definitely fugly. One of the title roles was being played by Marisa T. Karava, the only person I knew who wrote her middle initial on papers and who, if asked her name, would reply, "Marisa T. Karava." (I could therefore only assume that the "T" stood for "Tool.")

Marisa read Juliet's lines with about as much enthusiasm as I had for going to the dentist. I'd almost suggested to Mrs. Bloom that she'd made a terrible casting mistake, but then I realized I sort of *liked* reading the Nurse. To spice things up in class, I spoke every other word with a cockney accent. It threw people off, which was a good thing. Jed thought I was predictable, and I despised that label. I wanted to be spontaneous. Fun. Carefree.

Here's the scoop on Jed, my boyfriend: two years before, as a sophomore, he'd become the first underclassman in Bennington's history to be elected student body president. He'd held on to the title ever since. Jed excelled at the game of (high school) politics—patting the right backs, shaking the right hands, kissing the right asses.

I was the girl he could be himself around, loosen his tie around (literally; Jed wore a tie to school every day), even complain around. I'm not sure if it was *love*, but our relationship was definitely more than your typical high school fling. Jed understood me, which was what I liked most about him. Not that his father was nouveau riche or that Jed was a Dartmouth legacy or that his wardrobe consisted almost entirely of buttery pastels or even that he ran the morning announcements, which were pretty much his own television show that aired for ten minutes during homeroom.

Fact: At the Bennington School, a disgustingly posh preparatory on the outskirts of Manhattan (and by that I mean Long Island), the morning announcements are presented on televisions throughout the school—one per classroom—in this ridiculous sort of variety show that Jed hosts. One of the privileges of being student body president.

Typically, student groups wrote up their own messages and Jed performed them like monologues while the show filmed live in the video production room behind the auditorium. At Bennington, the morning announcements were a Pretty Big Deal, and Jed Brantley was a Pretty Big Deal for delivering them.

But he was an Even Bigger Deal for dating me.

Marisa had just butchered the balcony scene (*Romeo*. Pause. *Oh Rom-e-o*. *Wherefore* cough *art thou* yawn *Rom-e-o?*) when Mrs. Bloom glanced at the clock and flipped on the TV screen above the blackboard.

"Do you like being the center of attention? Are you blind?" Jed asked. He was wearing a ribbed sweater, hair swooped over his right eye in a way that made me want to brush it back. "Auditions for *The Miracle Worker* are this week and the Drama Club wants *you* to be there on Friday!"

I really shouldn't let him write his own jokes.

"Now, there's something important I have to say," he said.

My ears perked.

"Most of you know my girlfriend, Marni." A few kids turned around to stare at me. "Short blond hair, sort of pretty, nice gams."

Sort of pretty? *Gams?* I attempted to hide my eyes behind my fingers.

"I just want to say how much I've enjoyed dating you this past year," Jed continued. "You've been a great girlfriend."

A few girls "awwed," even though his little speech was definitely not aww-worthy. Some of the guys on the opposite side of the room rolled their eyes and I silently applauded them. I had no idea what Jed was doing.

"That being said, it's time to let you know that we're through. I've met someone else who's really great and, uh, doesn't like her friends more than me. Sorry. I'm sure you understand." Jed straightened a few papers on his desk and then said, "Hey, Darcy!" before the announcements were over and the screen turned blue.

Oh.

Shit.

No one looked at me, and no one made any noise. At all. The room was so silent I could hear myself breathe. I could hear the soft hum of Eric's iPod and the sound Mrs. Bloom's shoes made against the floor. My arms began to tingle and my stomach swirled like water in a toilet bowl.

"Can you believe that?" I heard Dara Hoebermann say.

"That effing *sucked*," Dana replied. "Even more than the time I ate a Popsicle for breakfast and my tongue was stained orange."

"That was *this morning*," said Dara.

I attempted to smile. Maybe I could play this off like it was all a big joke, like I'd known that Jed was going to do this. But I hadn't known. As the whispers started filling up the classroom, I could hear my own voice echoing, *Stupid, stupid, stupid,* in my head. And I tried hard—the hardest I'd ever tried—not to break down and cry.

After a few minutes, or what felt like minutes and were probably only seconds, the heads started to turn. I dug into my purse for my cell phone and quickly texted *911!* to Clarissa, Priya, and Lili. Supposedly, if we ever received a text like that during school, we would all leave class and meet up in the faculty bathroom—which no one ever used—by the student parking lot. I say "supposedly" because it had never happened before. An emergency, I mean. And this was *definitely* an emergency.

I clicked Send and raised my hand. "Can I use the bathroom?" I asked, trying to sound as desperate as possible, which wasn't very difficult. "It's important."

"He's a pig," Priya said, wiping her eyes with a Kleenex. "He *disgusts* me. If I wasn't on a diet that forbids eating bacon, I would totally fry him up and put him on a BLT. Like *that*."

By the time I arrived at the bathroom, Priya, Lili, and Clarissa were waiting for me with open arms. That's what friends are for, I guess. Being there to pick you up when you're down. *Way* down.

"Thanks, Priya," I said, trying to avoid acknowledging that Jed had made a mockery of me in front of the entire student body *and* that Priya was on a diet, which meant I would have to start one in a few days. (You can't let one of your best friends diet alone. It's inhuman.)

And the whole broken heart thing, too.

I felt completely out of control. Tears poured down my cheeks; my nose was raw and leaky; my throat burned and my chest throbbed with pain. Every muscle in my body was sore and weak and numb. I barely had the strength to hold a tissue.

"I'm sorry," I said, sniffling. "I just feel so awful."

Priya gave me a smile, or at least what I *thought* was a smile. Her eyes were hidden by a ginormous pair of black sunglasses that matched her hair, which was piled on top of her head like a plate of spaghetti.

"He doesn't deserve you," said Lili, rubbing small circles on my back. "You're much better off without him."

Lili was nothing at all like Priya, who was loud—life of the party—and the tiniest bit, well, dumb. Not that everyone has to be smart or anything, but while Priya had been blessed with the ability to fill out a halter top, Lili had been blessed with brains. Her mother had been born in Korea and her dad was Mexican, leaving her petite and slightly olive; there was a natural glow about her, and the result was stunning. Lili didn't seem to notice how pretty she was, though, which made her the easiest of all my friends to get along with.

"I guess," I said between sobs. Had Jed really dumped me like that in front of the entire school? Had our relationship meant so little to him? "It sure doesn't feel that way."

I blew my nose and averted my eyes from the mirror. I had never looked worse in my entire life. I felt like a wet, unwanted blimp. I glanced over at Clarissa, who had perched herself on the sink, the toes of her turquoise pumps dangling in midair. Once a week, Clarissa wore an outfit that was various shades of a specific color. That day she had followed in Picasso's footsteps and declared her "blue" day, choosing a navy blouse with eyelet lace and a sleek pair of low-rise jeans; a thick iridescent ribbon framed her forehead.

There are a lot of things I could tell you about Clarissa von Dyke: she spent five hundred dollars every month to get her hair highlighted; she used to drive a Lexus but then got an Audi; and when she was bored, she poked freshmen with safety pins in the hallway. But that's not the important stuff.

Clarissa was the kind of girl legends were made of. That sounds ridiculous, but it's true. She was a modern-day Helen of Troy, outrageously, insanely gorgeous— the kind of beautiful that propelled boys to carry her books and girls to pack celery and baby carrots for lunch.

It wasn't just that she was beautiful, though. Even I liked to think I wasn't a complete mountain troll, but I was still no Clarissa. No one was. Because no matter how hard anybody tried, that indeterminable X factor set her apart from all the other students at Bennington.

The four of us had been best friends since freshman year. Some random girls started calling us the Diamonds when we bought matching diamond pendants at the mall and wore them to school. At first we adopted the nickname as a joke, but then it stuck, and before we knew it, that was exactly who we were—at Bennington, anyway. *Diamonds*. Girls wanted to be us, guys wanted to date us (not Jed, apparently, but whatever), and Clarissa was our fearless leader. While I adored Priya and Lili, Clarissa was the one person I couldn't live without, the first one I'd ask to the movies if I had two tickets, the first one I'd go to with a problem. With her, I didn't care that I was the supporting role and not the lead; I was happy to be a part of the show.

Lili cleared her throat. "Clarissa," she murmured as if I were invisible, "say something."

"Are you okay, Marni?"

I shook my head. Jed had been my first real boyfriend, my first real kiss. Wasn't I worth an in-person breakup or, at the very least, a phone call? How long had he been seeing Darcy behind my back?

I started crying again. All I could muster was "No."

For Clarissa, that was enough. "You're gonna be fine," she said, slipping off the sink and holding out her hand. "I promise."

"I just want to go home," I slurred.

"You can't," Clarissa said. "You have to go to gov."

AP Government was our final class of the day. It was a smorgasbord of United States history with a focus on the Constitution and its amendments, the judicial system—mainly the Supreme Court—and debate. It was the most riveting class I'd ever taken, and not just because my father was a law professor and I'd been groomed to find that sort of stuff interesting.

Here was the problem, though: not only were the Diamonds in AP Gov, but so was Jed. *And* Darcy McKibbon, who wasn't full-on Goth but wore enough black eyeliner, bloodred lipstick, and witchy apparel to make people uneasy.

"No way," I said, folding my arms. "I won't go. I can't."

"You *have* to," Clarissa said firmly. "I'm going to fix this, and we all need to be there for it."

Clarissa had a knack for making problems disappear. Caught without a hall pass? No problem. Forgot your homework? Hand it in the next day. She was the golden child of the Bennington School—a million students rolled into a single perfect person. One smile and people bent over backward to help her. And, to a much lesser degree, help me. It wasn't hard being a Diamond, truth be told. It was very, very easy.

There's always a catch, though, and for me it was this: if our friendship had been a poker game, my cards would've been facing up on the table, while Clarissa's would still have been concealed, waiting for anyone—including me—to call her bluff.

Clarissa looked at me with a mixture of sympathy and expertly applied mascara. "Okay?"

"What are you going to do?" Priya asked, excitement spreading across her face.

"You'll see," Clarissa said, soaking up her chance to be secretive. "Rest assured: Jed Brantley is going to regret the day he ever messed with one of the Diamonds."

She walked over to the door and pulled on the metal handle.

"Don't do anything crazy," I warned, even though it was no use. Clarissa would do exactly what she wanted. She always did.

Clarissa tossed her hair like she was in a shampoo commercial. "No worries," she replied with a smirk. "I've got your back."

"Me too," added Lili, placing a hand on my shoulder.

"Yeah," Priya said. "Ditto."

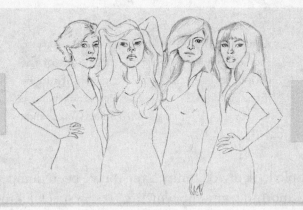

• EXHIBIT A •

I studied my three best friends as they stood with me in the faculty bathroom during the middle of first period, and smiled my first postbreakup smile. It didn't matter that I wasn't as smart as Lili or as funny as Priya or as beautiful as Clarissa (although truly, even now, that word doesn't do her justice). It didn't even matter that my boyfriend had cheated on me. We were a team. And unless something changed soon, this was who I would always be.

A Diamond.

Beautiful. Elegant. Unbreakable.

♦ 2 ♦

> A well regulated Militia, being necessary to
> the security of a free State, the right of the
> people to keep and bear Arms, shall not be
> infringed.   —*The Second Amendment*
>   *to the United States Constitution*

People look at you funny after you've been dumped on the morning announcements. It's a special kind of look—typically reserved for those who suffer catastrophic misfortunes or travel to foreign countries for inexpensive plastic surgery—that I never anticipated being on the receiving end of.

I was a Diamond. Things like this weren't supposed to happen to me.

And yet they were. Every step I took, someone was gossiping about how Jed Brantley had dumped me for Darcy McKibbon. It was the biggest scandal Bennington had seen since Mr. Unger, a former economics teacher, had been accused of embezzling money from the school to pay for a mail-order bride from Hong Kong.

By the time ninth period rolled around, I was a complete mess. The only place I wanted to be was in my bed, wearing a comfy sweatshirt, shoveling Ben & Jerry's Half Baked ice cream down my throat and watching *Days of Our Lives*. I had promised Clarissa I'd show up, though, and a promise was a promise.

To say that AP Government was run like any other class would be lying. First of all, since Mr. Townsen was hot, he garnered instant and unwavering attention from all his female students, and secondly, he was incredibly cool, which meant all the guys listened to him as well. A winning combination, really.

That week, we were in the middle of an in-class trial. A *mock* trial, if you will, as a large part of the curriculum was dedicated to dissecting legal procedure and its use in effecting United States law. It focused on the Salem witch trials of 1692. Not typical fodder for an AP Gov class, seeing as how the United States hadn't even been established yet, but Mr. Townsen believed it was one of the most primitive trials on North American soil—a warning to us all of what life might have been like sans our current government. (The Salem witch trials, as I'm sure you know, were totally bogus. They centered on these bratty little Puritan girls who pointed fingers at people for practicing witchcraft. Once folks were accused, their lives were pretty much ruined. It didn't matter that there was no proof. I won't get into a more detailed explanation, because (A) that's boring and (B) just Google it.)

15

We'd been given a packet of information to study over the summer and were expected to know it by the start of school.

"It's a dangerous thing to have a legal system without checks and balances," Mr. Townsen had told us on the first day of class, after the bell had rung and we'd settled into our new seats. "To hold trials without proper evidence and condemn people to jail—or worse, *death*—without proof. Don't you think, Ms. von Dyke?"

I'm pretty sure he called on Clarissa because the four of us were whispering together in the corner.

"Sure, Mr. Townsen" was her response. "Whatever you say."

Instead of recreating the trials, kids in class were portraying the prominent figures of the time, throwing them into our current legal system to be judged for their actions. The point was to see whether in today's world the Salem witch trials would be able to occur.

I was on the prosecution team, which consisted of the Diamonds; a girl named Sareep, who had a mustache and never talked; and Tommy Payne, this obnoxious kid who thought he was a reporter for the *New York Times* but was actually just a lame editor for the *Bennington Press*.

As I approached Mr. Townsen's classroom, I ran my fingers through my hair, attempting to pull myself together. I couldn't let Jed see how upset I was.

The room was arranged into a pseudocourtroom for

the trial. Our desks had been parted, leaving an open space in the center. Mr. Townsen's mahogany desk had morphed into the judge's bench, a stool pressed to its side as a witness stand. Metal chairs were grouped together for the jury; the rest of the desks had been separated into two distinct areas, with PROSECUTION and DEFENSE written neatly on loose-leaf paper taped to the floor.

The usual suspects were spread throughout the room, shuffling notes and getting ready for the bell to ring. Mr. Townsen stood in the middle of it all, looking incredibly dapper in a tweed suit and a crisp navy tie.

"Ms. Valentine," he said to me, motioning to the prosecution side. "Please take a seat."

I plopped into an empty desk next to the Diamonds, refusing to look for Jed. "I'm here," I groaned. Clarissa was studying her notes. "Can I go home yet?"

"Don't worry," Lili said, resting her head on my shoulder. "It's gonna be fine."

Priya nodded in agreement. "It doesn't even matter that Jed and Darcy are sitting next to each other," she said. "Holding hands."

"Priya!" Lili said with the intensity of a scream but the volume of a whisper. "Just. Stop. Talking."

"It's okay," I said. As long as I didn't see them, everything would be all right. I could pretend this had never happened, that I hadn't been humiliated in front of everyone I'd tried so hard over the past three years to impress, that my boyfriend hadn't thrown me away like the bag of chips you get at Subway that you

17

don't really want but take anyway because they come free with your meal.

To my left, on the defense side of the room, was Jenny Murphy. Jenny was Clarissa's archnemesis, a beautiful girl with perfect skin and pronounced cheekbones. Jenny was a member of nearly every major club, including mock trial, and had made a name for herself at Bennington as the anti–Clarissa von Dyke.

When I say that Jenny was Clarissa's archnemesis, I should clarify that statement. They used to be friends, back in the day, until Clarissa became, well, Clarissa, and Jenny Murphy stayed Jenny Murphy. She was always looking to take Clarissa down a notch, but it had never happened.

"Okay, guys," Mr. Townsen said, cueing us to be silent. "Does everyone remember where we left off?"

It wasn't as though we could have forgotten. The day before, Priya had sat in the witness stand dressed as Tituba, the West Indian slave woman believed to have started the witch hunt craze by telling some of the young girls "magical stories." Priya had taken her role way too seriously; she'd even come to school dressed for the part in an oversized skirt and a head scarf. On the witness stand, she'd spoken with an accent that was a cross between Elton John's and that of Sacha Baron Cohen's Borat; she'd been basically unintelligible and, after about five minutes, Mr. Townsen had asked her to sit back down.

"We're going to abide by all the proper rules and

regulations this afternoon," Mr. Townsen continued. "Marco, are you getting all of this down?"

Marco, a small boy with long, greasy hair, sat in the corner with a laptop on his knees. A modern-day stenographer. "Yup, Mr. T."

"Great." Mr. Townsen edged his way toward the bench, a pair of tortoiseshell glasses resting on the bridge of his nose, a black robe over his suit.

"All rise for the Honorable Judge Townsen," Marco instructed.

"Thank you, Marco." Townsen settled into his chair. "You may all be seated. Prosecution, you may call your next witness."

Tommy, who'd pretty much been steering the trial single-handedly, stood and cleared his throat. He had a nice-looking face—sharp where Jed's was round—a good complexion, and wavy black hair. The major difference between them was that while Jed was sure of himself, Tommy was *full* of himself, running around the school holding interviews with cafeteria workers, teachers, and select students, fretting over a newspaper that no one read.

"The prosecution would like to call—"

"Cotton Mather to the stand," said Clarissa, her smooth, clear voice sounding in the classroom like a wind chime.

Tommy looked at her, shocked. "Uh, Clarissa, what are you doing?"

"Sit down, Tommy," she said, pushing him gently

to his seat. The jury looked incredibly interested in what was going on. Sherry Something—a new student at Bennington as of that year—rubbed her hands together eagerly.

"What *is* she doing?" I whispered to Lili, leaning in for an explanation.

"Just watch."

"You do realize, Ms. von Dyke, that Cotton Mather has already been questioned by the prosecution," said Mr. Townsen.

Clarissa, sporting a smile that was both wicked and wonderful, simply replied, "Yes."

There were a few murmurs in the room. I wasn't sure exactly what Clarissa was up to—one never really knew—but I had the feeling it was something underhanded, dirty, and spectacular all at once. You see, the person playing the role of Cotton Mather, the seventeenth-century Puritan minister, was none other than the former love of my life: Jed Brantley.

If this were a horror movie, right then would've been the cue for the musical *duh duh duh!* It was also the moment that Jenny Murphy decided to pipe up. "Your Honor," she said, her voice startlingly brassy, "I object!"

Personally, I'd never gotten the impression that Mr. Townsen liked Jenny all that much. She was a very in-your-face type of girl, and while I understood why some teachers—the older, stiffer, highly medicated ones—adored her eager-beaverness, I liked to believe that Townsen could see right through her perfectly planned exterior. Perhaps if anyone else had been the defense attorney and objected, he might have acceded; what he did, however, was shake his head as if her mere presence bored him.

"Motion overruled, Ms. Murphy," Townsen said regally. Then, in his normal voice, he added, "Get on up here, Jed."

I braced myself to see Jed for the first time since that morning on Mrs. Bloom's television screen, clenching my fists so tightly my fingernails practically cut through the skin of my palms. A few seconds went by before Jed tottered forward, avoiding my eyes as he claimed the witness stand.

Bryan Jermaine, a lanky, dark-skinned kid who I think was on the basketball team, played the part of the bailiff. "Do you swear to tell the truth and nothing but the truth, so help you God?"

"I do," Jed answered.

To an outsider, Jed might have seemed calm and unconcerned. But I could tell he was nervous. Maybe he'd feel guilty and apologize or admit the entire thing was a joke and ask for my forgiveness. Deep down, I knew that if Jed wanted me back, I would say *yes*. How pathetic is that? Unfortunately, the more I thought about it, the clearer it became: this was no joke.

"Cotton," Clarissa said, getting into character by lowering her voice, "yesterday you described the strange behavior the four Goodwin children exhibited, behavior which *you* attributed to witchcraft. Is that correct?"

21

More than anything, I was shocked that Clarissa had been paying attention.

"Yes," Jed answered.

"Is there anything you would like to add to your statement?"

"No?"

Clarissa looked knowingly at the jury, then back at Jed. "Are you sure? Are you *really* sure?"

"Objection!" Jenny Murphy stood up from her seat. "Honestly. What is going on?"

Mr. Townsen gave a little hum. "Does the prosecution have a point?"

"Of course," Clarissa said, stopping in the middle of the room. "My *point* is that perhaps the Goodwin children are not the *only* ones under the influence of witchcraft!

"Ladies and gentlemen of the jury," she said coolly, "I would like to charge Cotton Mather, also known under his civilian name, Jed Brantley, with a crime. A crime of love." She located Jordan Durrel, one of the jurors, and winked. "Let us provide justice to Marni Valentine, who was disgraced this morning by Mr. Brantley and Ms. McKibbon, a known witch, for the entire world to see. Well, the entire school."

I inhaled sharply. In less than five minutes, my best friend had morphed a *mock* trial into a real one.

"They are being tried here today on one ruthless charge: Intentional Heartbreak. And I assure you, my fellow students, they are *indeed* guilty."

"Yes, girl!" Priya shouted. "Take 'em down!"

Tommy turned toward me. He was frowning. "Did you plan this?"

I shook my head.

"This is ridiculous!" Jenny shouted. Her lips were curled back, and the veins in her neck bulged. "Can we *please* get back to the assignment? I have all my notes right here," she said, waving a fistful of paper in the air.

Mr. Townsen looked thoughtfully at the class. I could only assume he was in Judiciary Heaven. "You've piqued my interest, Ms. von Dyke. Please continue."

Clarissa bowed her head. "Thank you." With two steps, she was right beside Jed, who fidgeted on his stool. "What would you say, Mr. Brantley, if I were to inform you that an eyewitness saw you kissing Ms. McKibbon outside the Burger Shack last Friday night?"

I actually gasped. That Friday night, Jed and I were supposed to go to the movies, but he'd canceled because he was "sick"—the stomach flu or something. He'd been at the *Burger Shack?* With *Darcy?* Gross.

"Can I plead the Fifth?" Jed asked.

Clarissa turned to me for help.

I shook my head. "Since the defendant has already answered questions from the prosecutor during this proceeding, he is no longer protected by his Fifth Amendment rights. Also, this isn't exactly a real trial, so . . . no."

"In case you're unclear, Mr. Brantley," Clarissa said, "you may *not* plead the Fifth."

"Eat him alive!" Priya bellowed.

Mr. Townsen banged his gavel. (Yes, he actually had a gavel.) "Order in the court!"

"Moving on," Clarissa said, an actual spark in her eyes. "What if I were to tell you, Mr. Brantley, that I have the pictures to prove it?"

Jed's entire face began to tremble. For someone who usually kept his cool, he appeared to be on the verge of collapsing.

"Let me tell you what I think happened," said Clarissa, turning to face the rest of the class. "I think you were growing tired of your longtime girlfriend, Ms. Valentine. Who looks totally cute today, by the way"—she smiled in' my direction—"and I think Ms. McKibbon, using her witchlike voodoo powers, perhaps even placing you under a hex or a curse"—she smirked in Darcy's direction—"intrigued you. You started seeing her secretly, behind Marni's back, but in order to protect yourself and your student government position—elections are, after all, in only a few weeks—being well aware that your relationship with Marni undeniably boosts your status, kept said relationship under wraps. But then you got anxious. Jumpy. Maybe Darcy threatened to leave you if you didn't come clean. *I don't know.* I *do* know one thing, though."

Jed's lips were moving, but no words came out.

"You got caught." Clarissa brought her hands down

on Mr. Townsen's desk in a smack that stung the heavy air. "What do you have to say for yourself now?"

At that moment, I noticed a strange look pass between Clarissa and Jed. It was something—fear, anger, determination—I couldn't quite place my finger on.

"It's true," Jed said. His lips looked dry, and I remembered that his tube of Chap Stick was inside my bag. He was never getting that shit back.

"Darcy and I have been, erm, *seeing* each other for a while now. Marni didn't know. I was going to wait until after the elections to say something, but Darcy threatened to tell Marni herself if I didn't do it first." Then he looked at me. It was a pitiful look, one that made my heart threaten to escape my rib cage, my blood quicken, and my eyes flood with tears. "I'm sorry."

Mr. Townsen banged his gavel (again). "That will be enough, Mr. Brantley. Please step down from the witness stand and take your seat."

Jed drifted toward the defense area and sat right behind Darcy, who shielded her eyes with thick fingers.

"Ms. Murphy," said Mr. Townsen, leaning back in his chair. "Thoughts?"

Jenny leaned over and whispered something into Jed's ear. I couldn't hear what it was, but he nodded, and then she rose. "With the understanding that I think this is absolutely ridiculous and completely irrelevant to the actual assignment," she said, "in light of Jed's testimony, the defense would like to enter a plea of guilty."

25

As quickly as it had begun, the trial was over. I clapped my hands lightly and looked at the Diamonds, who were beaming. Lili placed an arm around my shoulder, and Clarissa's smile was brighter than the sun. (Priya even put her sunglasses back on.) I wasn't sure what exactly I had won—I no longer had my boyfriend or my pride, after all—but it felt good not to, well, *lose*.

"Accepted," said Mr. Townsen. "Ms. von Dyke?"

Clarissa wasn't typically one for speeches; at the same time, she wasn't typically one for due process of the law. I was hardly surprised when she launched into a lengthy monologue, heels planted firmly on the floor.

"Marni Valentine is a wonderful friend and an even better girlfriend. What Jed and Darcy have done to her is unforgivable. Today, in this very room, we have a chance to make a decision. No more sitting back and crying to your friends about being dumped, girls, or storing up hatred and resentment alongside your testosterone, gentlemen.

"Nick," Clarissa said, approaching the jury. Nick Rosedale, a semihot soccer player, leaned forward. "How would *you* feel if you found out that Lauren, your girlfriend of eight months, was cheating on you?"

"Awful," Nick said. "That would suck."

"It was a rhetorical question, but good answer." Clarissa shifted her gaze. "Leigh Ann. Freddy Meyers dumped you last spring and started dating Betty Smith-Condenzo barely two weeks later. You must have been heartbroken."

Leigh Ann Stergman was sitting a few seats down from Nick. She wiped underneath her eyes and nodded.

"Derek," said Clarissa, resting her hands on her hips. "You've never had a girlfriend, have you?"

Derek Fishman shook his head. Everyone at Bennington knew that the closest he'd ever been to a girl was riding his bike, which he'd named Vanessa, to school every day. (True story.)

"Well, imagine someone cut the lock on your bicycle and stole it, and then, the following week, you saw that person riding *your* bike all over town. Wouldn't that *enrage* you?"

"Yes," Derek hissed. "Very much so."

Clarissa smiled. "Ladies and gentlemen of the jury. Everyone in this room has been dumped. Or will be. Everyone has had their heart ripped in two. This is the moment to stand up for yourselves. For *every single person* who has been cheated on, screwed over, or completely blown off. So, my fellow classmates, *do* something about it!"

Clarissa's speech shocked me mostly because she had single-handedly dumped more guys than all the girls at Bennington combined. Plus, I'd never heard her speak so passionately about anything that didn't have a price tag—including our friendship. I was touched.

Apparently, so was Mr. Townsen. "Let's turn to the jury for their verdict," he said. "Would you like time to deliberate?" He paused. "You're all required to be here anyway."

The room was quiet for a few seconds. Then came a

27

voice: "That won't be necessary." I leaned forward and saw that Sherry Something, now standing, was wearing a pair of Bedazzled overalls. What was she *thinking*? "We've already reached our decision."

"Go ahead," Townsen said, obviously intrigued.

Keith Rosen, who still had braces, passed Sherry a folded piece of paper. She opened it and began to read: " 'We, the jury, find the defendants, Jed Brantley and Darcy McKibbon, guilty of Intentional Heartbreak. Their punishment is no PDA—public displays of affection—on or around school property for the rest of the school year.' " She then crumpled up the piece of paper and sat back down.

Before her butt hit the chair, people started to cheer. It was a twenty-person class, so nothing too loud, but Marco whistled with his fingers and Priya shouted things like "Gotcha!" and "Mmm, mmm!" while Darcy closed her eyes and Jed sat completely still, like a statue. This certainly wasn't good for his reputation.

"Thanks, guys," I said as the bell rang and everyone began filing out of the classroom. There was one thing still bothering me, though. I turned to Clarissa. "Do you really have pictures of them kissing?"

"Oh, Marni," she said, taking my hands in hers. "Of course not. I would have told you if I did."

"So . . . how do you know they were at the Burger Shack together?"

"Does it matter? Jed *admitted* it, and we got him back. Just like I promised."

"You're right," I said, forcing a smile. "And all of those nice things you said, Clarissa—you really didn't have to go through so much trouble just for me."

"Of course I did. Boys will come and go, but Diamonds are forever. Right?"

"Right," Priya and Lili agreed simultaneously.

We were about to exit the classroom when Mr. Townsen blocked the doorway, resting one arm on the white frame. "May I have a word, ladies?"

Priya, Lili, and I gathered around Clarissa. "Absolutely," she replied.

"That was a very impressive trial," he said, unzipping the robe he'd worn (his regular clothes were underneath, don't worry) and placing it on a hanger. "Unconventional, but impressive."

"Thank you," Clarissa said.

"Have you ever thought of joining the mock trial team?"

"Uh, *no*," Priya blurted out before Clarissa could respond.

Lili elbowed her in the boobs. "She means *not recently*."

Townsen narrowed his eyes. "Well, you should. There aren't very many people who can relate the law to everyday life here at Bennington. You would be a great addition to the team. You all would." He looked at Clarissa, then at me. "Think about it."

"Townsen is *so* out of touch," Priya said once we were outside. She pulled her hair back with both hands and scanned the student parking lot. "I mean, seriously. Mock trial? I'd rather get run over by a My Little Pony."

"My Little Ponies aren't real," Lili said, taking out a compact and blotting her forehead.

"Duh," Priya said, "they're magical. And they *hurt*."

"Whatever," Clarissa said as we approached Priya's BMW. She had parked underneath an old tree, and the roof was sprinkled with sap. "I think we should do it."

"What?" said Priya, shocked. "You're not serious, right?"

"Actually, I am."

I didn't have much to add to the conversation. I was still speechless from the trial—from the entire day, really, which had started out like any other and ended in a cacophony of emotions. I felt ready to go home, crawl into bed, and never leave.

After a few seconds, Lili said, "Well, it could be kind of . . . fun."

Lili was already on the executive board of student government. She *would* say something like that.

Clarissa looked at me. I shrugged. After what she'd just done for me in AP Gov, defending my name and seeking revenge on Jed, there was nothing I could refuse her. Besides, I thought, it *would* make my father (J.D., NYU School of Law, '77) pretty happy.

"I'm game," I said.

"This is wrong in *so* many ways I can't even begin to count them," said Priya.

"That's just because you can't count," Clarissa spat. She leaned in closer, holding Priya's gaze and refusing to let go. "Come on. Everybody's doing it."

And really, that was all it took.

♦ 3 ♦

No Soldier shall, in time of peace be quar-
tered in any house, without the consent of
the Owner, nor in time of war, but in a manner to be prescribed by law.
> —*The Third Amendment*
> *to the United States Constitution*

Fast-forward three weeks.

Life after Jed (LAJ) was difficult. Once the reality
sank in—that we were no longer together, that he had
taken advantage of me and abused my trust—I was a
complete mess. I had no energy whatsoever. I even
slept with a box of tissues on the pillow next to me just
so I wouldn't have to get up in the middle of the night
to blow my nose.

Fortunately, the Diamonds were there for me, and
eventually the intense, stabbing pain of no longer having Jed in my life had morphed into a kind of numb-
ness, like my entire body had been soaked in a vat of
Icy Hot. I'd returned to Bennington after a few days of
bed rest (emotional rehabilitation, Clarissa called it)

and began to piece my life back together. I wasn't happy, but I was moving on—or trying to, at least.

As it turned out, mock trial was actually interesting. I had certainly spent enough time in courtrooms with my dad to feel comfortable in that sort of setting, and it was nice to be good at something the other girls weren't. Lili had only memorized the basic elements of our AP Gov textbook, while Priya and Clarissa could barely piece together three or four episodes of *Law & Order: SVU*. I, on the other hand, had a working knowledge of the Constitution and could even recite the decisions of the more famous Supreme Court cases by heart.

Plus, it was a great distraction from my nonexistent love life.

Now that the Diamonds were official Mock Trial People (MTPs), nearly every student at Bennington wanted in on the action. That afternoon we were conducting our own version of jury duty to choose twelve Bennington students to assist us during the trials.

Once the bell rang at the end of ninth period, I hurried to my locker.

"Hi, Marni."

I looked over my shoulder. Aaron Banke. Soccer Player.

"Hi," I said, turning back around.

Ever since I'd been dumped, a never-ending line of guys had appeared, trying to get my attention and take me out on the weekends. Although I was flattered, I couldn't bring myself to even think about dating anyone. Even though Jed had deeply hurt me, I still missed him more than anything.

I missed him waiting for me at my locker in the mornings and walking me to class, taking me out to (semi)fancy restaurants on Saturday nights and paying the bill, calling me up for no reason whatsoever, just to say hello, and I missed knowing it was him from the way he said, "It's me." I realize those may seem like tiny, unimportant things, but each one left a hole inside me the size of a penny; with all of them added up, I felt like a walking piece of Swiss cheese.

My only consolation was that life for Jed had turned out pretty tragically. After the trial, he'd been impeached from student government, falling from the Bennington stratosphere faster than I ever could have imagined. He didn't even eat lunch in the cafeteria anymore; it was that bad. And Darcy, who had always been on the outskirts of popularity, was looking sloppier and sloppier every day.

Clarissa said the entire situation was a classic case of "What Goes Around . . . Comes Around" (Timberlake, 2007); still, I couldn't help feeling that *I* was the biggest loser. At least I had my friends, I thought, slamming my locker. Then I turned around and saw Jed.

He looked awful. His usually gelled hair was longing for a trim, and his cheeks were sunken, like he'd lost a few pounds. The khakis he always wore (perpetually washed and pressed) were rumpled and frayed at the bottom, the collar of his shirt droopy and sad-looking.

I watched as he practically tripped over some freshmen in the hallway, eyes half shut, not bothering to look where he was walking. A few members of the football team passed by, and one of them (a kid named Paul Warden, hair the color of tomatoes) pushed Jed into a bunch of lockers; he crumpled to the floor, books spilling in front of him like a deck of cards.

"Loser," Paul spat as he whisked by. "Watch where you're going."

I'm not sure what came over me, but I went to help Jed. Without looking up, he slipped his hands into mine for support—it felt odd, to be holding his hands, because they felt so familiar but weren't mine to hold anymore—and stood. He leaned against the wall made entirely of blue lockers and breathed a sigh of relief.

"Thanks," he said, noticing me for the first time. When he realized that I had been the one to help him, he bent over quickly to collect his books. No hello or anything.

"Are you okay?" I asked. If anyone should have been acting weird, it was me. Not him.

Jed looked at me with one raised eyebrow. It was a look I'd seen hundreds, no, *thousands* of times before.

"I gotta go," he said, picking up his stuff and scurrying away. He didn't even look back.

"Where were you?" Lili whispered as I slid into one of the chorus room chairs. Priya was busily filing her nails and Clarissa was stationed at the front of the room, trading whispers with Mr. Townsen. I glanced at the clock—ten minutes before the potential jurors were supposed to arrive.

"Sorry," I said, dropping my bag between my feet. "I saw Jed."

Lili raised an eyebrow. "And?"

"Nothing," I said, not wanting to relive our brief encounter.

"Are you okay?"

"Sure. I'm fine." I gave an unconvincing smile. "I promise."

Lili squeezed my thigh. "I'm really proud of you, Marni."

"What about me?" Priya asked, looking up from her nails, which were starting to resemble pink claws. "Are you proud of *me*?"

"Uh, sure," Lili said, "but you weren't dumped recently."

"Thank *God*," said Priya, slipping her nail file into her purse. "That would effing *suck*."

I wiggled the fingers on my right hand. "Remember me? The girl whose boyfriend humiliated her on the morning announcements? I'm right here."

"Sorry. I forgot."

"Do you want an Altoid?" came a voice from behind me. I glanced over my shoulder to see Marcus Hall, whose glasses were *actually* held together with Scotch tape. Four different Altoids containers—peppermint, citrus, apple, and tangerine—were spread across his hands. "I have breath strips, too."

"No thanks," I said, even though I really *did* want a citrus one.

Just then, Mr. Townsen cleared his throat and addressed the group. "Hey, gang," he said. "Is everyone here?"

Aside from Marcus, the rest of the MTPs were seated toward the front of the room. Jenny Murphy was the farthest away, hair up and away from her face, lips twisted into a scowl; Sherry Something (I had never bothered to learn her last name) was next to her, dressed in a sweater that made her look homeless; Eric Ericsson, a pockmarked boy in my economics class, sat two seats over from Sherry, and next to him was a shiny girl named Karen, who was always *super-freaking-excited* about *everything*! Xo-Yeung, a Chinese kid who went by the name "Bob," was absent that day.

That was the entire mock trial team, aside from the Diamonds.

"Great," Mr. Townsen continued. The setup of the room was similar to how Townsen had organized our in-class trial. "We're selecting a jury today, which I'm absolutely *thrilled* about. We're only steps away from hosting real trials here at Bennington. Are you guys pumped or *what*?"

All the MTPs in the front row (sans Jenny Murphy) bobbed their heads, razzle-dazzled by our presence—Clarissa, Priya, Lili, and me—and the new, mainstream recognition for their club.

Jenny raised her hand and started speaking. "Mr. Townsen, for the last time—we didn't come in first place in speech and debate at last year's conference because we needed to *modernize*. I think we're perfectly fine how we are."

"I certainly see your point, Jenny," said Mr. Townsen, "and I do respect your opinion. But I *am* the faculty advisor and it couldn't hurt to . . . broaden our horizons. Until now, there haven't been enough members to even *have* a jury."

I didn't blame Jenny for trying. She was fighting to protect her turf (see *West Side Story*, 1957). But Jenny was no match for Clarissa, and she was *certainly* no match for the Diamonds.

As if on cue, the chorus room door opened. Face after face, jacket after jacket, shoulder bag after metrosexual shoulder bag of different-colored bodies rushed in. Students filled the empty seats in a matter of seconds.

"Welcome, everyone," Townsen said. "There's more room up front. Don't be shy."

It was an interesting group. Members of nearly every social subset were present, from Sharon Cho, president of the Key Club, to Monique French, a foreign student from Paris, to Molly Dephrym, who single-handedly ran GALATGFCADD (Gays and Lesbians and Their Gay-Friendly Companions Against Drunk Driving). More than a few guys had showed up as well, including Ron Tucker and Tre Lombardo, two of Priya's ex-boyfriends; Oliver Forsting, who had an Italy-shaped birthmark on his forehead; and Boyd Longmeadow, the metropolis of the Bennington theater scene (of which there was a small yet intimidating one).

"Look at all the freshmen," Priya muttered. "There's like a million of them. What whores."

Fact: Of all the students at Bennington, freshmen are the most impressionable.

It wasn't out of the ordinary for them to buy us gifts and attempt to sit with us at lunch. They reminded me of myself before I'd come to Bennington, before I'd been adopted by Clarissa, when I'd had stringy hair and awful clothes and eaten my lunch alone, when I would have done anything in the entire world to be liked and have friends. That was a time I never wanted to return to.

"They're everywhere," Priya continued. "Just looking at them makes me need to Purell."

"There *are* a lot of them," Lili agreed. "I only put up a dozen posters!"

A fake-blond girl approached us, and I put my hand out like a cop directing traffic. She pointed to the chair next to me, where my coat was draped. "Is this seat taken?"

I blinked. "Yes."

"Really? I don't see anyone sitting here."

I could have (quite easily) made room for her. I didn't, though. I was *not* going to let some random freshman show me up in front of my friends.

"Do you know who I am?"

The girl shook her head.

"Do you know who she is?" I pointed to Lili, then Priya. "What about her?"

Still no answer.

"Interesting," I said.

Just when I was about to provide Ms. Freshman with a (brief) education she would never forget, a pale hand shot across my vision like an arrow. The owner of said hand was none other than Elana Brockham, one of the more popular freshmen, a regular Diamond devotee, and proud owner of two fur coats.

"*Jesus* effing *Christ*, Jess," Elana said, pulling the girl away from me, "stop annoying Marni." Elana flashed me an apologetic half smile. "She's new."

"Whatever," Priya said. "Just get her out of my face or I'm *totally* going to heave. And I had tacos for lunch."

Meanwhile, Mr. Townsen was tapping on the blackboard. "Okay, guys," he said, "I really need complete silence in order to continue. Clarissa has a lot to tell you."

Clarissa gave a tiny wave at the mention of her name and everyone stopped talking immediately.

"Thank you," Townsen said, shifting his weight so that he was slightly tilted (see the Leaning Tower of Pisa, 1173). "Now, let me tell you all a little bit about our club."

Townsen recounted the in-class trial of JeDarcy—which everyone already knew about—and shared his hope of revitalizing the Bennington mock trial team.

"Serving on a jury is a privilege not to be taken lightly. If chosen, your decisions will affect the lives of your fellow students. Ideally, you will learn both about the law and about yourselves. I have no intention of holding your hands throughout this process. I will be observing, of course, and available to chat if you have any specific questions, but I am eager for you *all* to discover the wonder known as the United States legal system. Here, in this room, each and every opinion matters. You are all on an equal playing field."

Townsen spoke until his words were merely sounds and Lili had to pinch the underside of my arm to keep me awake.

"What's going on?" I asked.

"Clarissa just called the first twelve names," said Lili. "Go up there."

"To ensure fairness," Mr. Townsen was saying, "the prosecution will be selecting half of the jury, as will the defense."

For jury selection, Clarissa and I were the prosecuting attorneys, while Jenny Murphy and Eric Ericsson represented the defense. Lili had volunteered to be the stenographer (she was skilled at taking notes), and Priya fought Sherry Something to claim the title of clerk, which meant she was responsible for swearing in the jury and the witnesses.

"Welcome," said Clarissa, scanning the jury box (two rows of six chairs), "to what I'm *sure* will be the best part of your day so far. In my hand I have a series of questions, preapproved by Mr. Townsen. Please be honest in your responses. We want to find people who

41

are as excited as we are to bring *real* justice to the halls of Bennington. Let's begin."

In the second Clarissa took to open her file, Jenny Murphy extended one arm and said, "I would just like to add that—"

"Steffie," Clarissa said, cutting her off with a single word, "do you have a boyfriend?"

Steffie Jacobs was a sophomore with a good complexion and a round face. The year before she gave the Diamonds Christmas cards with personalized notes. (I'd thrown mine away, but it was a nice gesture.)

"Yes," Steffie said. Diagonal to her was Maria Patrinko, who would occasionally let me copy her physics homework; next to Maria was Jake Snider, a senior who Clarissa had kissed during the Halloween dance freshman year. According to Priya, Jake had "legit been in love" with Clarissa ever since.

On the far end was Adam Belling, who was in student government with Lili, and in front him was Patricia Kim, whose parents owned the nail salon Priya and I got manicures at every other Saturday.

"Let's say you were in AP Government on the day Jed broke up with Marni over the announcements. Do you think, as someone with a boyfriend yourself, you would have been *more* or *less* sympathetic to Marni?"

Steffie thought for a moment before saying, "Probably more. I think."

"I see," Clarissa said, taking a few determined steps and stopping beside Jake Snider, who was scratching the top of his head. "Jake. We kissed once. Do you think that makes you more or less likely to believe whoever I am representing is innocent?"

Jake blushed. "I guess *maybe* I would be more likely to, you know, vote in your favor."

"I would always vote in your favor," Boyd Longmeadow interjected. "As long as you were wearing something fabulous."

Clarissa chose not to respond. Over my shoulder, I saw Jenny scribbling furiously on a pad no larger than her palm.

I studied the remaining six jurors and then peered at the rest of the room. Everyone here was personally connected to the Diamonds in one way or another. It would be impossible to construct a fair jury. If the whole point of this newly envisioned student court was to make United States law accessible to the halls of Bennington, it was destined to fail.

Townsen was wrong. Everyone was *not* on an equal playing field. The only opinion that would truly matter was ours. *Diamond law.*

I glanced over at Clarissa, who was discussing the finer points of proving guilt beyond a reasonable doubt (I'd explained them to her the night before) while gliding her fingers through miles and miles of thick copper hair. I no longer had to wonder why she had been so eager to join mock trial. I knew.

In what seems completely unrelated but isn't (I promise), about two weeks earlier my mother had been operated on for carpal tunnel syndrome. How she got carpal tunnel I'll never know; she can't even turn *on* a computer, let alone use a keyboard for endless hours. The surgery left her wrists encased in two plaster casts and rendered her unable to do such basic things as eat with a fork and a knife, use the remote control, or be nice to me.

This meant one very important thing: I was in charge of walking Hot Dog (don't laugh; he's a dachshund, and my mother isn't terribly original), a chore that would ultimately change the course of my entire senior year.

("If you lose that dog, Marni," said Mom, propped up on the living room couch with a cup of apple juice and a straw that changed colors while she drank from it, the first day I was supposed to walk him, "I'm converting your room into a Yogalates studio and you'll be out on the street. And that's not a threat. It's a promise. I *love* Yogalates.")

So, after spending more than three hours listening to Clarissa grill prospective jurors, I returned home to take Hot Dog out around my neighborhood, which was when I ran into Anderson St. James.

Anderson St. James was gorgeous. He had a classic, all-American look, with enough rugged charm to find his way onto magazine pages or, better yet, onto a ranch in Montana with horses and flannel and dirt and sweat and spurs. His sandy hair was short, his smooth cheeks always the slightest bit red. He wore colored button-downs with khakis and wasn't afraid to wear jewelry, either; sometimes two or three silver chains dangled against the tanned skin of his chest. He was tall and broad and slim yet muscular; he sometimes wore faded loafers or plain white sneakers to school with his favorite band names sketched onto the canvas in inky script.

Anderson was Jed's complete opposite. Jed, forever pressed and cuffed, steamed, primped, hair gelled to one side, shirts buttoned all the way; Jed, who thought it was rude to wear sneakers unless he was in gym class, who tried just a little too hard.

• **EXHIBIT C** •

It's equally important to mention that Anderson was Clarissa's ex-boyfriend, and I wasn't allowed to talk to him. Literally. It was one of the rules our entire friendship was based on ("hos before bros," as Priya would say). Flirting with one of the Diamonds' former flames was a serious, serious matter—a crime that would *not* go unpunished.

It's funny to say that I "ran" into Anderson while he was actually running, but that was exactly what happened. I fell, and the first thing I did was drop Hot Dog's leash. "Hot Dog!" I yelled after the tiny dachshund as he scurried farther and farther away. Anderson sprinted, catching up with the dog and scooping him into his meaty, football-player arms.

I stood and wiped the gravel off my knees. Now I knew why Mom took her dog-walking so seriously: you never knew just *who* was around the corner.

"Here ya go," Anderson said, plopping Hot Dog onto the sidewalk and handing me the leash. He looked flushed from running.

"Thanks. My mother would've killed me if anything had happened to this dog."

Anderson laughed. It was rich and satisfying, like chocolate mousse. "Yeah, I've seen her walk him around the neighborhood once or twice. She gets really into it, huh?"

"That's an understatement." I felt myself starting to grin but stopped. What was I doing? If Clarissa ever saw me like this, she would murder me.

"So, how are you holding up?"

Anderson's question surprised me. I'd run into him a few times over the summer, after he and Clarissa had broken up, but I couldn't for the life of me re-member the last time we'd actually *spoken*. I searched

Anderson's face, waiting for the moment he would smirk, act distant, and jog away, but he didn't move an inch.

"Marni?"

"Fine," I said all too quickly. "I mean, I've been better, but I'm hanging in there."

"Yeah," he said, scraping his sneaker on the curb, "that whole Jed thing really sucked. I'm sorry."

I gave a tight smile. "I'm okay."

"Good," he said. "I'm glad."

"How've you been?"

He looked at me with soft eyes, the lines of his face and jaw so well defined I wondered if it hurt him to speak. "All right, I guess. You know"—he paused, and I waited for him to continue—"sort of lonely."

"I understand." If anyone knew about being lonely these days, it was me.

"Do you have a partner for the art project yet?" he asked.

Anderson and I took AP Visual Art, a class for seniors only, together. Anyone who'd taken basic drawing and painting classes could enroll; you didn't have to be the next Degas or anything like that. For our first big assignment, we were supposed to choose another student in the class and paint his or her portrait. It wasn't due until the end of the semester, and I hadn't given it much thought.

Until then.

I studied Anderson's face, tracing his features with my eyes. I imagined setting up an easel and being able to stare at him for hours and hours with a legitimate excuse.

"Why?"

Anderson looked confused. "Well, uh, I don't have a partner, and I thought maybe you and I could . . ."

"You want to be *my* partner?"

"Yeah," he said. "Everyone else in that class is totally lame."

"I don't know, Anderson. It's a little weird."

"Why? Because of Jed?"

I shook my head.

"Clarissa?"

I nodded.

"Don't be ridiculous." He stretched his arms behind his head. "Things are fine between us. It's a nonissue."

Anderson, not being a girl, obviously had no idea how long emotions could stay buried, especially inside someone as complex as Clarissa. I was about to decline his offer in favor of Diamond loyalty, but then I thought, *Why not?* It was just a school project. I didn't even have to mention it to Clarissa; it was *that* innocent. Besides, after everything I'd been through, I deserved to be a little selfish.

"Okay."

"Great! You're a really good artist."

Not true. It was kind of ridiculous that Anderson would be so excited to be my partner for a silly art project, but I would be lying if I said I wasn't flattered.

"So, what are you doing Friday night?"

"Why?" I said. "Are you asking me on a date?"

Anderson laughed again, but this time it was a tough, gritty chuckle.

"Sorry," I said, my heart pumping a mile a minute. "I didn't mean to—"

"Don't apologize. I just meant it'd be a great time to work on the project."

The project. Of course. "Oh, well, that sounds fine."

"Cool," Anderson said. We stood still for a moment, silence filling the space between us, before he turned. "I'm gonna finish running," he told me. "See you later, Marni."

"Bye," I called after him.

I took a deep breath. In a little while I would have to go inside, where I'd make dinner and feed it to my mom because she couldn't use her hands, and we'd watch a *Gilmore Girls* rerun, waiting for my dad to come home from work. I'd probably call Clarissa—maybe even Lili and Priya—to dish about JeDarcy and Townsen and mock trial. I wouldn't tell them about Anderson, though. And definitely *not* about Friday night.

Anderson retreated into the twilight, the sky a dark kind of blue, the sun drifting off to sleep in sparks of orange and pink. Suddenly, breaking up with Jed didn't feel like the worst thing in the entire world.

THE BENNINGTON PRESS
The New Face of Justice
By: TOMMY PAYNE

September 28—Lady Liberty received a face-lift yesterday afternoon when four Bennington seniors—Clarissa von Dyke, Priya Ramnani, Lili Chan-Mohego, and Marni Valentine—chose the jury for the newly envisioned student court, affectionately nicknamed The Diamond Court by students.

With the addition of the popular seniors to the team, the club's mission has changed from reenacting famous trials of the past to holding modern-day trials involving issues that affect Bennington students themselves.

"It's more or less peer mediation," says Mr. Townsen, AP Government teacher and faculty advisor for the team. "An alternative for students who want to settle their problems fairly and stay out of trouble."

But is this new version of the mock trial team really *fair*? "Of course it is," says Clarissa von Dyke. "It's more than fair. It's perfection."

Only time will tell. But one thing is for sure: even Capitol Hill has yet to see such beautiful lawmakers.

• **EXHIBIT D** •

♦ 4 ♦

The right of the people to be secure in their persons, houses, papers, and effects, against unreasonable searches and seizures, shall not be violated . . .   —*The Fourth Amendment to the United States Constitution*

Walking down the hall next to Clarissa was unreal. The way she moved was fluid and quick. People *dove* when they saw her. I'm talking leap-out-of-the-way, throw-yourself-against-the-wall dives where nothing mattered except getting out of her way. No one pushed her between classes or dared even to brush up against her. Once, sophomore year, Danielle Grazaldo was juggling a bunch of books and accidentally spilled some of her Poland Spring on Clarissa's skirt en route to the library. Two weeks later, she transferred. And that was just *water*.

I'd always wondered what it would be like if people were scared of me like they were of Clarissa. It wasn't the most admirable thing to aspire to—instilling fear in others—but ever since I'd become one of the

Diamonds, my life had been in a happy sort of limbo I couldn't seem to escape from. I was popular, yes, and people thought I was pretty and had expensive clothes (I mostly borrowed Priya's), and while that was certainly *nice*, I didn't stand out in any way whatsoever. I didn't sparkle. Clarissa was the gorgeous one, Priya was the fun one, Lili was the smart one, and I was, well, along for the ride. While a large part of me was satisfied simply to have friends who liked me, a smaller part of me wondered what it would be like for everyone to move out of the way for *me*—not for who I was standing next to.

I guess that was why I was so eager to join mock trial: because Clarissa wanted to. Because before I'd come to Bennington, I'd had nothing. Public school had been a disaster. I didn't wear the right clothes or have the right friends, or any friends at all, really. I was invisible. But then I enrolled at Bennington and Clarissa plucked me from a sea of nothingness and turned me into *something*, into someone. I still wasn't particularly special, but that didn't matter anymore. I owed her. I was a Diamond. I was not about to lose that for anything.

"Move," Clarissa said.

It was sixth period—time for lunch—and Scott Kirkpatrick was blocking my locker. Exactly one week had passed since we'd chosen a jury.

Scott, who had a squishy nose and a triangle of

pimples on his forehead, was so startled that he dropped one of his books and accidentally smacked his elbow on the locker next to him. I could tell by the look on his face that it hurt.

"Hi, Clarissa," he said. In what seemed like an afterthought, he said hello to me, too.

"Scott. You look *so* handsome today," Clarissa said. She was wearing a pink cashmere cardigan and a gray skirt. "Did you get a haircut?"

"Uh, no," he said, turning red.

"Really? Well, you look stunning. Like an Adonis." Clarissa arched her back and va-va-voomed her boobs. "Bye, now."

"Uh, bye," he said, scurrying away.

"You're cruel," I said, grabbing two binders and checking my hair in the mirror I had put up. "He probably thinks you like him now."

"That wasn't cruel," she said, reaching into her purse and applying lip gloss with her pinky. When she was done, she grabbed my arm and we began walking toward the cafeteria. "That was community service."

There were two cafeterias at Bennington, creatively named A and B. They were pretty much identical, except that A had tackier colors and *didn't* have a soda machine. B was only for seniors, with a few exceptions. (The Diamonds, for instance, had eaten in B since freshman year. We had our own table in the back corner, right next to a window overlooking one of the courtyards. We referred to it as Café Bennington, which, if you ask me, had a much nicer ring to it than "Cafeteria B.")

Usually people chose *not* to sit near us at lunch—admiring from afar, I'm sure—but that day Café Bennington seemed especially empty; all I saw were white walls, long tables, and about twenty or so pink lunch trays. A few recognizable faces stuffed their mouths with sandwiches, and Yolanda, an overweight lunch lady, stomped past us, her ginormous breasts threatening to flop out of her uniform.

Jed had lunch sixth period, too. At the beginning of school, he'd sat at our table (as a rule, boyfriends were only allowed to eat lunch with us after three consecutive weeks of dating), but he'd disappeared completely after dumping me. Over the past few days, I had spotted him in the courtyard with Darcy, and the thought of them together made me sick. And sad. At least he was smart enough to stay outside.

"What took you so long?" Clarissa asked, drumming her nails on the table as Lili sat down.

Lili motioned to the far end of Café Bennington, where there was a wooden box to leave suggestions for better cafeteria food (the most basic oxymoron ever).

"You did it?" Clarissa asked, flashing a smile. She turned to me. "I asked Lili to have student government approve turning the suggestion box into a place where people can file applications to have their cases heard at mock trial."

"Oh," I said. "Cool."

"*So* cool," said Priya, eating yogurt, something sixty

calories and blueberry, dipping her plastic spoon into the cup the way you'd dip your toe into a freshly drawn bath. Lili had taken out a crinkled paper bag and removed a sandwich—withery lettuce, sliced tomatoes, and what looked like turkey. Clarissa and I both had platefuls from the salad bar.

"This week was fine for just starting," Clarissa said, biting into a tomato, "but we really need to spice things up. This box is perfect. We can go through the applications and pick which ones we want to bring to trial."

"Everyone in student government thought it was a *great* idea," Lili added. "I just hope people actually use it."

"They will," Clarissa said with confidence. "Did you make the flyer?"

Lili nodded, reaching into her bag and pulling out a thin sheet of paper. "I haven't made copies yet, though."

I glanced over Clarissa's shoulder. It read:

Did your BFF trash-talk you behind your back and ruin your favorite dress?

Did your girlfriend cheat on you with the entire football team?

Fill out an application to have your case heard by the newly improved mock trial team! Put your best friend (or your worst enemy) on trial and have them get what they deserve: justice!

All trials held in the chorus room after school.

Clarissa von Dyke
Priya Ramnani
Lili Chan-Mohego
Marni Valentine

• EXHIBIT E •

"Perfect," Clarissa said.

We sat for a few moments in silence, eating slowly, until Priya finished her yogurt and burped. "Today in the bathroom," she said, "I heard Nicole Reynolds and Stephanie Grier talking about the Snow Ball."

"Oh God," Clarissa said, shaking her head.

Fact: Bennington's annual Snow Ball is like every single dance rolled into one; it's homecoming times a million and practically more important than prom. Every year, ten seniors (five boys, five girls) are nominated to the Snow Court as Ice Princes and Princesses. On the day of the dance, an Ice King and Queen are chosen. There's a huge pep rally in the gym and everything. Aside from winning a popularity contest, the people chosen as king and queen automatically become heads of the committee that organizes prom; they get to pick the location, theme, DJ, decorations. The whole nine yards.

The catch was that both faculty and students chose the nominees. Being well-liked didn't necessarily guarantee a spot on the Snow Court. Things like academic prowess and community service played pivotal roles in securing a nomination, which for the Diamonds— except Lili, of course—meant potential trouble.

"People are already thinking about that?" I asked. "They don't even announce the court for, like, another month or two, and the dance isn't until December."

Clarissa dropped her fork, shocked. Her two older sisters, Missy and Bronwyn, had been Bennington Ice Queens in their day; I knew she felt pressure to live up to their legacy, but it was silly, I thought, to take anything called the Snow Ball so seriously.

"It's *never* too early to discuss the Snow Ball," she said. "Honestly, Marni."

I sighed.

"It's easy for you to be so cavalier. This whole Jed thing couldn't have worked out better. You'll totally get the sympathy vote. It's *so* unfair."

Yeah, I wanted to say. *It's really unfair that my boyfriend cheated on me with some mannish girl who thought a black trench coat was appropriate to wear to school.*

"Sometimes," Priya said, "I have nightmares that Jenny Murphy gets nominated and I don't. Once, I woke up and my entire bed was wet. I thought I, like, peed in my sleep or something, but then I realized the sheets were soaked *with my own tears.*"

"Tragic," said Clarissa.

"Don't worry," Lili said, nudging Clarissa. "You've done community service, right?"

Clarissa shrugged. "I totally adopted two puppies from the North Shore Animal League, if that's what you mean."

"I thought you gave those away," Priya said, tilting her head.

"So? I still adopted them. I don't see *you* taking in any abused animals."

"I haven't worn real fur in *three* years—"

"Mock trial is a good start," I interjected. "I'm sure Townsen will put in a good word for you."

"True," Clarissa said, biting her lip, "but we need something bigger. Something that will be sure to impress the Snow Ball council. Well? Any ideas?"

"*I* know," Priya said, taking the straw from her drink and chewing on the end. "Okay, like, *I'm* really fashionable and *you're* really fashionable"—she pointed to Clarissa—"and *Lili's* really fashionable and Marni has a megaphone." It was true. I did have a megaphone. "So what if we stood outside and, like, made a booth or whatever, and we could all announce to people what doesn't work about their outfits, but not in an *American Idol* way, or wait—like, yeah, in an *American Idol* way but none of us would be Simon. We'd all be Paula, or like, Marni, you could be Randy and say 'dawg' or whatever—but we'd all be really nice and it'd be like we're *helping* people with their *fashion*. Community service. Right?"

"I mean, *Priya,*" Clarissa managed to get out. "No. That was retarded." She turned to me. "We *should* use your megaphone, though. I totally forgot about that. Lili, what do you think?"

"I don't have a formulated plan or anything," said Lili in a way that made me think she did, in fact, have a formulated plan, "but what if we organize a fund-raiser? Something that everyone at Bennington will want to attend." She paused. "The profits can go to charity."

"Yes," Clarissa said, folding her hands underneath her chin. "That's a brilliant idea." She looked so intrigued that, for a moment, I was upset I hadn't thought of the idea myself. "What *kind* of fund-raiser, though?"

"What about a fashion show?" Lili suggested. "We could hold auditions for any seniors who want to try out, pick models—guys and girls—and then get local stores to sponsor us with some clothes. We can donate all the money that we make on ticket sales to charity."

Priya, Lili, and Clarissa all squealed with excitement. I kept my mouth shut.

"Here's the question, though," said Clarissa. "We don't want the money going to just *any*body. We need a charity on the rise, something hip."

I wanted to raise the point that charities' goals were lofty—to fight disease and help mankind. *Not* to ride the wave of popular trends. I remember thinking, however, that such a comment would be lost on my friends.

"What about athlete's foot?" said Priya. "Or, like, being color blind?"

"I don't think being color blind really counts as a disease," said Lili.

"What—you think it's *normal?*"

"Oh, shut *up*, Priya."

"Guys, stop, we're not getting anywhere," Clarissa interrupted. "Any suggestions, Marni?"

"I don't know," I said, trying to think quickly. "We could always donate the money to homeless people."

"Oh," Clarissa said, throwing her hand over her chest as if she were about to recite the Pledge of Allegiance. "I've got it. What if we donate the money to homeless *trannies?*"

I laughed. Out loud and really hard. "You've got to be kidding me," I said. "We should donate it to the Salvation Army. They do a lot of great work for people who don't have a place to live or food to eat."

"No," Clarissa said, shaking her head, curls and all. "The fund-raiser should be specifically and *only* for homeless trannies. If a charity like that doesn't already exist, we should *make* one. It's *hysterical.*"

I didn't know what to say. "Lili, please talk some sense into her."

Lili lowered her glasses, sliding them down the bridge of her nose. "Actually, Marni, homeless trans-sexuals are a very specific minority who receive little, if any, help from the government. They're even discriminated against by *other* homeless organizations."

I opened my jaw and tried popping my ears. Maybe I wasn't hearing things correctly.

"Well, I love it," Priya added. "We can call them

Homies. It's 'homeless' and 'trannies' combined. Cute, right?"

"*So* cute," Clarissa agreed.

I thought I was going to explode. Then, from behind me, I heard the distinct sound of a throat being cleared.

Mr. Townsen.

"Hi, Mr. T," Clarissa said, her smile radiating like heat from a furnace. "What's new?"

"I just wanted to say you all did a great job with last Wednesday's trial."

He was talking about Vanessa and Margie. (*Solsti v. Taylor and Hirani,* in which Margie Taylor let Vanessa Hirani copy her chem lab, and Vanessa proceeded to hand in the same *wrong* answers to the same hawkeyed teacher, Mrs. Solsti, who caught them immediately.) Thanks to Clarissa's skills as a prosecuting attorney and my knowledge of U.S. criminal law for aiding and abetting, we had argued that Vanessa was guilty of cheating and Margie was an accomplice in the crime. The jury voted in our favor (hardly a surprise) and both girls were given two weeks of detention and a zero on their lab reports.

"Mrs. Solsti was very impressed with the four of you. She even mentioned the trial at yesterday's faculty meeting, and now all of the teachers who were skeptical about the new direction of the club want to use the mock trial team to settle any in-class issues." Townsen had a look on his face that people wore when they took a risk and ultimately succeeded. "And

Principal Newman wants to attend one of our meetings! Isn't that great?"

Clarissa fanned herself as if she were stranded in the Sahara without a drop of water. "Incredible," she said.

Mr. Townsen nodded enthusiastically. "Now we just have to make sure we have a bunch of trials lined up. We've gotta keep our momentum strong!"

"The executive board approved our use of the suggestion box," said Lili, "and after lunch I'm going to start flyering."

"Super," Townsen said, fixing his tie (green, striped). "Keep me posted. I really want you girls to have as much responsibility for this team as you can handle. Oh, and, Marni"—he smiled, seeming to notice me for the first time—"everyone was very impressed with your comprehension of the law. Great job."

After leaving Spanish, I was ambushed by Tommy Payne, the newspaper dweeb.

"Marni, can I talk to you for a minute?"

I shook my head vehemently. "No."

"Come on," he said, following me down the hall. "Just one minute."

All the "nonacademic" classrooms at Bennington were on one side of the building—art, music, dance, and the television studio—by the auditorium. I had chorus next (which Clarissa, Priya, and Lili took as well), my other elective besides AP Visual Art, and I wanted to drop my sketch pad off at my locker first.

"What do you want?"

"One or two quick questions," Tommy said, taking out a mini tape recorder and pressing Record. "Basically I need a quote from you about Jed Brantley."

Ugh. "In case you haven't heard, Jed and I broke up. I'm probably not the best person to talk to you about, like, his effort to get back on student council." I pursed my lips together and looked at my watch. "Gotta go."

Tommy clicked off the recorder and shoved it into his pocket. "I guess this isn't a good time."

I saluted him. "Bye now, Mr. Reporter." I took only a few steps before hearing his voice again.

"Oh, and, Marni?"

"Yeah?"

Tommy shifted his feet, his dark hair contrasting with the pale green of his eyes. "The article I'm writing isn't about Jed. It's about you."

THE BENNINGTON PRESS
Diamond Court Not a 'Flash in the Pan'
By: TOMMY PAYNE

October 5—The Diamond Court is stronger than ever in its second week, holding trials nearly every day after school.

For those of you who've been sleepwalking through the halls, the seniors who have taken their private nickname "The Diamonds" public with the Bennington mock trial team—Clarissa von Dyke, Priya Ramnani, Lili Chan-Mohego, and Marni Valentine—have kept the student body's interest high with their newly formed student court.

"Students are responding to the fairness of our trials," says Ramnani, "and the shortness of our skirts."

Any student who wishes to appear before the court may fill out a form in the cafeteria and schedule a trial of his or her own. "We'll hear *any* dispute," says von Dyke. "If you've been done wrong and want justice, come see us. You won't regret it."

After more than ten trials, it seems that von Dyke is telling the truth. The only individuals who may be regretting the court are those found guilty of wrongdoing. When this reporter attempted to interview some of the students who've been "sentenced" by The Diamonds, they were harder to open up than pistachio nuts. "No comment," said Vanessa Hirani, and she was not the only one. "Leave me alone, okay?" said Frank Ramirez. "Is my life some kind of joke to you?"

No, Frank. It most certainly is not. And so, my fellow students, I leave you with a final question: could The Diamond Court really be here to stay?

For this reporter's interview with Mr. Townsen, see pg. 5.

For yesterday's Diamond Court rulings, see pp. 10–15.

• **EXHIBIT F** •

◆ 5 ◆

No person shall be . . . deprived of life, liberty, or property, without due process of law;
nor shall private property be taken for public
use, without just compensation.
—*The Fifth Amendment*
to the United States Constitution

Anderson lived in a tiny cul-de-sac behind Tofu, the
overpriced Chinese restaurant my mother loved more
than me but less than Hot Dog. His house was three
stories tall and reeked of excess, ivy spilling down the
sides in tangles, soft cream siding, and red brick that
hugged the roof like an old friend.

I rang the bell twice. Anderson looked better than
ever when he opened the door.

Inside, he moved with familiar ease past a wall of
oil paintings and oak bookcases. I followed him
through a pair of delicate french doors, past the living
room, and into the den, which was set up like a minia-
ture studio. Two easels stood a few feet apart, and a
basket of brushes, charcoal pencils, and tubes of paint

rested by the far wall. A drop cloth (white linen) was spread across the floor.

"You really went all out," I said.

Anderson cocked his head. "It wasn't me. It was my mother."

I nodded. Certainly, if anyone knew about intense mothers, it was me. Upon further inspection, I noticed an assortment of vegetables—crudités, as they say—positioned on a tiny glass table, arranged to resemble a human face: cucumber eyes, carrot nose, lips of red pepper, and a broccoli wig. I was speechless, but in a good way. Anderson's mother was insane.

I felt right at home.

"So," I said, picking up a carrot and crunching it between my teeth. "Ready to paint?"

Anderson was in a navy T-shirt that left little to the imagination, clinging to every muscle on his chest, and a pair of faded jeans. "Sure."

I reached down and opened my sketch pad. What was the point of small talk?

Then I saw a guitar.

It was resting on a thin, metal stand, looking incredibly shiny, a leather strap draped down its neck and a heart-shaped pick tucked behind one of the strings.

"Is that yours?" I asked, glancing back at Anderson, who was squeezing a tube of reddish paint onto a wooden palette.

"Yeah," he said, nodding mindlessly.

"Do you play?"

"Why else would I have a guitar?"

Good point. "Can you play me something?"

Anderson's eyes glimmered like tiny lights on a Christmas tree. He wiped his hands on his jeans and crept toward his guitar. With one swift motion, he ran his thumb across the strings—the sound was beautiful, brassy—and turned one of the silver pegs at the top counterclockwise.

"What do you wanna hear? I know some Beatles."

"Slow ones," I said.

I rocked my head slowly as he started, his fingers surprisingly deft. He sang "Blackbird" and his voice was good and much different from his speaking voice. Wider, if that makes any sense, and lazy, like drippy molasses and sleeping dogs and apple pickers resting in the shade, fanning themselves with leaves. The music made me happy and sad all at once, and incredibly lonely, but I loved it.

He closed his eyes and continued with a few of my favorites—"In My Life," "Yesterday," "Julia" (why oh *why* wasn't my name Julia?)—and I closed my eyes, too.

"Wow," I said breathlessly when he was done. "You're incredible. Do you write any of your own stuff?"

Anderson rolled back his shoulders. "Yeah. Well, some."

"Can I hear"—*stay calm*—"one or two songs?"

"Maybe another time," he said, shifting the guitar back to its stand and sliding next to me on the couch.

His leg touched mine and he didn't move it; we sat there, speechless, staring at each other.

Questions that ran through my head included:

Why did you ask to be my partner?

Why do you play the guitar so well?

Why didn't I wear a padded bra?

I didn't get to ask any of them, though, because Anderson asked one first. "How do you wanna do this?" His breath was hot against my cheeks. I could barely remember my own name.

"What?"

"The portraits." Anderson pointed to the easels and the paint. "Do you want to paint me first, or . . . ?"

Oh. Right.

I willed my pulse to slow down. Anderson didn't want to kiss me. He wanted to paint my picture. And not in a *Titanic* kind of way.

"Whatever," I said. "I don't care."

Anderson went over to one of the easels and sat down facing me. He twirled a charcoal pencil between his fingers. "Why don't you sit back and, uh, lean your head against the window."

"Like this?"

He gulped. "Yeah, like that."

I made a few minor adjustments, twisting my torso, rotating my shoulders—did my breasts look bigger?— and stared out the window behind me. Anderson's backyard was dotted with trees, long and thin, short and fat. There was a stone patio, an expensive-looking set of wicker furniture, and even a pool. I glanced back at Anderson, who was busily sketching on the white canvas.

"Don't move."

"Sorry," I said, flexing my toes almost involuntarily. "This is weird, huh?"

He didn't look up. "Whaddya mean?"

"Oh, I don't know. Me, sitting here, posing for you." I felt a trickle of sweat run down my back.

"Not really."

"I just mean we haven't been together since—"

"Can you not," Anderson said, his eyes meeting mine with a flicker of something cold behind them, "move?"

My lower lip fell forward. "Sorry. I didn't realize you were so into this."

"I've always liked drawing. See those?" He pointed to the wall behind him, where a triptych of watercolor paintings were mounted in black frames. "They're mine."

The paintings were spectacular. They were of his house, the one I was sitting in, during different seasons: the first in autumn, with red, orange, and yellow leaves; the next in winter—roof, shingles, and lawn covered in white-white snow; the last in either summer or spring. I wasn't sure which, but the colors were sunny and warm and bright.

"I never knew you were such a serious artist."

Anderson scrunched his nose and looked back at

the canvas. "I guess there are a lot of things you don't know about me."

"Like what?"

"Well," he said, drawing the word out so that it took three times longer than it should have to say, "I like long walks on the beach and puppies that wear sweaters when it's cold out. My favorite vegetable is spinach, even though most people think it's gross, and I listen to Pink Floyd every night before I go to bed." He smiled with all his teeth. "Sometimes Wilco. Bet you didn't know all that."

"No," I said in agreement. "Anything else I should be aware of?"

"I dunno." He grinned. "You tell me."

I was suddenly aware that Anderson was flirting. With me. And even though it felt sort of nice, I couldn't help thinking about Clarissa, about how ex-boyfriends were off-limits. And also about Jed.

"You know, I should really get going." I stood up and brushed invisible lint off my jeans. "Maybe I can come back another time so you can finish—"

"No need," Anderson said, standing up himself. "I'm done." He turned the canvas around to face me. "See for yourself."

Other than in a mirror, there aren't many times in life when you stare at your reflection. I've heard that some movie stars don't watch their own films because they don't want to see themselves onscreen. Looking at Anderson's creation, though, the fine lines of charcoal so evenly blended, dark and light in just the right places, the shading, shape, and detail of my features so immaculately perfect, I couldn't understand why. Not because I'm vain or anything—at least, I don't *think* I am—but because the feeling of being part of something larger than myself was overwhelming. It might have been just a drawing, a sketch for a high school class, but to me it was art.

"What do you think?" Anderson asked.

I looked at him and felt everything strong inside me collapse. "It's beautiful."

◆　　◆　　◆

I'll be the first to say it: mock trial turned out to be fun. Like, *really* fun. After Tommy's second article, the suggestion box in Café Bennington overflowed with student requests to have their trials heard. The Diamonds would sort through applications at Clarissa's house after school and pick the best—i.e., the funniest—ones to schedule for trial the following week. We'd write up subpoenas and have freshmen slip them inside people's lockers, notifying them of when to appear before the Diamond Court.

Part of it was the power, sure. We had our (manicured) hands in every aspect of the court. The only thing we *didn't* control was whether the jury found the defendant guilty or innocent, but usually it was pretty obvious, and for the most part, the jury was filled with Diamond wannabes. All we had to do was drop a hint or two about what we *wanted* the outcome of the trial to be, and That was That. Then it was up to us—the Diamonds—to dole out the punishments as we saw fit. Mr. Townsen sat in the back of the room, taking notes and drinking it all in; most of the time he didn't say a word. He strongly believed that "we must learn to govern ourselves," a motto that proved easier with each successive trial.

Another part of it, though, was simply spending time with my best friends. Any excuse to spend more time with them—yes, even morphing the Bennington mock trial team into a court where students could settle their relationship problems and personal grievances in a professional manner that simultaneously served the Diamonds' best interests—was a good one. At least in my book.

"All rise for the Honorable Judges Valentine, Ramnani, Chan-Mohego, and von Dyke."

The entire audience in the chorus room—which was packed, by the way—stood at attention while Clarissa, Priya, Lili, and I sauntered forward, making sure our skirts swished just the right amount, and took our seats. Marco, our bailiff, looked like an overgrown string bean in a pair of green khakis and a green long-sleeved shirt. ("It makes me feel like there's a tree growing in the room," Priya said after she'd ordered him to dress that way, "and I *love* nature. Kind of.")

Once we were settled, Clarissa said, "You may be seated." The collective noise of seventy or so bodies sitting down filled the room. The trials were so popular that people had to sign up on a sheet outside the chorus room the day before to watch the proceedings. (There was even an alternate list.)

"Today's trial, *Goldstein v. O'Hara*, is about to begin. Are all parties present?"

I glanced around the room. There was Rosie Goldstein, a junior who played lacrosse (which, in my opinion, was totally lesbionic) and had teeth that reminded me of candy corn. Across from her was Erin O'Hara, also a junior, and one of Rosie's best friends.

The scenario: Two weeks before, Rosie's boyfriend, Mark (senior, blondish, semiattractive), showed up at school with a fist-sized hickey on his neck. Everyone assumed it was from Rosie. The following week, Erin walked into school with a matching one, and people start putting two and two together. (Side note: Why do people let other people give them hickeys in visible places?)

Clarissa, who, above all else, hated cheaters, was über enthusiastic about this case. I, on the other hand, was less than psyched. After everything that had gone down with Jed, and after I'd hung out with Anderson behind Clarissa's back, I felt (A) sort of uncomfortable and (B) sort of hypocritical laying down the law for Erin and Mark.

"Yes," said both the prosecution and defense teams. Jenny Murphy, whose lap was filled with books and notepads, simply nodded.

"Will the prosecution please call its first witness?" Lili said.

Eric Ericsson stood up and snorted. "Surely. The prosecution would like to call Kelly Silver to the stand."

Kelly, who couldn't have been more than five feet tall and walked with a limp, wobbled toward the witness stand. I wasn't particularly fond of Kelly; she talked too much, and most of what she said was unintelligible.

"Do you swear to tell the truth, and nothing but the truth, so help you God?" Marco asked.

"Ya, totally."

Eric adjusted his belt. His shirt—plaid, red—was tucked in and pressed. "Kelly. How do you know the defendant, Ms. O'Hara?"

"Thank you *so* much for asking, Eric. I know the defendant because we, like, go to school together."

"And you two are friends?"

"I wouldn't say that," Kelly muttered. "We, like, *know* each other. Not biblically or anything, though. Just because I kissed Amy Steinberg at a Halloween party last year *doesn't* mean I'm a lesbian, no matter what anybody says."

Eric turned to the jury. "Let it be stated, for the record, that Ms. Silver and Ms. O'Hara are *not* close friends. Also, she is not a lesbian." He turned back to Kelly. "Why don't you tell me about last Wednesday?"

Kelly leaned back in her seat. "Last Wednesday was wild. I mean, like, *crazy*. I had to stay after school because I get tutored in math—I'm, like, totally dumb about numbers, so whatever—and I was leaving school and walking to my car"—she smiled at the jury—"FYI, I drive a BMW"—she fanned herself with her hand—"and I'm, like, doing my own *thang* when I see these shadows where all the smokers hang out. Meanwhile, I'm totally on the phone with my BFF, Jenny, and I remember being like, God, Jenny, just *shut up* for a hot second, because I think I see a *ghost*. And I, like, legit thought it was a ghost. No joke. But when I got closer, I was like, Oh, that's not a ghost. It's Erin O'Hara and Mark Durango, making out, and I remember being like, *Awwww*, but then I was like, Wait, back that shit up, those two are *not* together! Mark is dating Rosie Goldstein, who, by the way"—she offered Rosie an apologetic frown—"is *such* a better person than Mark or that rabies-infected, Macarena-dancing *lady of the night* Erin." She paused. "And that's all I remember."

"No further questions, Your Honors." Eric returned to his seat as Jenny Murphy rose from hers.

"You may cross-examine the witness," Clarissa said.

"Thank you," Jenny said, taking a few steps, her heels clapping loudly on the floor. "Kelly. Isn't it possible that the people you saw kissing were *not* Mark Durango and Erin O'Hara, but two completely different people?"

Kelly blinked. "Are you saying I'm dumb?"

"Of course not," Jenny said. "I'm simply raising the possibility that you may have been mistaken."

"I'm not dumb, and I'm *not* blind," Kelly spat,

wiping the corners of her mouth. "I know what I saw. You're trying to cover this up"—she pointed at Jenny—"just like Watergate. I won't be silenced!" she screamed, pounding her fist on her thigh. "I won't!"

Clarissa banged her gavel on the judges' bench. "Marco, please remove Kelly from the witness stand."

Marco approached Kelly, offering her his hand. She refused it, choosing instead to leap from her chair and run out of the room as if she were being chased.

"What a nutjob," I whispered to Priya. Then, out the corner of my eye, I noticed that Clarissa's gavel was covered in what looked like rhinestones. "Does Clarissa have a Bedazzled gavel?"

Priya stared at me like I was as crazy as Kelly Silver. "What other kind of gavel is there?"

"Never mind."

"Eric," Clarissa said, asserting her control over the room, "you may call your next witness."

"Gladly," Eric replied. "The prosecution would like to call Mark Durango to the stand."

By the end of the trial, two things were clear:

1. Mark and Erin were fooling around behind Rosie Goldstein's back.

2. I shouldn't have drunk an entire iced coffee beforehand; I had to pee like whoa.

During the break, while the jury deliberated—this could take anywhere from a few minutes to an hour or so—I used the bathroom and found my way back to the judges' bench. Clarissa was chatting with Mr. Townsen, while Priya and Lili were debating the benefits of using pore-cleansing facial masks before bed.

"They just suck everything right out of you," Priya was saying. "Like a vacuum cleaner, but for your face. And who doesn't want that?"

"What do you think is taking so long?" I asked, sitting down.

Lili shook her head. "No idea. This one is pretty simple."

"What should their punishment be?" I asked. "No PDA?"

"Eh," Lili said. "It's been done."

"What about if, like, they have to walk around the school in handcuffs?" Priya suggested, smiling.

"First of all," I said, "I don't think we're allowed to demand that people wear handcuffs. Secondly, we want to keep Mark and Erin *apart*—not allow them to be together twenty-four/seven."

"You're right," Priya said, smacking her forehead. "What about, instead of handcuffs, they have to wear, like, friendship bracelets? Made out of hemp! They'd have to wear them every day"—Priya started laughing maniacally—"*or else.*"

Lili rolled her eyes. "No, sweetie. Just . . . no."

Clarissa chose that moment to reenter the conversation, slipping into her seat between Lili and Priya and wrapping her arms around them, pulling us into a tight clump. We called this our Deliberation Pose. The four of us would tilt our heads so that our hair covered our faces and, in soft voices, decide the fate of whoever was on trial.

"*Obviously* Emily and Mark are going to be found guilty," Clarissa said without even a hint of doubt. "Thoughts on punishment?"

We ran down the typical sentencing for cheating on a significant other.

"I don't know," Clarissa said, "this all just seems so . . . uninspired. Marni, what do you think?"

"What do you mean?"

"Exactly what I just said. What should their punishment be?"

I was confused. Usually, that was Clarissa's job. "You want me to decide?"

"Why not?"

She had a point. Why *not* decide? I had been cheated on. I knew the score.

"Think about it," Clarissa instructed, pulling us out of our huddle. "Fast. The jury is back."

As expected, the jury found Erin and Mark guilty of Cheating in the First Degree and of Being Skanky Exhibitionists Who Don't Know How to Properly Administer Hickeys.

"This is ridiculous," Jenny Murphy said, loudly enough for everyone to hear.

Clarissa shot her a death glare.

"That's all," said Jake Snider (juror no. 1), taking his seat. He passed the verdict over to Clarissa, who looked at me eagerly.

I cleared my throat. It was Now or Never. "On behalf of the court," I said, trying to invoke even the slightest bit of Clarissa's authority, "the Diamonds sentence Mark Durango and Erin O'Hara to no PDA on or around the Bennington School property. Mark and Erin are no longer allowed to be within five feet of one another at any time." I glanced at Clarissa for help. She did nothing except widen her eyes. It felt like a challenge. Nothing was going to change the fact that, for Rosie, her boyfriend and her best friend had betrayed her trust. I knew that much from experience. But I had the power to make her life a little easier, didn't I? What good was having that power without using it?

"In addition, Erin and Mark are required to wear clothing that exposes their necks for the next two months. If either is seen with a hickey, or a bruise that resembles a hickey, they will be required to do community service with Ms. Romano's special education class at the Bennington Cemetery on Saturdays. Erin and Mark are no longer allowed to eat lunch in Cafeteria B, and any student seen fraternizing with either individual will hereby be banished from Cafeteria B as well."

I reached over, grabbed Clarissa's gavel, and slammed it down as hard as I could. The sound was deafening. "Case closed," I said.

"That was amazing," Clarissa told me. We were in her car, driving toward my house. My hands were still shaking from the trial. "You were so in control."

"Really?"

She nodded, turning up the radio. "I was so impressed. I didn't think you had it in you."

I understood where she was coming from. I'd even surprised myself.

I thought about Erin and Mark and how the few words I'd uttered would, most likely, change the course of their entire year. It both scared and exhilarated me. Outside, the sky was darkening into night. We sped down Willis Avenue, the funky beats of MIKA blasting from the speakers.

"Doesn't it feel good? To lay down the law and know that whatever you say, people will follow it?"

"Yeah," I said. After this, there was no going back. I was addicted. I would stay part of the Diamond Court forever. "It does."

♦ 6 ♦

In all criminal prosecutions, the accused
shall enjoy the right to a speedy and public
trial, by an impartial jury of the State and
district wherein the crime shall have been
committed . . . and to be informed of the nature and cause of the accusation . . .

—The Sixth Amendment
to the United States Constitution

On the second Friday of every month, all the
Bennington seniors with social lives attend the *Sound
of Music* sing-along at the Roosevelt Multiplex, an
artsy cinema about twenty minutes away from my
house.

To this day, I'm still not sure how the tradition got
started or why the sing-along was an exclusively "senior" event. Maybe it had something to do with the
fact that it was, you know, a *Sound of Music* sing-along.
What underclassmen wanted to explain to their parents why they needed to be dropped off at the movies
wearing an outfit fashioned out of living room drapes?

I met up with Clarissa three hours before the movie

started to coordinate our outfits. I was going as the virginal nun-in-training (also known as a nunette), Maria, who taught the Von Trapp children the importance of sunshine, laughter, and singing in harmony. Clarissa was going as Elsa Schraeder, the vampy sexpot who tried to steal the Captain away from Maria and send the children away to boarding school (where—I'll say it—they probably belonged).

"So, how are you holding up?" Clarissa asked, standing in front of her mirror and adjusting her boobs so that they stretched the front of her dress to full capacity. (Clarissa didn't exactly have a sense of the time period, if you asked me.)

I looked at her blankly. I was sitting on the edge of her bed.

"With *Jed*," she clarified.

"I still miss him," I said, falling back and resting my head on her pillow. "But more the *idea* of him than anything else."

"I know what you mean," Clarissa said. "I was the same way right after I broke up with Anderson. It gets better, I promise."

I stared into the eyes of my very best friend (for better or for worse, that's what Clarissa was, how much she meant to me) and struggled with a response. Everything inside me screamed to tell her about my trip to Anderson's house and my confused feelings for him, no matter how upset she would be.

Then I heard it: "Laaaaadieeeesss," said the voice, high and chirpy. "The party has arrived!" Priya had suddenly appeared outside Clarissa's bedroom door, a six-pack of Coronas in one hand and a bottle opener in the other. I'd almost forgotten she was coming. "Oh, and Lili's here too."

"Very funny," Lili said, brushing past Priya and making her way inside. She was dressed as Liesel, I think, the eldest Von Trapp daughter, who fell in love with a Nazi but realized at the last minute that Nazis were totally lame.

"Who are *you* supposed to be?" Clarissa asked Priya, who was clad in a slinky black number that stopped in the middle of her thighs.

"I'm a nun," she said, lifting one of the bottles in her hand. (Clarissa's parents were out for the night, which was why we'd chosen her house to pregame.) "You really can't tell?" Priya turned to face Clarissa's mirror. "Oh," she said, "*duh.*" She reached down, grabbed a silver cross, and held it up to her chest. "How about now?"

"Oh," Clarissa said. "*Now* I see it. Totally. A nun." She looked at me and laughed. "Don't you, Marni?"

"Yeah," I agreed. "Totally."

Priya opened her beer and took a swig. "Whatever, Marni. Let's see who goes home alone tonight and who doesn't." She eyed my costume as though it were a garbage bag. "Then we'll talk."

"That's it!" Clarissa jumped up from her bed and grabbed my wrist. "We'll find you a guy tonight. Someone to take your mind off Jed."

I already have someone to take my mind off Jed. You dated him for almost a year.

"That's such a good idea!" said Lili.

"Brilliant," said Priya, who was busily squeezing fresh lime into her Corona and drinking up the fizz as it overflowed. "Brilliant."

Clarissa grabbed her makeup case. "Lili, hand me my brush."

"It's a fashion emergency! Code Blue! I mean, Red!" shouted Priya, swishing beer on her dress as she shimmied. "Aw, shit."

"You guys, I look *fine*," I said. I was no longer some clueless middle school transfer student in need of a makeover. I had spent *two* whole *hours* getting ready. What was the deal?

"Yes, you do," said Clarissa, pulling out a compact with twenty different-colored eye shadows. "But you don't have a boyfriend anymore. It's a whole new world out there," she said (*Aladdin*, 1992), "and starting tonight, you are officially on the prowl."

About an hour—and the rest of the Coronas—later, we all piled into Clarissa's Audi. I was the designated driver. Staring into the rearview mirror, I didn't think I looked *that* different. Sure, I was blushing, but that was because of the MAC blush; and sure, I was smiling, but that was thanks to the four layers of lipstick; and *yes*, my eyes were giving off an innocent, doelike vibe, but that was courtesy of Clarissa's shading expertise and not anything particularly new or interesting about *me*.

"Can we listen to something less annoying?" Clarissa whined, flicking off the radio. She was next to me in the passenger seat. I stared at her profile. Even with all the makeup in the world, I would never look like her.

"It's your car," I said. "We can listen to whatever you want."

"I love music," Priya shouted. "Turn it up!"

Clarissa glanced over her shoulder. "There's nothing playing, Priya."

I twisted the wheel and kept my foot on the gas, pulling into the parking lot. "We're here."

"Thank effing God," Priya said, tossing her empty Red Bull can out the window.

"Priya! Wait for a garbage," Lili said, getting out of the car and picking up the discarded aluminum from the ground. "You shouldn't litter."

Priya fluffed her hair. "Your *mom* shouldn't litter."

"Good one," Clarissa said. "I love Your Mom jokes." She grinned at Priya. "Or maybe I just love your actual mom."

We all laughed and started walking toward the movie complex. I imagined how I would direct this scene in a movie—probably in slow motion, with close-ups of our faces and then a pan out to the four of us walking side by side. An electric song would be playing in the background, and I would make sure the cinematographer spent a good amount of time focusing on each of us—Lili, in her maroon curtain dress; Priya, in her slutty nun habit; Clarissa, in her royal evening wear, looking like the voluptuous baroness she was; and me, a young Julie Andrews, heavily doused in liquid concealer but perhaps the prettiest I'd ever looked.

Take *that*, Darcy McKibbon.

Lili gasped. "Okay, don't look now, Clarissa, but you-know-who is standing right outside buying his ticket."

"Who?"

"Anderson," said Lili. "And Ryan and Duncan. Oh, and Tiger."

"Shit," Clarissa said, grabbing my arm. "What are they *doing* here?"

Obviously, the exact same thing we were.

This is as good a time as any to give you a rundown of Anderson's friends.

Ryan Brauer: a tight end on the football team with short chestnut hair, a forgettable face, an overly thick neck, and an even thicker personality.

Duncan Correy: another football player. I can't remember his position, but Duncan is actually a cool guy.

Tiger: also—surprise!—on the football team. Tiger's real name is Jeremy; his last name is Lyon, which sounds like "lion," and before I got to Bennington, someone started calling him Tiger for the goof. I have nothing more to say about that.

Anderson was definitely the leader of the pack, partly because he was the coolest of them, and partly, or even mainly, because he was the hottest.

"Do you want to leave?" asked Lili. "We could always just leave."

"Or we could pretend like we don't know them and walk right by. I mean, we *are* in costume," said Priya.

"You're wearing a black cocktail dress," I reminded her. "It's not exactly a disguise."

"Girls!" said Clarissa. "Let's not make this a bigger deal than it already is. Onward, shall we?"

Clarissa started walking with the sort of determination I'd come to know her for. "Hi, boys," she said as we approached the front door.

Inside, I could see that the Roosevelt Multiplex was all decked out. The hills were alive, so to speak, with cardboard cutouts of mountains and flowers strewn about the lobby.

Clarissa blinked. "Nice night for a musical."

"For sure," Ryan said.

Tiger nodded in our general direction. "Wassup, bitches?"

Priya clucked her tongue. "Don't *ever* use that word when you're speaking to me, okay, Tiger?"

"My deepest apologies," Tiger said, getting down on one knee and holding out his hand. He had on a Yankees cap (backward) and a shirt that said: *Don't hate me because I'm beautiful. Hate me because I f*cked your sister.* "Would you care to accompany me to this evening's queer-a-palooza—I mean, sing-along?"

Priya looked him up and down a few times. "You're not exactly dressed for the occasion," she said, seeming disappointed. "Where's your costume?"

"Oh, here," said Tiger, standing up. He reached into his pocket and pulled out a gigantic cross, which looked more appropriate for a 50 Cent video than a Rodgers and Hammerstein musical. "How about now?"

"Much better," Priya said, raising her own cross and clinking it with Tiger's. "We match."

"I cannot believe what you two are wearing," Lili said, pointing to Ryan and Duncan, who were in matching lederhosen and white dress shirts. "Where did you get those?"

"Lederhosen for Less," Duncan joked. "It's right next to Abercrombie at the mall."

"Be serious," said Lili.

"*You* be serious," said Ryan.

"My older brother had them left over from when he used to go to this," Duncan said, playing with his suspenders. He was wearing a tight green vest over his shirt and a tan belt. "Anderson has on a pair, too. He's getting the tickets."

We stood there momentarily, waiting. Then Priya said, "I'm going with Tiger to get our tickets." I reached into my purse to grab some money, but Priya *shushed* me. "It's on my dad," she said, flashing an AmEx Black Card.

This being my first sing-along, I wasn't exactly sure what to do. Where were all the booze (not that I wanted any) and the drugs (not that I wanted any) and the make-out sessions (which maybe I wanted but only with one boy in particular)?

"Do you like Duncan?" Clarissa whispered.

I had to admit he looked sexy in his over-the-top getup. "He's cute," I said, hoping Clarissa would leave it at that.

She, of course, did not. "How cute?"

"I don't know, Clarissa. Cute."

"Uh, guys?"

Clarissa and I broke from our mini conversation at the sound of Duncan's voice. "I can hear you," he said. "I'm standing right here, you know."

"Are you still dating that sophomore?" Clarissa asked, not the slightest bit fazed. "Rebecca?"

"Nah," he said, pulling at the bottom of his lederhosen to stop them from riding up. "Not anymore."

"Good." Clarissa opened up her purse and took out a pen. It was pink and covered in rhinestones. "She looked like she had palsy." A few quick scratches and I realized she'd written *my* phone number on his hand!

"There you go, Duncan. Don't sweat too much."

"Is this your cell?"

"Absolutely not," she said, tossing the pen back into her purse. "It's Marni's. She's single now."

"Clarissa!"

"Don't call after ten," Lili added. I shot her a quick glance—the traitor! "Marni likes to get her beauty rest."

Priya, who had returned with the tickets, added nothing, choosing instead to make the "Suck It" sign with her hands.

"You don't have to call," I said, trying to seem as apologetic as possible while still looking desirable. "Really."

Duncan scratched his chin and looked at me. It was the kind of look that meant he was trying to size me up, and by "size me up," I mean size up my boobs. *He really is handsome,* I thought, but there was no way I'd ever date him. He was Anderson's best friend.

"It's cool," Duncan said, mustering a smile.

Then I heard it. Him. "Yo, here are the tix," the voice said, low and husky, thrilling and divine. Anderson. Dressed in a snug pair of brown lederhosen, calves bulging, his white shirt open to reveal a tan, smooth chest.

"Oh," he said when he saw Clarissa, Lili, Priya, and me standing there. "Hi."

"Hello, Anderson," Clarissa said as though saying his name took a great deal of effort she didn't care to exert.

"How are you?" he asked. While the question was technically directed at Clarissa, it felt like he was asking me, too.

"Fine." Clarissa brought her arms in front of her chest and clasped her hands, one of her signature moves to show off her boobage. (I used it, too, sometimes, with less success.) "You?"

"Good," he said reluctantly.

Since their breakup, Anderson and Clarissa's conversations had pretty much all been like this: short, tense, awkward. I'd never really understood why; Clarissa was the one who'd dumped *him,* and she acted as if it were the most devastating breakup in the History of High School.

Usually, I didn't pay much attention to their infrequent interactions, but now—oh, but now!—I hung on to every word Anderson said like rungs on a ladder, trying to detect some cryptic message that meant *Marni, I'm in love with you.*

"Well, it's been *really* great catching up." Clarissa gave Lili a nudge and opened the lobby door. "But we don't want to miss our tea with jam and bread, if you know what I mean."

Anderson turned sideways, patting his boys on the shoulders. "Let's go inside," he said. "Bye."

About halfway through "My Favorite Things," when dogs were biting and bees were stinging, I had the sudden urge to flee. Not from the Nazis, though. Just outside.

"I'll be right back," I said, although over the sound of the music (no pun intended), no one could really hear me. "I have to pee."

Outside, it was raining—just my luck. The roof had an overhang, though, so I wasn't getting wet. I walked a little farther, ducked behind the corner, and leaned against the rough concrete of the building. How had life become so complicated?

"Hey there," said a voice. I immediately felt my heart leap. "Didn't anyone ever tell you it's dangerous for a nun dressed like that to be out by herself at night?"

Anderson.

In his lederhosen.

Talking to me.

"What are you doing out here?" I asked. Had he been about to ask me the very same question?

"I'm not exactly the hugest fan of musicals. Well, *movie* musicals."

"*The Sound of Music* is a classic."

"Mmm-hmm," he said, walking closer. "How've you been?"

I wanted to say: *Lonely*.

I wanted to say: *Confused*.

What I said was: "Oh, you know. Fine."

"It's been a crazy week," he said, sliding next to me and pressing his back to the wall. He was so close I could hear the rise and fall of his chest and the sound his lederhosen made when he shifted his legs.

"So, what's this I hear about you giving Duncan your number?" He frowned. "You never gave it to *me*."

"First of all," I said, "I didn't give my number to Duncan. Clarissa did. And second of all . . . you never asked for it."

"I'm asking for it now."

"Maybe I don't want to give it to you," I said, looking into his eyes. They were copper and gold and green and, most of all, blue.

My knees felt like rice pudding, and the wind gusted around us, spraying a few droplets of rain into my face and onto my neck. Anderson moved closer, his nose practically touching my cheek, his breath warming my entire body.

"Marni," he whispered.

93

There were tingles up and down my arms, and I thought a million things all at once.

Does he like me?

Is he going to kiss me?

Will I let him?

Do I have a Listerine strip?

Anderson was so close that he couldn't move any closer. One push and he'd be on top of me, up against me on the wall. Covering me entirely.

I tried to focus on his face, but all I could see were the muted light from the parking lot and the dark sky and his skin, his lips, his teeth, his eyes. Everything about him overtook me. I had to blink to make sure he was really this near and it wasn't a cruel trick of my imagination.

He touched my arm and my body surged, like a waterfall, as if every tiny thing inside me was rushing together in one huge jolt. "Just kiss me," I said, grabbing his lederhosen and pulling him to me. I felt his stomach pressing up against me. Then his lips were on mine, rough and soft and sweet and full. It felt as though everything, every question, was buzzing on the very tip of my tongue, waiting to explode. He kissed me harder and my face was wet from the rain but I kissed him back, and I moved my hands into his hair and he slipped his fingers down my sides, my back flat against the wall, our legs intertwined. I never wanted to stop kissing him. I never, ever did. He tasted like beer but it was a wonderful taste, really, and when I opened my eyes, Anderson was staring right at me.

Before I could say anything, what he said in his low, husky voice was "I guess I should tell Duncan not to call you, huh?"

For some reason Duncan made me think of Clarissa, my best friend, who would never do anything to hurt me and would be devastated if I ever told her what I had just done.

I held on to Anderson with both hands. This moment, I thought, in all its fragile glory, had been a wonderful mistake.

♦ 7 ♦

In Suits at common law, where the value in
controversy shall exceed twenty dollars, the
right of trial by jury shall be preserved . . .
—*The Seventh Amendment
to the United States Constitution*

On Sunday afternoons, the Diamonds brunched at
Bistro, an adorable pseudo-French restaurant in the
fancy shopping center near Clarissa's house. Not only
was the décor welcoming—high ceilings, oak-paneled
walls, ceramic jars labeled *Moutarde*, and tables far
enough apart to ensure our utmost privacy—but there
were free refills on all drinks, including iced coffee.

This Sunday, though, was different from all the
rest: I was thinking about Anderson. About the way
he'd kissed me, what—if anything—it meant, and
how soon we could do it again.

"And then I was like, 'I'll have *one* percent, please.' "
Priya opened her eyes so that her lashes touched her
forehead. "I mean, do I *look* like I drink whole milk?"

Priya was heavily makeupped that day, as usual, her
lips doused in a color she called sluttycappuccino. (As

far as I know, it was actually called mocha. "But when I wear it, I feel slutty," Priya told me while sampling the lipstick at Macy's. "And like I wanna have a cappuccino.")

Lili kicked me underneath the table. "That's awful," I said.

"I know. And *then* I was like, 'I'll have it with *Equal*, please. Not *Splenda*.' "

"What's the difference?"

Priya sighed heavily. "I don't like that kind of joke, Marni."

Lili finished her iced tea in a long, clean gulp and held out her glass for another. "Can we change the subject?"

We didn't have to. Clarissa chose that moment to slide into her seat—which had, of course, been left empty—and take a sip of my Diet Coke.

"Hi, girls," she said casually, glancing at her cell phone. Brunch was always at eleven-thirty, and that never changed. It was something we just *knew*, like $E = mc^2$ or cowboys = gay.

"Where were you?" Priya asked, pouting. "You're late."

I wondered if Clarissa could see right through me, if she could tell that I'd kissed Anderson—and not only kissed him, but *kissed* him—behind the megaplex.

"Whatever," she said, turning to me. "Did he call you yet?"

Clarissa's question startled me and I banged my knee against the edge of the table. "Did *who* call me?"

"Duncan," she said, stabbing her fork into one of my potatoes. "Who did you think I was talking about?"

With a sigh of relief, I remembered everything that had happened *before* Anderson had kissed me. "No, he didn't. Thankfully."

"Marni, this would be a good thing for you. Duncan is really sweet."

"Last year, in April, he told me I looked nice," Priya said, twirling the ends of her dark hair with her fingers. "It was a Tuesday."

"You remember that?"

"Of course," Priya said. "I always remember Tuesdays."

"Don't worry," said Clarissa. "I'll talk to Duncan tomorrow. I'm sure he's simply intimidated"—graceful hand flourish—"by your overwhelming beauty."

"Whatever," I said. "I think he likes you more than he likes me."

"Not true," said Clarissa. "Besides, I hear he has a really long . . . *tongue*."

Gross.

"But if you don't want me to say anything, I'll have the Professor do it."

Fact: The Professor is a nickname Clarissa uses for Lili. It's pretty self-explanatory.

"Absolutely," Lili said. "What do you want me to say?"

"Nothing." I wished I could explain that I didn't want any of them to speak to Duncan for me because I wasn't interested in him; I was interested in his best friend, the one boy who was off-limits. Then I thought of that Shakespeare line: "The lady doth protest too much" (*Hamlet*, 1599–1601), and realized it *did* seem a bit odd that I wasn't remotely interested in Duncan. Yes, Jed had dumped me, and *yes*, it was depressing and awful, but you only get to mourn for a short amount of time. I was kind of pushing it. Maybe if I at least *pretended* I was into Duncan, it would steer the Diamonds clear of any suspicion that I liked Anderson—at least long enough for me to figure out exactly what was going on between us.

"Fine. Say whatever you want to him."

"So you *do* think he's cute!" Priya exclaimed, accidentally knocking the butter tray onto the floor.

Clarissa smiled victoriously. "Don't worry, Marni. We won't embarrass you."

Too late. Just then my train of thought was interrupted by our waitress. The fallen butter tray had no doubt garnered her attention.

"What can I getcha?"

I assumed she was speaking to Clarissa, the only one without a plate in front of her.

"Hulluh?" The waitress, whose face was caked in too-light foundation, eyes close together and dull as pennies, looked at me for help. She had wispy sideburns and an unfortunate snaggletooth. "Can I . . . help you?"

Clarissa slowly turned her head. "Yes?"

The waitress, whose nametag said *LADY*, popped her gum. "What can I get for you?" Every vowel she said came out long and sticky.

Clarissa waved two of her freshly painted nails in the air. "Where's Raymond?"

Raymond was "our" waiter. He worked at Bistro every Sunday; since we had the same thing every week, Raymond would serve us without taking our orders.

"He's out today," LADY informed us. "Sooo, whaddya want? The eggs here are reeaally good."

"I *know* the eggs are good," said Clarissa. She sniffed the air and made a funny face, like she'd tasted something sour. "I'll just have my usual."

LADY started scribbling on her pad but caught herself. "And, uh, what's that?"

"It's"—Clarissa blinked—"my usual."

"Okaaaay, but, I'm new and I don't know what you usually order."

Clarissa gave her an eerie smile. "That's not *my* problem, is it?"

LADY, who had obviously never dealt with the likes of Clarissa von Dyke before, glanced around the table and popped her gum (again). She placed her hand on Priya's shoulder and leaned down. "Can you tell me what her usual is, hon?"

Not even Priya was dumb enough to get between Clarissa and her prey.

Part of me felt bad for LADY. In my mind, she lived

in a trailer park or a homeless shelter. She probably worked fourteen-hour shifts and lived off the tips she earned and the kindness of her customers. When she got home after a long day of work, she most likely removed all her piercings, set them on her dresser (which was made out of playing cards), and opened a cold beer. "If it weren't for the kindness of my customers," she would say to herself, petting her dog, who was covered in tumors she couldn't afford to have removed, "I'd have nothing."

The other part of me found this entire scene very amusing.

"I'd like to see the manager, please," Clarissa said. "Pronto. That means 'fast.' "

LADY grumbled and hobbled past us, dragging her bowling pin legs into the kitchen. A few moments later, a waifish man, Eric, came tumbling out.

"Hello, ladies," he said with familiarity. "What seems to be the problem?"

"We miss Raymond," said Priya, dabbing at the corner of her eyes with her napkin.

"I completely understand," said Eric, "but Lady is very nice, too, and I think if you just—"

"*Lady*," Clarissa said in a way that made LADY sound like anything but, "is a *tramp*. She was rude to my friends and refused to bring me my brunch."

Eric turned behind him to where LADY was leaning against the wall like a broken doll. The rest of Bistro was pretty full, mind you: couples and families were eating and chatting in every nook and cranny. For that moment, though, it seemed as if we were the only ones there.

"Is this true?"

LADY said nothing. She didn't move. She didn't even blink an eye.

"Let me get you your usual," Eric said once a few seconds had elapsed, trying not to make the scene any more awkward than it already was. "I remember what it is."

He turned toward LADY and scooted her away with his hands as if she were a disobedient terrier who'd just peed on the carpet. "And don't worry, girls. Brunch is on me."

Eric stepped backward into the kitchen and I stared at Clarissa with a humble expression. "You are *so* bad," I said.

"Awful," said Lili.

"The worst," Priya agreed.

Clarissa curtsied in her seat, and we all laughed. Then we finished up the food we no longer had to pay for.

Afterward, we gathered around Clarissa's Audi.

"What's everyone doing for the rest of the day?" Lili asked.

I had promised my father I would work on my college applications, but I didn't want to open that can of worms. Lili, I knew, was applying early-decision to Yale, and there was no way she *wouldn't* get in. Priya wanted to go to FIT, and Clarissa was a third-generation legacy at the University of Pennsylvania. I was the only one who had absolutely no idea what the next year held in store.

"I dunno," I said.

"In that case," Clarissa said, fixing her hair as the wind blew it around her head, "I have a few . . . *favors* to ask of you guys. Now that things are getting more serious with mock trial, we need to be as organized as possible.

"Professor"—Clarissa turned to face Lili, who was checking the time on her phone—"I was thinking it might be interesting to make our trials an option for people who receive detention or suspension. If people feel they are unfairly accused, they can bring their cases to mock trial and we can help dispute them. I have a conference scheduled with Principal Newman for next week."

"Okay," Lili agreed. "I'll mention it at our next student government meeting."

Clarissa looked at Priya. "I think it's about time for some coordinated outfits, don't you?"

"I like the sound of that," Priya said as though she'd just had a vision. "I'm thinking . . . balls. Tiny metal balls. Everywhere."

I laughed.

"That's not really what I had in mind," said Clarissa. "We should have a dress code, you know? Like judges' robes, only . . . more flattering. Think sexy but sophisticated. Last but not least," she went on, draping a lanky arm around my shoulder, "Marni."

At the sound of my name, I felt a tiny ping in my stomach; it was a ping of regret, of fear, even, and I wondered just how long I would be able to keep my kiss with Anderson a secret.

"You have the most important job of all. You know, like, the Constitution?"

What kind of question was that?

"Yes," I said.

"I thought it would be interesting if we made up our *own* version. Not the entire thing, but you know, like, the amendments. Those are the ones you add, right?"

Clarissa didn't have the most eloquent phrasing on the matter, but the constitutional amendments were in fact just that: additions to the original text to reflect society as it grew and changed.

"Yeah," I said. "What for?"

Clarissa obviously had a plan.

"The Constitution is great and all," she said, "but it can always be made better."

That, I thought, *is the understatement of the last few hundred years.*

"If we can add a few amendments so it relates specifically to everyone at Bennington and the point we're trying to get across, I think it will be a *huge* success."

"What exactly *is* the point we're trying to get across, Clarissa?"

Lili nodded; I could tell she was wondering the

same thing. Priya, no doubt, was wondering how to get her hands on dozens of tiny balls.

"We're trying to *help* people, Marni."

"Since when have you ever cared about helping people?"

The question was out of my mouth before I could even think about what I was saying. I instantly regretted it.

Clarissa lifted her arm from my shoulder and brushed her red-red hair from her eyes. I could tell she was offended. "If you don't want to help, Marni, you don't have to. Priya, Lili, and I have it covered."

"No, I do," I said, tucking my hands into my back pockets. "I'm sorry. I didn't mean it like that."

"Good," she said. The conversation was over. For now. "Maybe your dad can be of some assistance."

Yeah, maybe. And maybe Darcy McKibbon will win Ice Queen.

Clarissa clicked open her car door and got behind the wheel. "See you tomorrow, ladies. Brunch was fabulous."

With that, she drove off, out of the parking lot, and down the street, the same way she'd come.

Alone.

"Do you need any help?" Dad asked, looking up from the desk in his study. It was his private sanctuary, decorated in rich, nutty colors—walnut, chestnut, acorn— with exquisitely crafted bookshelves and the framed original copies of his many degrees.

In my hand was a heavy book called *The Constitution for Dummies* (Smith, 2000). Mom and I had bought it years before as a birthday present; it had a copy of the Constitution and all its amendments (circa 1999) and explained how each one affected our daily lives.

"No," I said, leaning against one of the bookshelves. "I'm okay."

Dad lowered his reading glasses. "What do you have there?"

I flashed the yellowish cover. "For an assignment," I said, trying to be as vague as possible. Dad loved to volunteer his help for my school projects—especially anything government-related—and always made things *more* difficult than necessary. "I've pretty much got it covered."

Dad scribbled on what I could only assume was a student's paper. "Does this have anything to do with your recent membership in one mock trial organization?"

"Yeah," I said. "It's just something I'm helping Clarissa with."

"Well, don't work *too* hard on it," Dad said. "College applications are coming up pretty soon, you know. Georgetown's deadline is November first."

"I know, Dad."

Georgetown was my father's alma mater, and it was his dream for me to attend college there, too.

"I'm just saying, Marni"—he smiled a tired, tight-lipped smile—"this is a really important time in your life. Don't go spending all your time with Clarissa un-til *after* you've been accepted to college. Okay? I'm glad you joined mock trial, though. That will look great on your application."

It's funny how little parents know. "Sure, Dad."

He stopped me before I could make my exit. "How's Jed doing these days?"

I hadn't told my parents about Jed. I was too em-barrassed. How did you tell your parents that the boy you'd been seeing for nearly a year broke up with you in the most scarring way possible?

"He's fine."

"Tell him I said hello?"

"Okay. I'm gonna go now," I said, expecting to see him staring at me concernedly.

But he was already back to work.

THE BENNINGTON PRESS
The Weekly Roundup

By: TOMMY PAYNE

Below are the highlights from last week's mock trial rulings. For a full listing of case files, please see pg. 12.

Please note that this reporter neither supports nor condemns the following rulings. He is merely a messenger.

CASE FILE:
Tabitha Walton
v. Jake Cooley
[*The Diamond Court,*
October 11]

Facts: Tabitha, a senior at Bennington, wants to annul her relationship with the defendant, Jake Cooley, her boyfriend of four days; as it turns out, Jake is a terrible kisser. If Tabitha had known, she never would have agreed to date him, or bought him a Starbucks gift card. When he asked her out at the movies, it was dark and she couldn't make out the size of his tongue, which—during their first kiss—filled her entire mouth and rendered her unable to breathe.

Issue: Can the Bennington community pretend she never had this lapse in judgment?

Holding: Considering the relationship's short duration, the court ruled in favor of Tabitha. Everyone at Bennington will act as though she never dated Jake in the first place. Now all female students are aware of Jake's oversized tongue and may request to see and/or measure it before agreeing to date him. Jake also must repay Tabitha for the gift card.

CASE FILE:
Blair Jerome
v. Greta Arlington
[*The Diamond Court,*
October 13]

Facts: Blair and Greta, both juniors, have been best friends since the fourth grade. Recently, however, Greta has allegedly been hooking up with the entire soccer team and garnering a poor reputation for herself and the general female population at Bennington.

Issue: How can the court stop Greta from being so promiscuous?

Holding: The Diamond Court rules in favor of the plaintiff, requiring Greta to stop hooking up with any and all student athletes. Additionally, Greta is not allowed to be seen within five feet of any boy who plays an extracurricular sport, nor is she allowed to hook up with anyone who is not her steady boyfriend of at least one (1) month.

CASE FILE:
Helen Watson
v. Sherri Stillman
[*The Diamond Court*
October 14]

Facts: Last week, Helen, a senior, found an e-mail from Sherri in the e-mail account of her boyfriend (Mark Heillman, a senior) that clearly indicates Sherri has (sexual) feelings for him.

Issue: How can the court ensure that Sherri respects boundaries?

Holding: Making a move on another person's significant other is a terrible offense; not only should all girls with boyfriends (and girls who may acquire boyfriends in the future) steer clear of Sherri, but she is allowed only limited access to the Bennington computer lab—with a teacher present—and if she is ever found in a similar situation, she will be asked to turn over her laptop to the Diamonds (but only if it's a Mac).

CASE FILE:
Gus Carver
v. Yolanda Washington
[*The Diamond Court,*
October 15]

Facts: Gus, a senior and one of the editors of *LYLAP,* Bennington's poetry magazine, is bringing his girlfriend, Yolanda Washington, a freshman, to court for cheating on him.

Issue: How can the court put Yolanda in her place?

Holding: Considering that "Yolanda should have been thankful a senior was paying her any attention in the first place," the Diamond Court rules in favor of Gus, requiring all upperclassmen to shun Yolanda and deny her access to Cafeteria B, the courtyard, and the senior parking lot. Also, for the next three months, Yolanda is no longer allowed to wear red lipstick, low-cut tops, or any other clothing meant to attract attention from the opposite sex. If she violates any of these restrictions, Yolanda will be up for further inspection by the court.

· EXHIBIT G ·

◆ 8 ◆

Excessive bail shall not be required, nor excessive fines imposed, nor cruel and unusual
punishments inflicted.

*—The Eighth Amendment
to the United States Constitution*

On Monday, for the first time ever, I didn't eat lunch
with the Diamonds. I would see them all later at mock
trial, and I needed some time alone. To think.

At the beginning of school, Mrs. Donaldson had
informed members of the AP class that if we ever
wanted a quiet place to do some sketching during our
off periods, we should feel free to use the art room and
the materials. (The only perk of being in AP Visual
Art, I suppose.) Before I knew it, I found myself standing outside the door to the art room.

I was sketching within minutes. Because Anderson
was on my mind, and also because our project was due
in the near future, I started recreating his face from
memory; once I started, I couldn't stop. I stared back at
a crude version of the boy I was currently obsessed
with. It didn't really look like him at all. It had eyes, a

nose, and a mouth, but they could have belonged to anyone. The only thing that remotely resembled Anderson St. James was his name written across the top of the page in fancy script.

· EXHIBIT H ·

Then I began doodling funny things across the border; on his face, I drew thick glasses and a top hat. I was chuckling out loud when I heard footsteps behind me. I turned around, expecting to see my crazy art teacher, but there he was: Anderson. In the flesh.

"Hey."

I threw my arm over the picture but it was too late. I could tell by his expression that he'd seen *ANDERSON & MARNI 4 EVA* written across the page.

"Listen," I said, arching my back to show off my lady lumps (Black Eyed Peas, 2005), "about Saturday—"

Anderson put his fingers to his lips, motioning for me to be quiet. The room was empty for now, but he was right—anyone could walk right in.

Anderson sat down next to me. "What are you doing tomorrow?"

"Night?"

"Day."

"I'll be at school. . . ."

"Wrong!" he said, X-ing his arms and making the noise of a game show buzzer. "Try again."

"In class?"

"Nope. One more try."

I had no idea what he wanted me to say. "I'll be . . . with you?"

"Ding ding ding!" Anderson threw his arms around me.

There has never been anyone in the history of the world more beautiful than you, I thought.

"Come with me? I have to go into the city to buy a new guitar," he said.

I had never skipped school. Not once.

"You want me to go with you?"

"Never cut class before?"

I gave a faint smile. "Something like that."

"You're not *actually* cutting class," Anderson said playfully. "You're ditching a day of school, which is totally different."

"Oh? Is that how it works?"

"Yeah," he said. "Just have your parents write you a sick note."

I could hear my mother's nasal voice in my head: "There's no way on God's green earth I'm letting you run off into Manhattan with a boy, Marni," she would say, taking a drag of her cigarette. (My actual mother didn't smoke, but Daydream Mom smoked like a chimney.) "Think of all the homeless people. *And the terrorists.* Do you want to get blown up for one measly day of pleasure?"

"Marni?"

"If you pick me up," I said, formulating a plan, "will you call the school and pretend to be my dad? That way the attendance office won't call my house looking for me, and my mom won't get suspicious."

"Totally," Anderson said. There wasn't the slightest hint of anxiety or hesitation in his voice. "That'd be awesome."

"Okay," I said. What the hell? "Let's do it."

Anderson got up from the stool and leaned his arms on the table. "Then we can talk about . . . everything."

"Yeah," I said. "That would be cool."

The bell rang, and the hallway was suddenly bursting with energy.

"See you tomorrow, Marni."

"Where have you been?" Clarissa asked me after school. I was waiting by her locker, as usual, my bag slung over one shoulder.

"What do you mean?"

"Lunch, Marni. You know what? I got my nails done yesterday. Do you mind?" She glanced toward her locker and recited her combination.

"I was working on my art project," I said, opening the locker for her. Inside, everything was stacked neatly, with a different-colored binder for every subject. A picture of the Diamonds was taped to the back of the door. "Sorry."

"Well, you missed a *whole* lotta shit."

"Like what?"

"I don't know if I should tell you."

"Oh, come *on*," I said. "Tell me."

"Let's just say that Nicole Reynolds threw apple juice in Stephanie Grier's face and called her a backstabbing, heartless wench."

"No way!" Nicole and Stephanie were best friends, but they were on the periphery of the Bennington social sphere. "I wonder what happened."

"Oh," Clarissa said, nudging her locker closed with her elbow. "I'm sure we'll find out."

Once we reached the cafeteria, Clarissa handed me one of her binders and withdrew a key from her pocket. She used it to open the mock trial application box, removing a dozen or so folded scraps of paper and perusing them briefly until she stopped on one.

"*Look* at *this*," she said.

I grabbed the paper; it was filled out in black pen, the ink still wet.

Name: Nicole Reynolds
Cell: XXX-XXXX
Dispute: XXXXXXXXXXXXXXXXXXskankXXXXXX
XXXXXXXXXXXXballsXXXXXXXXXXXX
XXXhedgehogXXXXXXXXXXXXXXXXXX

• EXHIBIT I •
(text replaced for legal purposes)

"Is Nicole's cell phone number on there?" Clarissa asked. I nodded, and she motioned to my bag with her free hand. "Call her, will you?"

The last time I'd spoken to Nicole Reynolds was freshman year, honors English, when she came back from the bathroom with a pee trail running down her pants.

"I don't want to call her," I said. "*You* call her."

Clarissa gave me a you're-being-annoying look and said, "Fine. I'll do it myself."

THE BENNINGTON PRESS
Diamonds Become a Bennington Staple
By: TOMMY PAYNE

October 20—In what has become the shocker of the school year so far, the Diamond Court (formerly known as the mock trial team) has maintained its grasp on student life at Bennington. If anything, over the weeks, the court has grown stronger, dropping many of the original mock trial members and enhancing the reputations of the judges (aka the Diamonds—you all know who they are) each passing day.

"It's hard to be so fair and look so good while doing it," says one anonymous freshman. "You don't want to cross them or you'll be, like, socially eliminated."

What started out as an interesting experiment has quickly morphed into the most intense extracurricular activity at Bennington. "We hold trials nearly every day after school," says Lili Chan-Mohego (see "Chan-Mohego Officially Takes Over Presidency," Oct. 10), "and the chorus room is always filled with onlookers." Since the trials have been open to the Bennington public, there has been an outstanding drop in attendance at many other activities. "We used to have around twenty-five members," says Sharon Wu, president of the Key Club, "but now we're lucky if two or three show up to a meeting."

Even this reporter has seen a drop in staff at the *Bennington Press* over the past few weeks. "People are interested, I think, to see what happens," says Clarissa von Dyke, judge. "It's like watching a car wreck; you don't want to see the damage, but it's impossible to look away."

Damage is certainly the right word. The students on the receiving end of the Diamonds' negative rulings are finding themselves more or less ostracized from the Bennington community.

"It's not anything official, really," says one anonymous senior on the football team. "There's no teacher being like, 'Don't like this person,' or 'This person's a loser, so don't talk to them,' but, like, the Diamonds know what they're doing. If you did something wrong, you need to be punished. It's just like in the real world."

So, readers, beware: Be nice to your friends. You never know who's gonna take you to court these days.

• **EXHIBIT J** •

"What about this one?"

"Nah," Anderson said, shaking his head.

I scanned the long, cluttered wall of Sam Ash on Forty-eighth Street and pointed to another guitar a few feet away. It was light-colored and had a pearl rosette around the center. "That one looks nice."

It was just before noon, and the store was practically empty. I should have been in calculus, but instead, Anderson had picked me up, parked his Jeep at the train station, and taken the LIRR with me into the city. Other than during the few seconds it took to hand the conductor our tickets, he'd held my hand the entire time.

"You can't choose a guitar just because it looks

nice," he said, lifting the one I had pointed to and strumming a chord. He made a face. "It has to feel just right in your hands. Like an extension of your body."

"That's creepy."

He laughed. "Yeah, you're right. But it's true."

I had never seen so many guitars in one place. Acoustic ones hanging from the walls. Electric ones propped up in the corners. Special ones on display in the middle of the room.

After an hour or so, Anderson had narrowed his search down to two: a dark mahogany one from Martin & Co. and a sea green Takamine. Dressed in a tight pair of corduroys and a black sweater, he sat on a stool, playing them both. "These are like the designer jeans of guitars," he told me.

I tried to imagine what Jed would do if he ever stumbled into a music store, and laughed. I picked up the mahogany guitar, letting the strap fall around my neck, and dragged my thumb across the strings.

"How do I sound?"

"Great," Anderson said, even though he frowned.

I sighed. "I wish I could play."

Anderson studied me as if I were the Eliza Doolittle to his Henry Higgins (*My Fair Lady*, 1956). "Here," he said, standing up and motioning to the stool. "Sit." Anderson brought his arms around my shoulders. "Your hands go like this. And this. Then take your arm and bring your two fingers together—good—and then strum."

This time, when I played, it made me smile.

"Do it again," he said, only I couldn't make one continuous sound.

"Sorry."

"It's okay. You just have to find your rhythm." He leaned forward. "Put your hands on top of mine."

I moved slowly, lining up our fingers so that they matched perfectly. His hands were warm, as if he had just taken them out of the oven, and so was his breath. I felt his cheek press against mine; the scratchiness of his stubble grazed my ear.

"See how this feels."

Anderson started playing, and my arm moved back and forth with his. After a few moments, he began changing chords; my fingers followed, shifting across the strings. It felt as if I were actually playing.

"That," I said when he stopped and removed his hands, "was incredible."

Anderson gave me a quick kiss on the cheek. "Glad you think so." Then he signaled one of the salespeople behind the desk. "I'll take this one."

Later, we walked uptown, toward Central Park. The air outside was crisp but it wasn't cold enough for gloves. We split a hot pretzel as we walked, the sun fading in tired rays across the sky.

Around Columbus Circle, we went into the park, shuffling down strips of pavement, surrounded by walls of wiry branches and leaves beginning to color red and yellow around the edges. Up ahead, a pair of mothers pushed enormous strollers, and joggers whizzed by as fast as taxis. When I saw an empty bench, I plopped down and dragged Anderson with me. He rested his new guitar case on the grass next to us.

We sat like that for a while, people-watching in silence. I couldn't help sneaking glances at Anderson, at the funny way he pursed his lips and the soft creases beneath his eyes. Finally, when he put his hand on my knee, I said, "So?"

"So," he repeated.

"Here we are."

"Yup. Here we are."

"What are you thinking about?"

He looked at me with those eyes and I felt as though my skin were translucent and he could see everything hidden inside me.

"Oh, you know," he said. "How pretty you look today."

I felt myself blush. I was wearing hardly any makeup. A soft green cable-knit scarf was tied around my neck, my jacket (brown, leather) snug and zipped.

"What are *you* thinking about?"

I wanted to say: *I'm thinking about how quickly life changes, about how a few months ago I would have dreamed of a date like this with Jed and now I'm here with you.*

I wanted to say: *I'm wondering why I can't stop thinking about you, if this is even a date at all, and, if it is, why you want to date me in the first place.*

But what I said was: "What are we doing, Anderson?"

His hand was still on my knee, and I tried hard not

121

to move. I didn't want him to pull away. "Sitting on a bench," he said.

"I'm serious. Why did you ask me to come with you today?"

"Because I like you, Marni. I like spending time with you."

"You do?"

"Don't you like spending time with me?"

"Sure," I said, "but I'm trying to figure out what's going on between us, you know? The other night at the movie theater was, well—"

"Hot?"

I rolled my eyes. "I was going to say 'intense.' And unexpected."

Anderson stretched his free hand behind my ear, cupping my neck. "Look, Marni. I like you. A lot. Is that so hard to believe?"

Yes, I thought, but I didn't say it out loud.

"It's complicated for me," I told him. "You know how upset Clarissa would be if she ever found out I was with you today, let alone if we started, well, you know."

"What?"

"You know," I said, studying his face for any sign that I was misreading the situation. "Dating."

"Marni," Anderson said, tracing my cheek with his fingers, "not everything has to be so serious. You can't make your decisions based on what Clarissa wants." He kissed me softly. "What do *you* want?"

It was a difficult question for me to answer. I wanted to be well-liked. I wanted to have friends who admired me and parents who believed in me. I wanted people to think I was funny and smart and beautiful, that I was slightly mysterious and intriguing, older than I actually was. I wanted to enjoy the rest of my time at Bennington, attend a college that would allow me to try and fail, and hopefully discover a passion for my future in the process. But most of all, I wanted for someone to care about me, to want to spend time with me, to love me. Once, I had believed Jed was that person. I was wrong. But sitting there in the middle of Central Park on a school day, I truly thought that someone could be Anderson—if I let him.

"I think," I said, "that I want to be with you. To try, at least."

Anderson kissed me again, harder this time. "Good," he said, "because that's exactly what I want."

"But, Anderson," I said, taking his hands and pressing them to my chest, "we have to keep this a secret."

He frowned. "Clarissa is your friend, Marni. She wants you to be happy."

"Not if that means dating you. I can't even begin to imagine how awful she would make things for me if she ever knew."

"So where does that leave us?"

"Right here," I said, gripping his hands even tighter. "If we're smart about it, if we don't tell anyone, I mean *anyone*, and we're careful not to raise any suspicion at school, I think we could have something really special. It's worth a shot, right?"

I was shocked by my sudden confidence. Anderson

looked deep in thought; I had never been so attracted to anyone in my entire life.

"If that's really what you want," he finally said, "then I'll do it. But at some point the truth will have to come out, Marni, and the longer we wait, the harder it will be."

This time, I leaned over to kiss him. "Let's cross that bridge when we get to it," I said. "Okay?"

He reached over to pick up his guitar. "Okay."

We rose from the bench, and before it got too dark and too cold outside, Anderson took me home.

Later that night, I received a call from Duncan, Anderson's best friend, asking me out on a date.

"What do you *mean* you're not gonna go?"

The Diamonds were lounging in Café Bennington before first period, and Clarissa was *not* happy. With me. We were seated around a small table, bags underneath the tiny metal chairs, coffees in hand. It was the day after I'd played hooky with Anderson, and I was leafing through some notes for a math test I had to make up after school. Nicole and Stephanie's trial was later that afternoon.

Priya was wearing a poncho the color of sandalwood, threaded with specks of teal and asparagus green. Her hair was down, wet with mousse and flowing every which way. "This latte is R.E.G.," she said.

"What does R.E.G. stand for?" asked Lili, looking the slightest bit frazzled.

"Really Effing Good," said Priya. "Funny, right?"

"Hysterical," Clarissa said, rolling her eyes and sloshing her latte (soy) in its paper cup. (Clarissa was beyond lactose intolerant. "If I even *smell* milk, I start farting," she'd once told me.)

There was something regal about her that day; I wasn't sure if it was her posture (straight), her complexion (flawless), or her outfit, which included a fantastic pair of skinny jeans and a plum collared shirt unbuttoned just enough to be risqué but not raunchy.

"Now, tell me again why you're reneging on your promise to go out with Duncan."

"It wasn't a promise," I said. "I'm sure Duncan will understand."

"And *what*, pray tell, is this elusive reason *why*?"

Lili placed her drink onto the table as three freshman girls walked by. They saw us, stopped, whispered, and ran. I had to admit: inspiring fear in others was kinda fun. "Is it because of Anderson?" she asked.

If I were a cartoon, this would have been the moment my jaw unhinged and skydived to the floor. "What?"

"His band is playing at the Ghost House next Friday," said Lili. "Duncan probably wants to go to that and you said no, right?"

"Wait," Clarissa interjected. "Anderson has a band?"

"Apparently," I said.

"Let me get this straight," Priya said. "Duncan asked you out on a date to see Anderson's show, and you said no in support of Clarissa?"

Despite that being as far from the truth as possible, I nodded.

Priya swooned. "You are *such* a good friend."

Clarissa looked at me with the kind of smile she usually reserved for when a college guy asked for her phone number. "Marni, that *is* really sweet of you. I'm touched, honestly, but you need this date. I want you to find Duncan and tell him that you'll go."

I was about to argue with her, but then I realized that Clarissa was basically giving me her blessing to see Anderson play. If hanging out with Duncan beforehand was the only downside, I would be an idiot not to take advantage of the situation.

"If you really think I should . . . ," I said.

"You know," said Priya, "I bet everyone is gonna go to Anderson's show and then to Ryan's Halloween party. They're on the same night."

"We should all go," Lili said. "It would be fun."

"It doesn't sound all that appealing to me," Clarissa said.

"I know, I know!" said Priya, raising her hand as if she were in class and (thought) she had the right answer. "We could invite guys, too. Anderson will already be there, and Duncan and Marni, so it will be, like, a quadruple date!"

"And who is *my* date supposed to be?" Clarissa asked. "I'm not exactly going to walk up to Anderson and start making out with him. We're broken up, remember?"

"You never know," Priya said, flicking her hair back

with her fingertips. "Maybe you'll rekindle your romance at the gig."

That might have very well been true, but this was *my* super-secret semiboyfriend we were talking about! I struggled to hide my annoyance as Clarissa finished her latte.

"I'll think about it," she said.

Just then a white-haired girl I recognized from the first jury selection smushed her face against the glass wall, peering into Café Bennington. When she saw us, her eyes lit up; she entered timidly, at a snail's pace.

"Can we help you?" Priya asked.

Clarissa turned around. "Arlene. There you are." She glanced at the clock hanging a few feet away. "You're three minutes late. That's unacceptable."

"S-sorry, Clarissa," the girl said, rocking her scrawny legs back and forth. "I walked."

"Can't one of your parents drive you?"

Arlene shook her head. Her eyes looked watery; I wondered if she was about to cry. "They both leave early for work."

"Well then," Clarissa said carefully, "tomorrow you should get a taxi." She turned her attention back to the table. "Oh, I forgot to tell you guys. I have a new personal assistant. Her name is Arlene." She pointed to the girl. "Arlene, these are my best friends. If any of them ask you to do something, just do it, okay?"

"S-sure, Clarissa," Arlene said, wiping her nose with the back of her hand.

"That's disgusting." Clarissa reached into her bag,

pulled out a tissue, and threw it at Arlene. "Do you have the files I gave you?"

"Absolutely." Arlene took out a purple folder and handed it to Clarissa.

"That's all," Clarissa said. "Oh, and, Arlene?"

"Yes?"

Clarissa tilted her head. "I appreciate you." Then she pointed to the door.

"What," Priya said once the girl had disappeared, "was that?"

"Since when do you have a personal assistant?" Lili asked.

"She came up to me the other day and wanted to help."

I laughed. "Help what?"

"Don't be jealous," Clarissa said.

"Believe me, I'm not."

First period was about to start. I reached underneath my chair, grasping the handle of my bag, when Lili said, "What's this?"

In her hand was a piece of paper from Clarissa's folder. Lili examined it for a few seconds and then passed it around the table. Printed in a single row was a list of half a dozen names; I immediately recognized them as the six jurors Jenny Murphy and Eric Ericsson had originally selected.

"That," Clarissa said once we'd all had a chance to read it, "is a list of people I want *out* of mock trial."

Priya raised her eyebrows. "Why? They're just on the jury. It's not like they actually *do* anything."

Lili gave Priya a crazy look. "You're not serious, are you?"

"What?"

"The jury does more than we originally thought," Clarissa said, taking the piece of paper and laying it in front of her. "If they don't vote in our favor, then we *lose*. And we can't afford to lose."

I cleared my throat. "Is this because of what happened on Monday?"

Fact: On Monday, we'd had our first mistrial. Due to a lack of evidence, the jury was unable to determine whether Sean Martin (junior) was guilty of two-timing his girlfriend, Lexa Roth (senior), with an unnamed redhead who attended the Friends School, another prep school on Long Island.

It wouldn't have been a big deal, except that Clarissa actually *liked* Lexa (they'd had bio together sophomore year) and had pulled out all the stops during the trial, expecting Sean to be found guilty. Sean was friends with Jenny Murphy, though, and also with some of the jury members Jenny had picked; Clarissa was convinced that his personal connections had swayed the vote. Clearly, she was upset.

"I'm not going through all the trouble of reenvisioning this mock trial team to have Jenny Murphy's lackeys mess everything up," Clarissa said. "They've *got* to go. Then we can replace them with people we *know* will vote in our favor."

"You do know that's, like, illegal," I said to Clarissa, making sure I understood her correctly. "Townsen is never going to allow you to kick people out just because you don't think they're going to vote in your favor."

"What about kicking them out if they're fugly?" Priya asked. "Do you think he would allow that?"

"No," said Lili. "We would need solid evidence of them, like, breaking school rules or doing something that would prove them incompetent and biased jurors. And we don't have that, because it doesn't exist."

Clarissa smoothed the collar of her shirt with her fingers and tucked back the fiery waves of her hair. "Well," she said, "not *yet*."

I had the feeling Clarissa was gearing up for something *huge*, but I didn't know what. While I was certainly concerned, my pending date with Duncan overshadowed my mind like thick, dark clouds on a rainy day.

I found him in the hallway before sixth period. He was wearing a light blue oxford shirt and khakis, his black-brown hair parted at the side.

"Hi," I said. "I got your message last night."

His eyes widened. "And?"

"How about Friday night? You can take me to see Anderson's show, and then we can go to Ryan's party afterwards."

"Cool," he said. "I mean, great. I mean, I'm looking forward to it."

He sounded so sincere that I wanted to take him by the shoulders and whisper the truth into his ear, but I couldn't. I was doing this for me. For Anderson. So I channeled Clarissa and blew him a kiss, acting as casual and carefree as possible.

"Pick me up at seven," I said. "Bye."

Then I made my way to class.

♦ 9 ♦

The enumeration in the Constitution, of certain rights, shall not be construed to deny or disparage others retained by the people.
—*The Ninth Amendment*
to the United States Constitution

Once Anderson was officially in my life, everything was different.

I no longer spent hours obsessing over Jed and how I "Used to Love Him" (Fiona Apple, 2005); my grades improved; I was happier, healthier, and more fun to be around. I didn't even push any freshmen in the hallways. Well, I *hardly* pushed any freshmen in the hallways.

Really, I let Clarissa, Lili, and Priya take the lead. I loved the trials; don't get me wrong. Sitting next to my best friends and laying down social law was the highlight of my day. But looking back, I'm not sure I could even tell you what most of them were about. I thought only of Anderson, of the way we stared knowingly at each other in the halls, the time I spent with him in the early evenings at his house. I still felt incredibly guilty about lying to Clarissa, but I was In Love. What was I supposed to do? All I wanted was for her to start dating someone. Anyone. Then, once I was sure she was really over Anderson and her feelings wouldn't be hurt, I could tell her. He and I could start dating out in the open. No more sneaking around. It wasn't the best plan ever, but it was all I had.

After listening to Anderson practice his new guitar for what seemed like forever, his show was only a few days away. I couldn't *wait*. Nothing else even crossed my mind until the Diamonds helmed a trial that, for multiple reasons, would have tremendous consequences.

Reason No. 1: It was the first trial for which Mr. Townsen would *not* be present. Since the daily number of applications we received sufficiently outweighed the amount of time we had at mock trial meetings (no one—me included—ever wanted to stay past five o'clock), and since Townsen was thoroughly impressed with our work, the Diamonds were now allowed to hold after-school trials any day of the week. "I trust you girls to follow the letter of the law," he'd told us. Lili and I would be serving as judges, while Clarissa and Priya represented the prosecution and the defense, respectively.

The only person this pissed off was Jenny Murphy, whose other extracurriculars made it impossible for her to attend additional meetings. Eric Ericsson and

Sherry Something were also unable to attend the new meetings, as were three of the jury members who, along with Jenny Murphy, were Mathletes.

Clarissa immediately replaced the jurors with three of her choice—Michelle Adalgo, Robin Berningham, and Eileen Smith, freshmen girls who worshipped the ground she walked on. She also began planning character-assassination plots for the remaining jurors—Michael Tompson, Nicole Morrey, and Joy Darling—who she felt were working against her.

Reason No. 2: This was the first trial that Principal Newman would be attending. Unlike most school administrators, Principal Newman was a moron. Two years earlier, he'd forgotten the name of our school at an assembly. ("Welcome, Barmingham students!") He was old and tired and didn't do much of anything. How he'd held on to his job for so long was beyond me, though I think the parents of Bennington students actually preferred a principal they could easily manipulate over someone they, well, couldn't.

Principal Newman would be observing the trial before (potentially) approving the plan to let us—I mean, mock trial—dole out punishments for certain students *instead* of the dean.

Reason No. 3: I'd finally finished the new version of the Bill of Rights Clarissa had asked me to write. Supposedly, Priya had finished her robes, and Clarissa insisted that all four of us wear them. Now that we were holding trials completely on our own, without

Townsen, it was important for us to "look as fierce as possible."

Knowing Priya, I hoped they weren't see-through.

I arrived for the trial almost ten minutes early. Priya and Lili were in tow, along with three iced coffees (french vanilla) and once iced latte (mocha). Directly across from the chorus room was a faculty bathroom, which we weren't supposed to use, but that had never stopped us before.

Clarissa was already inside, applying her lipstick at the mirror. "There you are."

Priya took a black valise from underneath her arm. "Here are the outfits," she said. "They're not so much *robes* as they are *really amazing dresses with sleeves*, so be careful with them."

Priya unzipped the garment bag and withdrew the robes one by one.

Mine fit like a second skin. The black material wrapped itself around my waist and fell just below the knees; the sleeves were long and billowy. For something so low-cut, it was surprisingly conservative. I was impressed.

Priya twisted her shoulders like a Vegas showgirl. "If you're going to have a *trial*, you'd better do it in *style*."

Clarissa fixed her hair in front of the mirror and adjusted her pendant. She looked like she belonged on the cover of a magazine called *I'm Gonna Punish You*. "Does everyone have their diamond on?"

I glanced down at my neckline. Check.

"Marni, do you have the modified constitution?"

I reached into my bag and pulled out the pages I'd printed off the computer. "I'm not sure if this is exactly what you had in mind." I had altered only the first ten constitutional amendments, which made up the Bill of Rights; they were the ones most people knew.

"Marni," she said once she was done looking them over. "These are amazing. So funny."

"Really?"

"This must have taken you *hours*," said Lili.

"Let me see, let me see!" Priya said, doing the Hokey-Pokey with her hands. "I wanna see!"

"I'm happy to help," I said. And I *was*. It's not often I can put my semiobscure knowledge of the Constitution to use (while exhausting my father's personal library). Clarissa turned her attention back to the mirror. "What should we *call* it? We need something really . . . you know. Jazzy."

"What if we called it the Diamond Rules? Marni made them with us in mind, and we *do* want people to follow them, or at least pretend to," Lili suggested.

"*The Diamond Rules*," said Priya. "Classy."

Clarissa smiled. "I like it."

Outside the faculty bathroom, things were less serene. A bunch of kids rushed past us, no doubt trying to find last-minute seats for the trial. I hadn't gotten far before I heard the voice of a boy I liked to pretend did not exist.

Tommy.

"Wait up, Marni!" he said. "I need to talk to you."

I hadn't forgotten that Tommy was supposedly writing an article about me.

"What do *you* want?" Clarissa asked, stepping beside me and scowling.

"To apologize," he said. Tommy loosened the neck of his shirt (light purple, a daring color for any high school guy to wear, let alone one without a girlfriend). "Sorry I bothered you the other day, Marni."

"Apology accepted," Clarissa said for me. "Now, if you don't mind, the club for dork-ass virgins who aren't going to get laid for at least the next five years"—she sniffed the air—"and who smell bad is meeting in the *band* room."

Tommy crossed his arms. "I guess *this* isn't a good time to talk about the article, either?"

"What article?" asked Clarissa.

"I'm, uh, trying to put an article together about Marni, and—"

"About Marni? Why?"

"That's sort of what I wanted to talk to you—I mean, her—about."

Clarissa grabbed hold of his shirt and practically threw him inside the chorus room. She moved so quickly I barely had time to blink. I'd never known she was so strong.

"I'll give you something to write about."

"Totally in conclusion," Priya said in her closing statement, which was more coherent than I'd expected,

"Joy Darling, a juror and a terrible dresser, has been accepting, like, bribes in turn for her vote. You've heard from three brave"—Priya motioned to the sophomores sitting together a few feet away—"and fashionable witnesses who have each admitted to paying Joy off. Now it's up to *you* guys to, like, decide her fate." Priya curtseyed. "Thanks."

I had never been less prepared for a trial. Usually, Clarissa and I knew beforehand the details of the case from the application and discussed a game plan. This time around, there was no application; Clarissa had organized the trial herself, and I knew from our conversation in Café Bennington that it was totally bogus. It was also the first time I'd stepped out from behind the judges' bench and was acting as the prosecution. (Clarissa wanted to ensure that everything ran smoothly for Principal Newman.)

Joy Darling, who was definitely *not* the kind of girl who would ever accept a bribe (she had bangs, for crying out loud), sat next to me, on the verge of tears. The girls who had supposedly bribed her—Liza Vorla, Sheila Covington, and Mary Black—would have done anything to get on Clarissa's good side. Who knew what she'd promised them in return for lying.

"Thank you," Clarissa said. Lili was next to her, a serious expression on her face.

I turned to Joy, who was dabbing her right eye with a tissue.

"Marni, the defense may present its case."

I didn't *have* a case. No one could refute the girls'

statements except for Joy, and frankly, it was highly unlikely that anyone would believe her.

"Joy," I said softly, tapping her shoulder. "What do you want to do?"

She stopped with the tissue and stared at me blankly. One eye, I realized, was smaller than the other and slightly wonky. Her cheeks were red and puffed out like a chipmunk's.

"Do you want to testify?"

"What's the point?" she asked. I couldn't think of one. "Clarissa is out to get me." Her eyes started to water. "I just don't know what I did wrong. Do you?"

"Uh, no," I said, crossing my legs. I didn't even have any paper in front of me to shuffle. What a disaster. "If you don't want to take the stand, Joy, I'm not sure what else there is to do."

Joy took a fresh tissue from her pocket and blew into it so hard I thought her nose fell off. "Whatever you think is best," she said.

The room had been silent the entire time, and Clarissa repeated my name. "The defense may begin."

I stood up. At this point there was no way Joy would be found innocent, but at least for Principal Newman's sake, I wanted to give some semblance of a proper trial. "Joy Darling would like to assert that the allegations against her are false. She does not have any proof, but since the evidence is entirely circumstantial and based on witness testimony, it's up to you, the jurors, to decide who is telling the truth."

I looked at the jury, the eleven students I had helped

139

Clarissa pick (Joy had no alternate), and couldn't help cringing. Carrie May had her cell phone in her hand, and I could tell she'd been texting the whole time. Emmy Montgomery was applying lip gloss even now, as I spoke, and Ronnie Yelman was ogling Clarissa as if she were a filet mignon at Henry's, the most expensive steakhouse on Long Island. The only people who were paying attention were Michael Tompson and Nicole Morrey, who knew something was fishy and would no doubt be Clarissa's next victims.

As frustrating as it was, I couldn't really be mad. I had assisted Clarissa every step of the way; so had Lili and Priya. I'd issued just as many punishments as Clarissa. The sudden power of the mock trial team was our responsibility, too. And while I didn't really care what happened to Joy Darling (sorry, Joy), I had an icky feeling she was only the first of many to come.

I turned to Clarissa and Lili, who were fixing their robes. "The defense rests."

Once the trial was over, we took a ten-minute break for the jury to deliberate.

"Wonderful job, girls," Principal Newman bumbled, approaching the front of the room. His tie was crooked and one of the buttons on his dress shirt was undone. "Incredible."

"I'm *so* glad you liked it," Clarissa said, pointing to Kathy Shiblay, the mock trial team stenographer. "Kathy could make you a copy of the transcript if you like."

Principal Newman adjusted his glasses. "No, no, that won't be necessary. It was like I was in a real courtroom," he said. "It gave me chills. Well, either it was the trial or the ice pack I'm using for my knee"—he pointed to his right leg—"but I definitely had chills. Brrr!"

"So," Clarissa said, "Principal Newman, do you think you'll approve the proposal from student government?"

"Well, Ms. von Dyke, I do need to think about it," he said, "but I can't imagine why not."

Clarissa smiled with both rows of her teeth. "Wonderful!"

"I should be running," Principal Newman said, reaching out to shake each of our hands. "Stop by my office sometime this week, girls, and we'll discuss all the details."

Once he was out of earshot, Lili raised her eyebrows. "That seemed promising."

"Definitely," Clarissa said, turning to me. "You look sad, Marni. What's wrong?"

I wanted to say: *Aren't we taking this a little too far?*

I wanted to say: *What did Joy Darling ever do to us?*

But I couldn't. What I said was: "Nothing. I'm fine."

People started taking their seats again, visibly eager to hear the jury's verdict. Out the corner of my eye, I saw Joy devouring a chocolate bar and full-on crying.

"Good," Clarissa said. "Because we have a trial to finish."

After Joy was officially found guilty and removed from the jury (I never knew a person could produce that many tears or have such severe camel toe), I said good-bye to the Diamonds and headed toward the student parking lot.

"Hey, Marni. Wait a sec."

Tommy was running to catch up with me.

"If you think I'm going to sit down for an interview with you right now, you're out of your mind." I continued walking down the senior hallway, past my locker, and out the back exit. Tommy stayed right by my side.

"Nah," he said eventually. "I'm okay for now."

"Stop," I said once I'd reached my car. It was dark now. Bright lights filled the student parking lot as if it were a football stadium.

"Stop what?"

"Following me."

"I'm not following you." He pointed to the ancient red Buick wedged next to my Ford Taurus. "That's my ride. I'm not that creepy, Valentine."

Tommy opened his door and slipped into the driver's seat. He started his engine and pulled out of the cramped spot. "But that guy is."

I snapped my neck and peered into my car. Someone was sitting in my passenger seat, with a backpack in his lap and an outrageous grin.

"Hi," Anderson said.

"You scared me," I said, climbing inside and shutting the door behind me.

"You shouldn't leave your car unlocked. Some guy could sneak inside after football practice and have his way with you." He leaned over to kiss me; I closed my eyes and felt the tip of his tongue brush against my lips.

"I thought we were going to be careful," I said. "Tommy saw you."

"He doesn't know it was me."

"Maybe he does." I could hear the paranoia in my own voice. "What if I was giving one of the girls a ride home? They would have seen you in my car and—"

"Okay, okay, I get it." Anderson took my head in his hands and kissed my nose. "It won't happen again."

"Thanks."

"So."

"So . . ."

"Wanna come over?" Anderson wiggled his ears. "I'll be good, I promise. Or I can be bad," he said, lowering his voice. "Whatever you want."

"Well, when you put it that way . . . ," I said, coaxing the gas pedal. "Let's go."

THE BENNINGTON PRESS
Diamonds Team Up with Student Gov't

By: TOMMY PAYNE

October 28—It's official. The Diamond Court has joined forces with the Bennington Student Government, uniting two of the most powerful student groups on campus.

Principal Newman had this to say: "It's a very exciting time here at Bennington. Students are taking justice into their own hands, and we have decided to support them, providing the necessary backing for them to succeed."

Although Dean Meyerson still has his job, the mock trial team will now be allowed to issue detention and suspension for students who break school rules.

"It gives us a lot more cred," says Lili Chan-Mohego, current student body president and mock trial member, "and allows us the opportunity to really deliver justice to the halls of Bennington."

But there are some who voice a different opinion. "One group having so much power is *not* a good thing," says an anonymous senior. "It eliminates the idea of checks and balances our current government has in place."

When questioned, Mr. Townsen, faculty advisor for the mock trial team, had this to say: "Perhaps this does place a great deal of power in the mock trial team's hands, but these students have shown they are more than capable of being fair to their peers."

Let's hope the power doesn't go to their heads.

♦ 10 ♦

The powers not delegated to the United
States by the Constitution, nor prohibited by
it to the States, are reserved to the States respectively, or to the people.
—The Tenth Amendment
to the United States Constitution

If you're in high school on Long Island, the Ghost
House is *the* place to be.

It's this tiny coffeehouse about twenty-five minutes
from where I lived, the sort of place that, if you didn't
know it existed, you would never find. The lights are
perpetually dimmed; the walls are adorned with fantastic artwork; and every table has a blue candle that
flickers and burns a scent I can never quite describe—
rain, sea, salt—while paper cutouts of ghosts and
ghouls (female ghosts) hang from the ceiling and sway
in unison. On the weekends there are always live
bands. It's the perfect spot to go for a good time, which
is why, I suppose, Jed never took me there. ("Oh,
Marni, it's so loud. Don't you think? Honestly.")

"Here we are," Duncan said, opening the door and whisking me inside. "Wow, it's really packed."

It was Friday, the night of Anderson's show, and Duncan had picked me up twenty minutes earlier in his shiny Rav4. He was wearing a worn pair of jeans that weren't too tight and a striped button-down; his hair was gelled and ocean-wavy; and if I weren't head-over-heels obsessed with his best friend, I might have entertained the possibility that this *was* in fact a date.

But, of course, it wasn't.

Before I knew it, Clarissa and Lili were in front of me. "Hey," I said as Clarissa grabbed my hand and sat me down at a table that said RESERVED. Her skin dazzled with glimmery body lotion. Lili was standing next to her in a corduroy skirt and a gray sweater. Priya was nowhere in sight.

"Do you want something to drink?" Duncan asked, sliding his hand on top of mine. I had the urge to shake it off immediately, but let it rest there for a moment. "I'll go up to the bar."

"I'd love an Iced Blaze."

"Cool," he said. "Lili? Clarissa?"

Lili ordered a regular coffee with skim milk. Clarissa, without blinking, ordered: "a nonfat soy latte, no whip, with one Equal and a hint of vanilla. Stirred. *Soy*," she repeated. "No milk."

"Uh, sure," Duncan said, obviously wishing he had a pen and some paper. "Be right back."

Once he was out of earshot, Clarissa squealed like a fifth-grader. "So?"

146

"What?" I asked.

"Come on, Marni," Lili said, pushing up her sleeves. "You're on your first date since—"

"Your boyfriend tragically dumped you in front of the entire school," Clarissa finished. "I want *all* the details."

"There's nothing to tell. It's not exactly a *date* if your best friends are at the same table."

"Don't worry," Clarissa said. "At Ryan's party you can have him *all* to yourself."

I was about to make some sort of joke, but then she said, "I'm *so* happy you're out with a nice guy, Marni. You deserve it."

The only reason I'd agreed to go to the show with Duncan in the first place was to appease Clarissa, and in turn see Anderson, so it wouldn't kill me to at least *pretend* I was having a good time.

"You know what's amazing?" Clarissa's eyes jumped from table to table in an intricate ballet.

"What?"

"Look around," she said. I did. There were a few people I didn't recognize, but mostly it was the familiar Bennington crowd. People were chatting and having a good time, waiting for the lights to dim (as if the room could get any darker) and for the music to start. "Notice anything?"

"I don't see JeDarcy. Is that who you're talking about?"

"Sort of," she said. "They're not here."

"Thank God," I said, relieved. Being stuck in a

coffeehouse with your boyfriend trifecta—ex, pretend, and secret—wasn't exactly a winning situation. "Jed hates this place, anyway."

"That's *not* why he isn't here," Clarissa said with an I-know-something-you-don't-know smile. "Take another look around."

After a few minutes, I realized what she was getting at. None of our trial "victims" were here, meaning they didn't dare show their faces. As I continued to peruse the crowd, I realized that everyone, in some way, was staring at me. At us. There was a sort of force field around our table that no one dared to penetrate.

Before I could comment, Duncan was back, accompanied by Ryan, drinks in hand.

"Hey," Ryan said, taking a seat. "Are you guys stoked for my party? It's gonna be awesome. I got a keg and everything." Ryan's older brother was twenty-four and still lived at home; he was always available to buy booze. "And, of course, liquor for the ladies."

"Is your drink good?" Duncan asked softly.

I nodded. "Thanks."

"Here you guys are!" a voice called from over my shoulder. I turned around and there was Priya, in a shimmery gold lamé top and black jeans. A sheepish-looking Tiger was right behind her. "Is this some table or what?"

Tiger, I noticed, looked incredible sweaty; his hair, which at some point in the evening had probably been spiked up, limped to the side. Clarissa raised one eyebrow suggestively and tilted her head toward the bathroom.

Gross.

Priya sipped what looked like a glass of water. "I guess it's good to know people in high places, huh?"

"I'll drink to that," Clarissa said, making no move to touch her latte.

Duncan pointed to her drink. "Did I get you the right thing?"

"Oh, I think so," Clarissa said in a saccharine tone. "I'm just waiting for Arlene to test it and make sure it's not poisoned."

I laughed but, since I had Iced Blaze in my mouth, wound up spitting onto the table. I quickly wiped my napkin across the surface. "You're not serious, are you?"

Clarissa looked shocked by my question. "Of course," she said, motioning to the rest of the coffee-house with one hand. "I don't want to end up like Caesar, Marni. That's what happens to people in positions of power."

"But no one except the barista even touched your drink," I said. "Well, and Duncan."

Clarissa shrugged.

After a minute or so, I was forced to realize a certain truth: Clarissa thought she was important enough that someone at Bennington would actually try to *poison* her. Just then Arlene showed up at the table, her hairline dotted with sweat.

"I'm *so* sorry I'm late," she said, panting. "I was waiting for my mom to come home so she could drive me, and—"

"Next time take a cab," Clarissa said, pushing her latte to the edge of the table. "Now, taste this for me and make sure it isn't poisoned. Or roofied."

"I'm sick," Arlene said. "I probably shouldn't."

Clarissa made an actual hissing noise, like a snake. "If I wanted your life story, Arlene, I'd text you, saying, *Dearest Arlene, I value your friendship so much and care so greatly about what you think! Come over to my house as soon as you can. . . . We'll have a sleepover and braid each other's hair and make brownies in my Easy-Bake oven!* Did I send you a text like that?"

Arlene glanced at her phone as though she half expected one to magically appear. "No? I mean, I don't think so, Clarissa."

"Then drink up."

The entire table watched Arlene take one sip, then two. "It tastes fine to me."

Clarissa took back the drink. "That's all. Oh, and, Arlene?"

"Yes?"

"I appreciate you."

Arlene backed away from the table slowly until I could no longer see her. "Whoa," said Ryan with disbelief. "You're, like, evil."

Clarissa smiled and raised her glass. "To senior year," she said.

"To senior year," we all repeated, and as we did, the lights dimmed. Anderson was about to begin.

Everyone clapped and cheered, a few of Anderson's buddies yelling things like "Yeah, St. James!" and "I want your balls, Anderson!" as a joke. (I think.) Clarissa grabbed my hand underneath the table, and I suddenly remembered that she was his ex-girlfriend; it was probably hard for her to be there, with Anderson getting all the glory, her own face masked by the dark lights and shadows thrown by the candles. I thought about how I would feel if Jed were up there, about to play his own music (the very idea was ludicrous). I'm pretty sure I would have cried.

"Are you okay?" I whispered.

Clarissa squeezed my hand. "I'm just glad you're here with me."

That was the amazing thing about Clarissa. She could act so rude and superior all the time but really, inside, she was a little girl.

Anderson's music was incredible. The first thing he played was "I Hope You Don't Kill Me in My Sleep," a funktastic song about trying to break up with a girl who won't take no for an answer. (I had to keep reminding myself it wasn't about me.) I was surprised by how smart his lyrics were; he sounded like a real musician, not just some arrogant high school kid who'd picked up a guitar and thought he was the Next Big Thing.

The other guys were awesome, too—a drummer

named Jared and this guy Marshall on bass. (Anderson introduced them.) Anderson looked hot underneath the lights; he was born to play music in front of a crowd. I knew then and there, as he kissed the mic and sang about love and death and heartache and sex (I wondered, *How does he know about all these things?*), that no matter what, he was The One, and that night we would take our relationship to the next level (aka get freaknasty with it).

"Thanks so much for coming out, guys," Anderson said into the microphone. "There's one more song I'd like to play tonight. I've never played it for anyone before, so it might totally suck." He laughed, and I wanted to melt, like the candle on the table, and have him scoop me into his arms and reshape me. "But I don't think so. It's about this girl who's really special to me, and who, you know, changed my life. It's pretty deep."

He gave a quick nod to Marshall and Jared and began tapping his foot on the stage. "Here goes. It's called 'Into Your Eyes.'"

> *I used to wear these colors proud*
> *But they're fading*
>
> *I used to live my life out loud*
> *But that noise is grating*
>
> *Hold me close so the moment won't pass*
> *The weekend flies by and we're right back in class*

If only we could be honest
But we promised
I hope you've got a plan
'Cause these secrets are killing me

I used to hold my head up high
But not since I dissed her

So I let you pass me in the hall
With a wink or whisper

Kiss me hard and our secret is out
My guitar chords ring doubt after doubt

If only we could be honest
But we promised
I hope you've got a plan
'Cause these secrets are killing me

Everybody here's got a problem with us both
So I paint and you write
And we savor the night
As we make our faithful oath

But if my heart breaks, I can't take it
So I look into the stands
As my heart beats with the band's
And I see right through her eyes
Right into yours

I see over their helmets into the lights
But if I look right into their eyes, I can see all my
   nights before me

I sink into my groove
They're all looking at me
Waiting for my move

Everybody here's got a problem with us both
So I paint and you write
And we savor the night
And we make our faithful oath

But if my heart breaks, I can't take it
So I look into the stands
As my heart beats with the band's
And I see right through her eyes
Right into yours."

· EXHIBIT L ·

When it was over, the lights went from extra-dim to regular-dim and I sat motionless in my chair.

"I never knew Anderson was so intense," Duncan said.

I imagined that when Anderson saw Duncan and me together, a ball of jealousy would grow and burst inside him, exploding through his pores, out every inch of his body. There would be a brawl, perhaps, and Duncan and Anderson would trade punches over me, and somehow, in the middle of it all, Jed—who wasn't even at the show but would appear magically out of thin air—would get pushed between them and they would (accidentally) punch his head off. He would be rushed to the hospital, but there'd be nothing the doctors could do for him; Darcy would cry rivers and oceans and I would say, *It's okay, I'll handle it,* taking his head and wrapping it in a box with a beautiful bow to give to Darcy as a present. Clarissa and the girls would videotape the exchange and Anderson would be waiting for me in a horse and buggy and we would ride together into the darkness and I would lose my virginity to him.

"Me either," I said.

"Let's go." Ryan got up from the table. "We gotta beat the crowd."

I felt for my purse and Clarissa grabbed my hand. "I'm just going to steal her for a moment, okay?" she told Duncan. "We'll be right back."

Clarissa dragged me toward the bathroom, parting the throng of people with a simple gesture. Once we were inside the ladies' room, she leaned against the door. "That song," she said, "wasn't it . . . incredible?"

You mean my song?

"Yeah," I said. "It was."

"I think it was a sign." She looked ethereal, hair over her eyes, skin perfect and milky and clear. "I think Anderson wants me back." She lowered her voice slightly. "And I think I want him back, too. I'm going to tell him at the party tonight. I mean, how could I not, after hearing that song? He said I *changed* his *life*."

Clarissa did a little jump, and all I could think of was how much I wanted to punch her in the face.

155

I'm sure I don't have to tell you how crazy house parties are, and how dumb it is to throw them while your parents are away. But Ryan had been doing this since he'd gotten his braces removed, and his parties were perfect to the very last detail.

They were *not* open to the general Bennington public; you had to be invited. Very A-list. And since the invention of the Diamond Court, that list had been getting smaller every day. This left tons of room for drinking, dancing, smoking, and general naughtiness in practically every corner of Ryan's not-so-humble abode.

Debauchery at its finest.

While I certainly wanted to have a good time, I had one goal in mind: getting to Anderson before Clarissa did. She might have been my best friend, but I wasn't about to let her misinterpretation of a love song lead to the loss of my secret boyfriend. Clarissa was the girl who'd dumped Anderson and broken his heart; she was the girl who could have any guy she wanted at the snap of her fingers. (This is actually true; I've seen her snap her fingers and make a guy fall in love with her. His name was Dennis Abramson, and it was the ninth grade.)

She didn't need Anderson. Not like I did.

The party was going strong by the time we got there. Ryan lived in a tremendous mansion in a ritzy neighborhood. The house was set back at the end of a long, winding driveway with foreboding trees and granite statues everywhere. During the day, the ambiance would have been romantic; at night, it was a bit scary.

Inside, a makeshift bar was set up in the corner, bottles standing like soldiers at attention; some type of electronica was blasting through strategically placed speakers.

"Can I get you a drink?" Duncan asked.

"Sure," I said. "Vodka and some kind of juice?"

"At your service," he said. I took the opportunity to fix my face in the bathroom. I was pleasantly surprised. My makeup hadn't smeared, and my hair was finally at the point where I didn't look like an eight-year-old boy; I was wearing just the right amount of lipstick, my boobs looked perky, and after a quick touch-up, I was ready to go.

"Hi, Marni," Rebecca Steade, a pretty blond lacrosse player, said to me as I left the bathroom. "You look gorgeous. *So* effing fierce. Like a mountain lion."

"Thanks," I said.

I sauntered over to the bar. "Let me," I said, grabbing a cup with reddish liquid from Duncan. There was no ice and way too much alcohol.

"I didn't get a chance to tell you before," Duncan said hesitantly, "but you look, like, *really* pretty."

"Aww," I said. "That's sweet."

"Wanna dance?"

I finished my drink in one gulp and handed it back to him. "Maybe later?"

"Sure." Duncan nodded. He seemed disappointed, but not devastated. "I'll get you a refill."

By the time I found who I was looking for, I'd had three more drinks, two of which I'd taken from other people while they weren't paying attention. I would say, looking back, that I was pretty drunk. Not enough to stumble and fall or throw up all over myself, but the sort of drunk that makes you feel tingly all over and so numb that everything—lights, sounds, people—in the world (or in my case, the house party) seems beautiful.

There he was, leaning against the wooden railing of the staircase: Anderson. He was chatting with Amy Spanger, who (supposedly) was addicted to painkillers, (supposedly) had had two nose jobs, and (supposedly) had made a YouTube video in which she humped her dog to the sound track of the movie *Xanadu*, had posted it for five minutes, and then had taken it down. Beer in hand, he excused himself and walked toward me with the sort of swagger that made me want to rip his jeans off and sew them into a jean pillow that had *I HEART ANDERSON* written in big swirly letters. Just kidding. It was the kind of swagger that made me want to Do It.

"Hi," he said. We were standing closer than we'd ever stood in public. I could smell his breath on my face—sweet, intoxicating.

"Hi."

"Follow me," Anderson said, scanning the hallway. He opened the first door he saw and dragged me inside.

It was a closet. Pitch-black. I didn't mind at all. I grabbed his collar and pulled until he was on top of me.

"You were incredible tonight," I said, taking a breath. "That song . . ."

"You liked it?"

I ran my fingers across his face, tracing the wispy feel of his eyebrows; the strong, straight slope of his nose; his cheeks; and his lips, wet from mine. "I loved it." And then, because I had to, I asked, "It was about me, right?"

"Mmm," he said, and then he kissed me. That was all I needed to hear.

If you had told me that I was going to lose my virginity in the hall closet of Ryan Brauer's house, jocks crushing Coors Lights on their foreheads and playing beer pong a mere few feet away, Kylie Minogue singing, "La, la, la," in the background, I would not have believed you.

But there I was, kissing Anderson, my arms wrapped around his neck, when I felt something hard against my leg. At first I thought it was a sneaker, or a hanger (we were, after all, in a closet), but when I shifted my weight and it was still there, I realized that it was neither of those things.

"What are you doing?" he asked between kisses. He was still on top of me, but my fingers were clawing at his jeans. I unzipped them. I couldn't see anything, it was so dark. The heat between us was incredible.

"Hold on," he said, reaching underneath my arms and tugging at my sweater. Before I knew it, his hands were behind my back, slipping off my jeans and resting on my hips, just above my underwear.

159

"Are you sure?" he asked.

For that moment, there were only two people in the world: Anderson and me. Everything else faded into black and white, into gray, into nothingness.

"Yes," I said, and then his face was in my breasts, and I felt him in my hand. "Wait," I said, resting against his chest, which was bare and exposed, tense beneath my fingertips, his shirt crumpled on the floor. "Do you have a condom?"

"Yeah," he said, which surprised me. I heard him reach into his jeans and rip the foil. He kissed me again, slipping off my underwear, and I thought, *This is it. This is everything I've ever wanted.*

Then the light flicked on, and I was blinded by my nakedness, and his nakedness. The door flew open. Before I could move (there was no time to do anything but freeze), a sea of faces stared down at me— Duncan's, Priya's, Lili's, Ryan's, faces I had never seen before, shocked faces—and in the center of them all was Clarissa's, eyebrows arched in surprise, mouth pulled together in a tiny O that said a million things and nothing at once.

And I remember thinking: *My life is over.*

◆   ◆   ◆

The next day, nobody returned my calls.

When I stopped by each one of the Diamonds' houses on Sunday afternoon, they were conspicuously "unavailable." I even went to our regular brunch at

Bistro, but they were nowhere to be found. By Monday morning, what had happened at Ryan's party was all over school. For discretionary reasons, I won't repeat the gossip here, but know that it was awful, and that by third period, the entire school was under the belief that there was a sex tape of me, Anderson, and a live chicken floating around the Internet.

AP Lit with the twins was the worst.

"I heard she has 'I heart Anderson' tattooed across her back," Dana said while Mrs. Bloom drew stick figures of Romeo and Juliet on the board. "And underneath that, 'I heart balls.' "

"I heard that Lili and Priya never even liked her," said Dara, "and the *real* reason Jed dumped her is because she has warts. Not the kind on your feet, either."

The Diamonds weren't at lunch; they didn't show up for government, either.

Nobody was outright rude to me, but everyone stayed far, far away. The only human contact I had that entire day was two seconds with Anderson after art class, when he whispered, "Call me later, it's gonna be okay," into my ear and fled down the hallway before I could follow.

After school, Duncan was waiting for me at my locker with an incredibly peculiar expression on his face.

"Hi, Duncan," I started, "I'm really—"

He held up his hand. "Whatever, Marni. I'm just here to give you this."

Duncan handed me a thin slip of paper, which I

161

immediately recognized (I'd helped design them, and conceived the entire text): it was a subpoena, the kind the Diamonds slipped into peoples' lockers if they were supposed to appear at a trial.

"It's for today," he said, leaving before I could reply.

That was okay. I didn't feel much like talking.

There were more people in the chorus room for my trial than for all the previous ones combined. People were clumped around the doorway, balancing on their toes to see inside. To see me.

Clarissa, Priya, and Lili looked formidable and gorgeous in their chic black robes; I thought about mine lying in its garment bag somewhere, and about how—now more than ever—all I wanted to do was put it on and stand beside them.

Members of the jury scowled at me. Neither Mr. Townsen nor Principal Newman was anywhere to be found. Only the Diamonds and me, separated by a judges' bench and an apology.

Clarissa looked stone cold. "You are being charged with multiple offenses, Ms. Valentine, including First-Degree Backstabbing with Intention to Hurt, Second-Degree Being a Huge Slut, and Third-Degree Fugliness. How do you plead?"

Despite everything, I couldn't help laughing at the ridiculousness of the entire scenario. "Is this for real?"

"We need your answer," Priya said.

"Why didn't you return any of my calls?" I asked.

"Please note that the defendant refuses to answer

the question," Clarissa said stiffly, "which automatically enters a default plea of guilty."

I could tell I needed a better tactic. "Look, I have absolutely no desire to talk about this with you guys in front of all these people"—I glanced around the room—"but you're making it impossible to do otherwise, so here goes: I'm sorry." I locked eyes with Clarissa. "This thing with Anderson just . . . happened. I didn't tell you because I didn't want you to be upset. I don't want to lose your friendship over something like this."

For a moment Clarissa's face softened, but then she said, "So you admit to having a secret relationship with Anderson behind my back, and behind Priya's and Lili's, too?"

I felt my heart fold itself in half. "Yes," I said, because really, what else was there to say? Someone behind me whispered, "Slut," and someone else whispered, "Dumb tranny," which I hoped wasn't about me (but probably was), and before I knew it, Clarissa slammed down her gavel and said, "The Diamond Court finds you guilty of all the above charges." Apparently, she didn't even need to check in with the jury for this one. "You betrayed our trust and you're never to speak to us again. If you see us in the hall, look the other way. Delete our numbers from your phone, and forget our e-mail addresses. Don't sit next to us in class." She leaned forward and scowled. "From this moment on, Marni, you no longer exist."

I was speechless. Lili stepped down from the bench

and walked toward me. She looked the same as always, only there was something meaner, something crueler, that lay just beneath her skin. "Hand over your necklace, Marni."

My hand involuntarily went to my collarbone, where my diamond pendant lay against the base of my throat. "You can't be serious," I said, waiting for her to apologize for this outrageous scenario.

"Give us the necklace," Lili said. "Now."

Slowly, I reached behind me and unclasped the one tangible item that proved I was a Diamond, the daily reminder of who my friends were and what my place at Bennington was.

I dropped it into Lili's hand and held on to her fingers before letting go.

"Case closed," Clarissa declared.

PART TWO

I prefer liberty to chains of diamonds.
—*Lady Mary Wortley Montagu*

◆ 1 ◆

Any student has the freedom to pass notes, post flyers, and talk shit about his or her BFF in retaliation for said BFF talking shit about him or her first, as long as the above individuals do not include any member of the Diamond Court. —*The Diamond Rules*

A week or so later, the shroud of mystery around me had evaporated and everyone was just really, really mean.

Now that I'd been publicly stripped of my Diamond status, no one complimented me in the hall or told me I looked pretty or asked where I'd bought my dress or shoes or bracelets or [insert accessory here]. It was even worse than when Jed had dumped me, because then I'd still been a Diamond; now I was a *nobody*. Clarissa didn't yell for me to hurry up so we could walk to class; Priya didn't pull me aside on my way to Spanish to tell me about what Todd Jericho had said to her during physics; Lili didn't sit with me at lunch and listen to me complain about JeDarcy or help me with my calculus. I was alone. The one person I had was Anderson, and we only had art class together, which was nice—don't get me wrong—but it wasn't everything.

Fact: It's amazing how fast one's social life can deteriorate in private school.

Since all the days at Bennington pretty much sucked, it's hard to distinguish them from one another. My memory of those first few weeks is like a watercolor painting done by a four-year-old. One day, though—November 12, a Tuesday—stands out because it was quite possibly the worst day of my entire life. Among other things, it was the day I went to Principal Newman for help and he denied me. (It was also the day I discovered that one Starbucks Frappuccino exceeds the amount of calories you're supposed to have for an entire meal.)

That morning, when I arrived at school, I avoided Café Bennington and headed straight for my locker, where I found my first surprise: someone had written *SLUT* across the blue paint in black Sharpie. I tried rubbing it off (I even spat on my thumb), but that didn't work. I willed myself not to cry, because it would only make things worse.

First period was AP Lit, which meant morning announcements. I tried to ignore the twins as much as possible ("Marni looks like someone dipped a baseball bat in a jar of *butt ugly* and smacked her with it, and then made, like, an omelette with the rest of the *butt ugly* jar and fed it to her for breakfast.") and actually found myself relieved when Mrs. Bloom turned on the television.

Lili's face appeared on the screen and she began to read the pressing news. (After Jed's impeachment, Lili had replaced him as student body president. Go figure.)

"And, as you've all been waiting for, the votes for Snow Ball top twenty have been tallied. We now have your official top ten guys and top ten girls. Remember, seniors, only five of each make up the Snow Court, so vote wisely. You'll be hearing more from me about this in a week or so, when you'll be handed your ballots in homeroom and asked to turn them in by the twenty-third."

The screen went blank for a second and then turned blue. In white lettering, it read *GENTLE-MEN*, and a list of ten names appeared. My eyes immediately focused on Anderson's name, which was no surprise. Ryan, Duncan, and Tiger were there, too; Jed was on the list, which shocked me for a second because of his plunge in popularity, but then I remembered that faculty members picked five of the ten names. Even though he was no longer student body president, pretty much every teacher at Bennington was a Jed Brantley fan.

I hadn't had a chance to take in the other names when a new screen flashed *LADIES*, and before I knew it, I was staring at the list of potential Ice Queens. There were Clarissa, Priya, Lili, Jenny Murphy, Kara Rudolph, Sharon Wu, Leslie Durall, Ali Roberts, Anna Ford, and . . . *me*. I inhaled sharply and looked again. My name was on the list, at the very bottom, in what seemed like smaller print.

"Look," said Dara from behind me, not even trying to whisper, "*Marni* is on the list."

"OMG," Dana said. "Clarissa is gonna be so effing pissed."

I had no clue how I'd been chosen. Everyone hated me. Unless the list had been compiled before the Closet Incident, a time when my name was uttered in sentences that didn't also contain the words "cheap," "skizank," or "monkey whoreface."

The other possibility was that a teacher had selected me. The problem, however, was that I had no clue which faculty member liked me enough to have done so.

Being nominated for Snow Court may sound like a good thing, but it wasn't. As soon as my name was announced, the girls who hated me did so even *more*, and the girls who were on the fence in *von Dyke v. Valentine* were immediately tipped over, landing directly in Clarissa's lap.

In AP Bio, someone threw a paper airplane at me (believe me, I know), and someone tried to trip me in the hall. Then, thirty seconds later, someone else actually *did* trip me. I thought it was Buck Harrison, a junior on the soccer team with silly-string hair, but I wasn't sure.

Sixth period I had off; I usually went on a Dunkin' Donuts run with Clarissa, but since that wasn't exactly on the day's agenda, I decided to make a pit stop at

Principal Newman's office and see if he had time for a little chat. There was only so much a girl could take.

"He'll be with you in a minute," said Ms. Rose.

Fact: Ms. Rose looks like a carnie. Her teeth resembles a chessboard (alternating black and white) and I swear her left eye is made out of glass. Her hair is practically glued to the top of her head and then puffs out around her shoulders like a dress from the eighties.

She was also Principal Newman's secretary.

"Thanks," I said, sitting down in a beige chair.

While I waited, I thought about Anderson. Things hadn't exactly been easy for him, either. Three days earlier, someone had hot-glued the edges of his locker overnight. (We thought it was Paul Warden on the football team.) One of the janitors had to slice through the glue with a razor blade.

At least we had each other.

"He'll see you now," Ms. Rose said, gnawing on one of her fingers as if it were a chew toy.

Inside Principal Newman's office were fancy pictures of Bennington in brown frames. Windows overlooked the football field. Principal Newman sat in a tall, leather chair, leaning back and staring at the ceiling.

"Hello?"

"Marni"—his gray eyes met mine with a smile— "how are you?"

"Oh, I've been better." I took a seat in front of his

desk and launched into my Diamonds spiel. It wasn't that I wanted to get the girls in trouble, per se, but I wanted them to be stopped. If anyone had the power to pull the plug on the Bennington mock trial team, it was Principal Newman.

Too bad he was a total kook.

"Oh my," he said once I had finished, looking terribly displeased. "How horrible for you." He blinked and noticed a jar of candies at his side. "You simply *must* have one of these, by the way," he said, taking out a pink sucker and skipping it across his desk. "They're outrageous."

I slipped it into my pocket. "I'll try it later," I said. "Back to what I was saying, Principal Newman—"

"Oh no," he said, rubbing the creases of his forehead with withered fingers. "I can't hear any more about that, I'm afraid. Not today."

"What? Why not?"

"Because, my dear, you have no proof."

A minor detail.

Principal Newman shook his head. "You are making very grave accusations against three fine young ladies, Ms. Valentine. Where is your evidence?"

I shrugged. The only evidence I had was my personal knowledge of the Diamonds' agenda and my experience on the team with them.

"What do you think Clarissa would say if I called her into my office right now?"

"Probably that I was lying," I said, trying to imagine the scene. I barely could. "But I'm telling the truth.

172

Clarissa, Priya, and Lili are *not* who you think they are. They're using the mock trial team to—"

"Marni," Principal Newman said, cutting me off. "Get your head out of the clouds! You'll only wind up wet, and with cloud dust on your face. I've seen a great deal in my years here at Bennington. I try not to get involved in minor disciplinary matters unless I get multiple complaints and really, really have to. Parents get so huffy and puffy, you know?.So much drama. If you can support your case with solid evidence, come back and see me. Until then, however, I must insist that we speak of this no further."

Fact: Once the clock hits two-forty-five, the student parking lot at Bennington becomes a madhouse.

Outside, it was the sort of weather I loved—sunny but cool, and the slightest bit windy. I felt dejected that Principal Newman had basically dismissed my case, but determined to garner some "evidence" and go back to him. The only problem was how in the freaking world I was going to do so.

I'd parked in a pretty secluded spot, nowhere near Clarissa or Priya (Lili didn't have a car), underneath a cluster of trees that slouched like a bunch of elderly women with scoliosis. That hadn't stopped someone, however, from spraying my entire car with shaving cream—at least, I thought it was shaving cream— spelling "loser" on one of the sides.

"Fuck!" I said out loud, banging my fist on the hood in frustration and getting shaving cream all over my arm.

I dropped my bag on the pavement and stood staring at my Taurus. I could either drive it home and explain to my mother that everyone at Bennington hated me, or go back into school—an equally awful proposition—and secure a bunch of paper towels (how many would I need?) to wipe the entire car clean right there in the parking lot.

"Whoa."

I turned around. Tommy, in his chinos and his tucked-in shirt and his skinny black belt. I immediately noticed the marble notebook underneath his arm and the pencil behind his ear and came to the conclusion that he wanted to write an article about my sad social state—to jump on the I Hate Marni bandwagon and ride into the sunset.

"Leave me alone, Tommy," I said. "I'm not in the mood."

"Not in the mood for what?"

The sun reflected off his glasses, forcing me to squint. "For anything, really."

"Can I help?"

"Yes," I said. "Do me a favor—just *leave* me *alone.* Don't write anything about this in the paper." I motioned to my car with my free hand. "People don't exactly need any more reasons to make fun of me right now."

Tommy opened his bag and dropped the notebook he'd been holding inside. "How are you gonna get home?"

"I don't know. Why do you care?"

"Because"—he took a set of keys from his pocket and jingled them in the air—"I was going to offer you a ride."

"It's okay. I'll be fine."

"Come on. Let me drive you home, and later, if you want, I can help you clean this baby up." He gave a half smile. "It wouldn't even take fifteen minutes."

"I don't know," I said. Knowing Tommy, he probably wanted me to owe him a favor so that the next time he wanted to write an article about me, I'd feel guilty enough to cooperate.

"It's the least I can do," he said, this time smiling an entire smile, one that showed all his teeth and hinted at the pink of his gums.

I glanced back at my car, which was officially the Biggest Mess Ever. "Okay," I said, grabbing my bag off the ground. "But no talking."

Tommy drove an even older car than I did (a '98 Buick), which at a school like Bennington was a rarity. Everything about it reeked of Tommy: stacks of papers and colored folders littered the backseat, pens and pencils were strewn everywhere—the dashboard, the floor, the seat cushions—and the interior, a washed-out leather that once, perhaps, was a burgundy color, smelled like burnt coffee. A vanilla-scented air freshener (which definitely did *not* work) hung from the rearview mirror.

After a few minutes, Tommy said, "Am I allowed to speak yet?"

"Whatever," I said as we made our way down Dover Avenue. I didn't live far from Bennington. I should have just walked.

"I'll take that as a yes," he said, one hand on the wheel, the other fiddling with an old Bob Marley cassette. "So, how are ya?"

"Just make a right here," I said, pointing to the green sign that said JOHN STREET, "and then—"

"A left on Clover," he finished. "I know."

Was Tommy stalking me? Did he park his car outside my window and keep detailed surveillance notes about when I left the house and snoop through my garbage to see what sorts of things I was throwing out? What if the phones in my house were tapped and he'd known all along that I was seeing Anderson and *he* was the one who'd tipped Clarissa off that we were in the closet at Ryan's party?

My expression must have given me away. "I'm a reporter," he explained. "I know everything."

"You're not a reporter, Tommy."

"Oh no?"

"You write for the *Bennington Press*. It's not exactly the *Times*. Or even the *Post*."

Tommy didn't say anything, and before I knew it, we were in my driveway. He shifted the car into park and the two of us sat together, listening to the music on his radio.

"I'm sorry," I said. "You can't take anything I say right now to heart. I'm a mess. My life is . . ."

"Difficult." He moved his hand toward my shoulder, as if to give me a comforting pat, but then seemed to change his mind.

"Yes. Difficult."

"If there's anything I can do to make it easier, just let me know."

I was taken off guard by his kindness.

"So," I said, leaning against his window and staring at my house. The kitchen light was on; I could see the outline of my mother moving back and forth between the windows. "The other week, when I was with Duncan—what did you want to talk about?"

"Do you really want to know?"

The sky outside was losing its brightness, and Tommy looked older, somehow, and more handsome than I'd expected.

"I asked you, right?"

"Yeah," he said, shifting in his seat. "You did. I wanted to ask you about writing an article for the paper."

"You wanted *me* to write an article? About what?"

"You know," he said carefully, "about being a Diamond."

"I thought *you* were the one who wanted to write an article about *me*."

"I did."

"What made you change your mind?"

Tommy took off his glasses and rubbed them with the bottom of his shirt. There were slight purple bags underneath his eyes; I wondered how late he stayed up writing articles now that there was an issue of the paper coming out nearly every other day.

"When Jed dumped you, I was going to write about it." He said this unapologetically. "It was, as I'm sure you know, a pretty big deal. I thought if I published an article about it, maybe got a few quotes from you and Jed, people would start actually *reading* the paper. It seemed pretty foolproof."

"But you never wrote that article. I would have heard about it. Or read it."

"You're right."

"Why not?" I asked, but it took only a moment for me to realize the answer.

Clarissa.

"When Clarissa turned our trial around that day in Townsen's class, I realized there was a lot more to the story than just your breakup," said Tommy. "People actually stopped talking to Darcy and Jed after Clarissa more or less told them to. When Jed was kicked out of student government, I was like, '*Damn*. There's something explosive here.' "

"Which is why you started writing about the mock trial meetings?"

"It was history in the making! The most popular girls at school putting their peers on trial . . . I mean, *what*? And the fact that Townsen endorsed it, and the entire faculty actually seemed to approve of what was going on, well, it was incredible journalistic fodder." He paused. "Sorry. I know it's a sensitive topic for you."

178

"Don't worry about it," I said. "If *my* entire life was a student-run newspaper, I would have exploited the kids I went to school with, too." Tommy widened his eyes, and I quickly added, "That came out wrong. It's not your fault my friends are power-hungry bitches."

Tommy laughed. It was a nice laugh, and it made us seem like we were friends instead of two random people inside a musty car.

"Anyway," he said, "I wanted you to write an article about what it was like to *be* a Diamond. An insider's perspective. I figured you'd say no, but of all the girls, you'd be the best one for the job."

"You wouldn't want to hear from von Dyke herself?"

"People can't relate to Clarissa," Tommy said. "They can relate to *you*."

My cell phone picked that moment to start ringing; I dug into my bag and saw that it was my mother calling. I didn't answer.

"Do you have to go?"

"Sort of," I said. "I'm sorry I can't help you. Pretty much everyone at school thinks I'm a huge loser. I don't think anyone would want to hear what I have to say about Clarissa von Dyke."

"That's where you're wrong," Tommy said, slipping his glasses on. "Now would be the *perfect* time to write something! A tell-all. An exposé about the Diamonds, what they're *really* like. It would help people see you in an entirely new light. You could explain your side of the story, and—"

179

"I can't," I said before he went any further. "I'm sorry, Tommy, but no."

Tommy rested his elbows on the steering wheel. "Why not?"

"Because," I said, "I'm not exactly guilt-free. I did something awful to Clarissa and I'm not going to compound that by writing an article about how terrible she, Priya, and Lili are. I still believe that with time, they'll come to their senses." I opened the car door. "You understand, right?"

"Sure," Tommy said, deflated. "Of course."

"Thanks for the ride." I was about to leave when Tommy pressed his hand against the window. "Marni?"

"Yeah?"

"Here," he said, reaching into his pocket and removing a business card. He handed it to me, and the card stock felt heavy in my fingers. What senior in high school had a business card?

TOMMY PAYNE
THE BENNINGTON PRESS
Editor-in-Chief
XXX-XXX-XXXX
XXXXX.XXXXXX@XXXXX.XXX

• EXHIBIT M •
(personal information removed for privacy)

"What's this for?"

"If you change your mind."

"I won't," I said. "But thanks."

◆ 2 ◆

Boys have the right to carry pepper spray for self-protection, and girls to carry condoms for the same reason.   —*The Diamond Rules*

Two days after Tommy drove me home, things started to get a little more interesting.

1. SHARON WU, ONE OF THE FEMALE TOP TEN FOR ICE QUEEN.

Sharon had a gentle elegance that I admired; she was the type of girl who proofread her papers twice before handing them in and always knew the right answer in class but would only raise her hand occasionally (to give other people a chance).

In some people, these qualities might come off as pretentious, but in Sharon they were charming. Which is why I found it odd when she sat with me at lunch. Now, I'd gotten over eating in my car after the first day I was put on trial—so uncomfortable—but I wasn't ready to eat in the same cafeteria as the Diamonds. Since the weather was still nice, the courtyard was open during lunch periods. That was where I found myself eating: alone on one of the wooden benches (*In Memory of Zachary Drydan, Class of '74*), watching a few freshmen play wall ball, leaves sprinkled at my feet.

"Do you mind if I eat with you?" Sharon asked. I could tell from the way her blouse was untucked and her sweater hung the teeniest bit lopsided that something was wrong. I motioned for her to sit.

We didn't say much at first. I ate my sandwich like a mouse, overchewing the bites until they were mush and swallowing them down with a bottle of Poland Spring. Sharon had a salad of some kind in a plastic container; she moved it around with her fork a few times before speaking.

"I'm sorry about what happened to you," she said.

"Why are you sitting with me? Not that I mind or anything, but it's sort of social suicide to be seen with me these days."

Sharon looked at me like I had something stuck in my teeth. "You didn't hear?"

I shook my head. I wasn't exactly on top of my gossip these days.

"Clarissa, Priya, and Lili put me on trial yesterday."

I couldn't believe it. Sharon? What could she have possibly done wrong—gotten too many good grades?

"They claimed I embezzled money from Key Club, and also that I have terrible personal style." She touched her neck. "They even made fun of my pearl necklace."

I refrained from making a joke. "Did you steal?"

"Of course not! But Steffie Young, the treasurer, said there was money missing and that she saw *me* take it, which is a complete lie. And now Mr. Paulsen thinks it's true, and he asked me to step down as president, and I've *already* filled out my early application to Brown." She wiped her eyes. "And now I have an appointment to see Dean Meyerson. What if I get expelled?"

"Why would Steffie lie?"

"I don't know," she said. "All I know is that now *she's* going to be president and *I'm* the one who looks like a thief."

"I'm not sure what to say, Sharon. I'm really sorry."

"Oh, Marni, it was awful. Clarissa said I wasn't allowed to give my own testimony, and the jury—as soon as I saw that Emmy Montgomery was on it, I knew I was done for. She's hated me forever."

"Gosh," I said.

"Was it like that when you were part of the team?"

What could I possibly say: that I was majorly responsible for the current state of Bennington mock trial? That I had actually made up the Diamond Rules *myself*?

"I think," I said, "things have gotten really out of control."

Sharon nodded. "I went to see Mr. Townsen. Do you know what he said? *File an appeal.*" She laughed, but it sounded more like she was choking. "As if that would do any good. He really thinks those girls are doing a great job. Someone needs to expose them for who they truly are."

That gave me an idea. "Maybe you could come with me to Principal Newman," I said. Surely he would believe *Sharon*, who had never been friends with Clarissa or the Diamonds. Surely—

"I don't think so," she said, tilting her head so that her hair fell over her eyes like a veil.

"Why not?"

"I don't want to make life harder than it already is," she said, sighing. "If those girls find out I went to the principal, who knows what they'll do to me?"

"But if nobody does anything at all, nothing will ever change."

The bell rang, signaling the end of the period.

"You're right," Sharon said, getting up from the bench and tossing her salad into the garbage. "But I'm not the girl for the job. Sorry."

I could hardly blame her. The Diamonds had the support of the Bennington faculty and administration; challenging them was a nearly impossible, Herculean proposition. Nobody wanted to speak out against them for risk of being ostracized.

But *someone* had to do it.

2. THE MUSIC DEPARTMENT'S FIRST-SEMESTER CONCERT, *SNOW AND BLOW!*

In case you don't remember, Priya, Lili, and Clarissa all took chorus with me. Ever since life at Bennington had turned into a tragedy of Shakespearean proportions (complete with lust, betrayal, and confusing language), the idea of spending time in close proximity to my ex–best friends had scared me.

The sad part was that I'd always enjoyed concerts in the past. The Diamonds would stand on the top riser and look cool—without even trying—while Priya made bets on how far she could hike up her skirt without anyone in the audience noticing. (Mid-thigh.) The orchestra would soar and the band would blast; everyone in the room was really making *music*. How exciting! Now it was more dreadful than an episode of *Everybody Loves Raymond*.

Every day since I'd been punted to the bottom of the Bennington social scene, the Diamonds had done something new and cruel to me (or instructed their minions to do so). It started off with leaving rotten fruit in my locker and ice cream sandwiches that melted and destroyed nearly all my notebooks. They quickly enlisted helpers in each of my classes who would volunteer me to read out loud, write my name on the board before the bell rang (in calculus, for example, each day there was a new equation with my name next to the equals sign plus the words "fat whore," and each day Mrs. Friedman would get flustered, demand to know who wrote it, and erase it with a sigh when nobody fessed up), and leave unidentified sticky substances on my seat that I would have to clean up with paper towels from the bathroom.

What would they try next?

The night of the concert, the chorus room was totally nuts—sopranos flirting with basses, altos gazing over their sheet music, tenors flirting with tenors—and in the center of the room were the Diamonds, gorgeous as usual, sitting by themselves and barely speaking at all.

Instead of making any unnecessary drama, I waited in the bathroom (for nearly ten minutes); my plan was to miss the lineup and then, at the very last moment, slip into my spot on the risers. The concert would have already begun. Clarissa and the girls would never make a scene in front of an auditorium full of parents and school administrators.

At least, that's what I'd thought.

The whole thing went down like this: the choir filed in row by row until the risers were filled with knees and elbows and torsos. Ms. Ariana stepped onto a tiny wooden platform and tapped her baton on the music stand in front of her.

It was time to begin, and I made my move.

While Ms. Ariana shuffled through her binder, I crept down the side aisle of the auditorium and hopped into place, brushing Clarissa's shoulder with my own and startling her.

"What are *you* doing here?" Her skin looked airbrushed underneath the white-hot lights. The Diamond pendant around her neck sparkled, a painful reminder of all I had lost.

I ignored her, staring into the audience as though someone I knew were there.

"Clarissa just asked you a question," Priya said, breathing sticky air onto my cheeks. "Or has your skankiness taken over your hearing and made you, like, deaf?"

I tensed my shoulders and pretended not to notice them. Lili narrowed her eyes until each was as small as the slit you deposit change into at a public telephone.

Ms. Ariana raised her jiggly arms, which was our cue to begin the first selection, Fauré's Requiem. I listened to Clarissa's voice—airy and hollow, like a flute—and thought, *Everything is fine. You're standing next to Clarissa and nothing bad has happened. Yet.*

At the end of the requiem, Clarissa poked me with her index finger. Hard.

"Ow," I said, turning. "What was that for?"

She poked me again.

"Okay," I said. "You've made your point. You can stop now."

But she didn't. "Oh no," Clarissa said, pressing her lips together. "This is only the beginning."

Before I knew it, while the audience was clapping and Ms. Ariana was preparing for our transition into an eight-part version of "Shenandoah" in which Jeremy Baxton and Michelle Wang had featured solos, I felt Clarissa's hand on the small of my back.

A slight push was all it took.

I tumbled forward, my hands jetting out to brace my fall, smacking into the girl in front of me. My necklace, a string of freshwater pearls my grandmother had given me for my fourteenth birthday, came loose and broke apart, flying everywhere and hitting the floor in a crescendo of tiny clinks.

I remember staring at the ceiling, bathed in light. All I could see were dozens of colored circles; when I blinked, they didn't go away. My head ached and so did the back of my neck.

Eventually, with the help of Ms. Ariana, I rose to my feet. There was a buzzing in the audience, like hundreds of tiny fireflies were trapped inside the seat cushions. When I looked up at the Diamonds, smiles had devoured their faces, the whiteness of their teeth magnified and overwhelming.

For the first time since my relationship with Anderson had been exposed, I felt neither sorry nor regretful. I felt angry.

I didn't finish the concert. I left the auditorium and never looked back. After two or three minutes, I found myself out of breath, walking down the hill toward the main road that ran parallel to Bennington's property. My car was parked at school but I felt like being outside, surrounded by fresh air and open space. It was nighttime. The sky was dark and heavy.

Within moments, I heard the distinct crunching of tires. I turned my head to see a familiar car rolling alongside me, a familiar face at the wheel.

"Need a lift?"

The car came to a halt. I placed my hands on the roof, palms flat, and ducked my head inside. The interior smelled like chamomile and raw ginger and dirty socks. "I was told never to take a ride from strangers," I said.

"Oh?"

I studied the driver and felt the urge to jump inside. "But it's a good thing I don't listen to everything I'm told."

Anderson's smile was like the tide; it washed over me until everything I felt was clean and new. My life would never return to what it once was. No more Café Bennington or midnight phone calls or texting during class. No more hugging or gossiping or laughing or having a life more perfect than that of anyone else I knew. Clarissa, Lili, and Priya were serious about hating me. There was no going back. Only forward.

It was then that I let the Diamonds go, feeling them rush through my fingers like tepid water from a faucet.

Later that night, I was about to go to bed when I saw light peeking out underneath the door to my dad's study.

Inside, my father was still in his work clothes—a cream-colored shirt and a dark tie, hair brushed to the side.

"Dad?"

He looked up from his book. "Marni? Why aren't you in bed?"

Dad and I usually ran on different schedules; it was rare that we had solitary moments without Mom yelling for one of us to clean the dishes or cook dinner or change the TV channel. I lifted a stack of papers and settled into the black leather couch I'd used as a hiding place for Milky Way wrappers when I was younger. "I couldn't sleep, I guess."

"Me either," he sighed, motioning to the clutter on his desk. "Too much work."

"Need any help?"

Dad raised a thick eyebrow. "Don't you have school in the morning?" He glanced at his watch and whistled. "It's late."

I shrugged.

Dad studied me with focused intensity. "Here," he said, reaching into a ceramic mug on his desk (*BEST DAD EVER!*) and tossing me one of his favorite red pens. "You know what to do."

We worked in silence for what must have been an hour, the only sounds in the room coming from the scratching of pens and the flipping of pages and the coupled heaviness of our breath. I had graded approximately fifteen papers (only two A's—I'm pretty tough) when Dad leaned back in his chair and said, "What ever happened with your foray into mock trial?"

It seemed childish to beat around the bush. "I'm not on the team anymore."

"Would you like to tell me about it?"

Not really, I thought. I knew he would be disappointed in me. Before I knew it, though, I found myself dropping the pen to my side and recounting the

190

traumatic events of the past few weeks. (Not the part about almost losing my virginity, but everything else.)

After a few moments of waiting, he said, "You reinterpreted the Bill of Rights?"

I nodded. *Sort of.*

"And the people at your school, they voluntarily show up to this court you helped create?"

"I know it sounds crazy," I said. "I hardly believe it myself."

Dad cupped his hands behind his head. "I'm so proud of you," he said in an almost-whisper.

It wasn't exactly the response I'd been expecting. "For what? I lied to Clarissa and hurt her feelings. Priya and Lili, too. I helped punish kids at school who didn't do anything wrong. I probably deserve all of this."

"You've made a few mistakes," Dad agreed, "but that's life, Marni. And the important thing is that you actually *did* something."

I didn't understand.

"So many people wander through their days," he said, "doing what is expected of them and nothing more. Sometimes much less. But you have so much going for you. You used your knowledge to create something that made a difference at your school. Maybe it didn't work out like you expected, or for the right reasons, but if you can do it once, you can do it again."

Dad stood up and crossed over to his bookcase. He grabbed something as thick as a dictionary and placed it in my lap. I sighed. It was *The Constitution for Dummies*,

191

the book that had helped me create the Diamond Rules, which had propelled my very own downfall.

"Use it," Dad said, and I looked at him curiously.

"For?"

Dad locked his jaw, and his ever-ruddy cheeks tightened. "Why was the Constitution created in the first place?"

I never liked when Dad asked me questions he already knew the answers to. "To protect the rights of the people," I said.

"The important part of what you said is 'protect.' After freeing themselves from the reign of the British, our founding fathers created the Constitution to *protect* the rights of the people, not *exploit* them."

"No offense, Dad, but what's your point?"

"My point," he said, "is that every answer you will need is in this book. You must remind your friends that this country is a *democracy*. It sounds to me like they are running your school amuck mostly because no one is there to stop them."

"They're running the school because they're *popular*, and I was popular, too, until I screwed it all up."

"Then fix it," Dad said. He stepped closer and crouched on the floor, staring at me eye to eye. His breath smelled like butterscotch candies. "Take back the control."

"How?" I asked, my fingers folding into fists.

"By doing what every important man and woman in our country has done before you," Dad said. "By fighting."

The next day, I arrived at school early. I walked through the halls until I reached the technology room, where the *Bennington Press* staff met before and after school.

Tommy was there, alone.

I approached him and dropped *The Constitution for Dummies* onto the table. It landed with a smack. Tommy glanced up from the layout he was working on.

"Remember that article you wanted me to write?"

The circles underneath his eyes seemed to pulse. "What about it?"

"I'll do it."

"Really?"

"Yes. If *you* do something for *me*."

By that point, Tommy's mouth was opened slightly, as if he were about to take a bite from a thick sandwich only to realize it had suddenly vanished from his plate. I had his full attention.

"Here," I said, flipping open the book—which I'd stayed up all night rereading—and pointing to the pages I'd dog-eared and decorated with Post-its. "Read this."

Tommy's reactions were stock-exchange swift: confusion, skepticism, fear, and, ultimately, what I interpreted as utter rapture. It could also have been constipation, though. Tough call.

When I couldn't wait any longer, I said, "So? What do you think?"

Tommy stared at me but said nothing. He slipped

the hardcover monster into his backpack and jumped to attention.

"I'll have to cancel today's newspaper meeting," he said.

Then he smiled.

> Everyone has the right to refuse housing a
> foreign exchange student unless the afore-
> mentioned foreign exchange student is hot.
> —*The Diamond Rules*

While the idea of forming a rebel group of vigilante
misfits to battle the girls I used to call my best friends
and overthrow the stronghold they had on the
Bennington student body had never occurred to me
before my father/daughter chat, once the (proverbial)
seed had been planted, I felt it grow and blossom into
the sort of idea that inspires millions. Or if not millions, hopefully one or two others.

This was an endeavor I had to be smart about.
Secretive. Discreet. Which, apparently, was *not* my
specialty.

Enter Tommy.

My loserdom was still new, like a fresh cut. Tommy,
however, was secure in his lameness. Dorks trusted
him. Ugly girls adored him. The Diamonds had yet to
prosecute him. For this plan to work—and yes, I *will* tell

you what the plan was, give me a minute—I needed a buffer to convince others to join up with our cause.

Mostly, this was because the kids at Bennington hated me. The popular ones, of course—my former friends who had discarded me like unwanted carbohydrates—despised me. The other group of people (including JeDarcy, the Audio-Visual Squad, the Chess Team, the French Club, the Spanish Club, the Korean Club, the wannabe mafiosos, band kids—except Anderson—the entire orchestra, and the Drama Club) equally hated me. I was a Diamond. Well, an ex-Diamond, but still: for the past three years, I'd been absolutely horrible to them.

Most recently, I'd been on the opposite side of the judges' bench; I'd worn my pretty robe, glossed my lips, and agreed with Clarissa & Co., handing out judgments like Halloween candy and making life for Bennington's lower class worse than they ever imagined it could be.

People were happy to see me disgraced. And how could I blame them? I deserved it. But I wanted to change. To reverse the many wrongs I had helped perpetuate. All I could do was try and hope that Tommy had enough clout as an outcast to convince our potential recruits that I wasn't the person they believed me to be.

The only problem was, what if they were right?

More people at Bennington than I could count had suffered at the hands of the Diamonds. Part of me wanted to invite them all to join our crusade, but that was impossible. As Tommy reminded me, we needed to keep this quiet. We had to be selective.

We decided to invite four individuals, plucked from the four corners of the social stratosphere, to meet with us and hopefully join our cause. (There weren't actually four corners. Just go with it.)

NAME: Boyd Longmeadow
ROLE: President of the Bennington Drama Club

I think Boyd's downfall was pretty much that he wanted to *be* Clarissa von Dyke, while Clarissa wanted him to die a slow death (by jazz hands). Boyd was the sort of boy who everyone knew liked other boys but, since we attended the kind of private school where a clique of girls could call themselves the Diamonds and lay down social law, had not come out of the closet.

We chose Boyd because, well, he was dramatic, and because he had a really high-pitched scream that sounded like a whistle. And also because he could cry

197

on command, which is an important weapon in preparing for a revolution.

Boyd had suffered a huge blow when the Diamond Court was first getting started. He'd asked Clarissa if he could be an honorary Diamond; she'd said no, of course, and told everyone that Boyd wore thong underwear to school. (This may have, in fact, been true.) Either way, it didn't make life easy for him.

NAME: Mike Samuels, aka "Turbo"
ROLE: Semiprofessional Skateboarder

Mike was someone who'd pretty much slipped under the radar during my time at Bennington. He had the appeal of a surfer, complete with bleached-blond hair, manufactured tan, and a vocabulary consisting of words like "dude," "radical," and "kewl." (I'm not sure how I knew that it was spelled "kewl" and not "cool." But I did.)

Mike called himself a semiprofessional skateboarder, which I later found out simply meant that he fell down a lot and had anointed himself with a skater name: Turbo. At another school, Mike might have been popular. But at Bennington, where popped collars and football helmets reigned supreme, Mike was a total joke.

In one of the Diamonds' first rulings (*Rockford v. Samuels*), Emily Rockford, a well-liked junior, had claimed that Mike told her she was "hot" at a house party and it had made her uncomfortable. The Diamonds ruled in her favor and told Mike that he was no longer allowed to attend any parties thrown by Bennington students. The last I heard, he'd shown up at Ryan's party that fateful night Anderson and I were "Gettin' Jiggy Wit It" (Will Smith, 1998); not only had he been turned away, but Tiger had punched him in the stomach and poured a cup of beer on his head. (I didn't have the best night, either, but come on. That sucks.)

NAME: Monique French
ROLE: Foreign

Monique would have been pretty were it not for her mustache. She'd been born in Paris but had traveled all over Europe and lived in six different countries by the time she was fourteen. Her father was some sort of diplomat; she'd moved to Manhattan when she was fifteen and then to Long Island, where she'd started at Bennington as a junior. That was never good. I had a hard enough time starting at Bennington as a freshman, and my only savior from social oblivion was Clarissa. At sixteen, it's pretty hard to make new friends, especially if you carry a baguette in your backpack and speak with an accent. Monique knew, like, ten different languages, though, and served as the student body liaison between the foreign language department and all the different clubs.

Monique would be an advantage if we needed anything to be translated (you never know) and also if we needed anyone with a mustache.

NAME: Jenny Murphy
ROLE: Byotch

Then there was Jenny, who you already know about.

There's not much else to say. She was probably the first person at Bennington to hate Clarissa and, for some reason, one of the few to be left alone by the Diamond Court. (Jenny had quit the mock trial team soon after the Diamonds took over, yet had never appeared before the court herself.)

Jenny was an enigma and would definitely be the hardest to persuade, seeing as how she *hated* my *guts*.

There were others we could have asked, I suppose, but it was a delicate situation. We needed people who were trustworthy and had nothing to lose. People who weren't afraid—like Sharon Wu—of ending up worse off than when they began. I debated mentioning my idea to Mr. Townsen but thought better of it. *He* was the one who'd supported Clarissa from the beginning, who'd given her the unrestricted ability to usurp the Bennington mock trial team and hypnotize them into becoming her Bedazzled army of followers. Even though he supported Clarissa without question, there was no way I could depend on him to do the same for me.

Especially when I would be battling her to the finish.

I left it up to Tommy to do the talking on my behalf. Two days later, we decided on a time and place to meet. We couldn't meet at school, for risk of being overheard, and I suggested Anderson's house.

"That's an awful idea," Tommy said. We were standing outside the back entrance of the school. "What if he overhears us?"

I hadn't come right out and said I wanted Anderson to be a part of whatever it was we were doing, but I figured Tommy would understand. Anderson's friends had stopped talking to him, and the football team was extra-hard on him during practice. (They took the term "physical" to the extreme; there wasn't an afternoon when Anderson came home without a new bruise.) Besides, I wanted him around more than anything.

I gave Tommy an "And I Am Telling You [He's] Not Going" look (*Dreamgirls*, 1981) and he shrugged and said, "Whatever. I'll make sure everyone is there by three-thirty. The rest is up to you. As long as you write the exposé, of course, and I can print it in the paper."

"Of course."

Tommy was all business.

Now I just had to go find Anderson and convince him to let the biggest losers at Bennington convene at his house for the sole purpose of destroying the Diamonds.

Piece of (chocolate) cake.

In a strange twist of fate, Anderson was all for it. The conversation went something like this:

ANDERSON
(*looking like a supermodel*)
Marni, love of my life, the most important person in my
entire world! No, my *universe*!

ME
(*becoming thinner with every single word I say*)
Oh, Anderson!

ANDERSON
(*taking off his shirt to reveal a chiseled torso*)
Do you know that Michael Jackson song "The Way You
Make Me Feel"?

ME
(*panting, and suddenly in designer clothes*)
Yes! Yes, I do!

ANDERSON
(*panting back at me*)
Well, you make me feel like that!

ME
(*slightly confused but still panting and still in designer
clothes*)
What?

ANDERSON
(*with feeling*)
Kiss me!

ME
(*with tongue*)
Mmmggah . . .

Okay, so maybe I took a *few* liberties with that
transcription, but Anderson *was* fully supportive of

any extracurricular meeting with the sole purpose of dethroning Clarissa, Priya, and Lili.

"I'll tell my mom to make some snacks," he said, giving me a quick kiss before heading off to class. Anderson was slowly warming up to public displays of affection; whenever he touched me in front of other people, my insides went gooey, like a brownie taken out of the oven a few minutes too soon.

When I arrived at Anderson's, the gang was all there—sort of. Monique was perched on his den sofa as if it were a piano and she a sultry lounge singer in her prime; she was wearing a long, flowy dress that could have easily been mistaken for a muumuu. (It was cow print.) An unlit cigarette dangled from her lip.

"I smoke now, *oui?*" Her lips were smothered in purplish lipstick.

"You can't smoke in here," Anderson said. He was at the other end of the room, reclining in an oversized suede chair. "Sorry."

"Eeet's okay," Monique said, removing her beret, tossing the cigarette inside, and positioning the cap back on her head.

"Where's Tommy?" I said to no one in particular. Mike was admiring Anderson's guitar. His pants were baggy and littered with holes, and he was wearing a T-shirt that said *Death 2 Posers*.

"He went to the bathroom," came a voice from the other room. The timbre—nasal and high—could have been linked to only one person. Boyd. "I hope he's not taking a poop, because that could take forever."

On first glance Boyd looked like most any other Bennington guy: a slim pair of chinos, a starched oxford shirt, a comfortable tie. On closer inspection, though, his outfit was trademarked with his own personal flair. A shiny belt peeked out from the top of his slacks. Plus his tie was pink enough for a flamingo to envy.

Boyd must have noticed me staring, because he looked down at his chest and laughed. "Oh, this? It's reversible." He flipped over his tie; on the other side were the Bennington colors, blue and white. "It's like, if I wear it on this side, I'm *bo*-ring, but if I flip it over"—he made it pink again, effortlessly—"I'm am-*a*-zing!"

Anderson pinched me, and I applauded. "Wow!" I said. "That's so, um . . ."

"Diva? I know," Boyd said, setting a tray of drinks down on a metal coffee table with an intentionally tarnished finish. "Refreshments!"

Monique twitched her nose in the air. "Martinis?"

"Nope. Fanta, Fanta," Boyd sang, and then, suggestively: "Don't you wanna?"

I reached for two glasses—for Anderson and me. It was then that I noticed Jenny Murphy huddled in the corner, pressed against the wall as though she were a light fixture. "Jenny?" I called from across the room.

Her face twisted into an awkward hello. "Are you

planning on keeping us here forever? I have things to do, you know."

I returned Anderson's pinch.

"Uh, so, Jenny," he said, "do you want to see one of my paintings?"

"I didn't know you were an artist," she said, looking intrigued.

"I'm a *fart*ist," said Boyd.

Anderson got up from the chair; without his body to lean against, I fell into the empty spot. "These are all mine." Anderson motioned at the long wall with enough artwork to be a small museum.

"Dude," Mike said. "Kewl. Also, can you guys call me Turbo?"

I let Anderson show off for a few minutes, until Tommy appeared in the doorway, cheeks flushed, hair damp around his ears.

"I hope you washed your hands," said Boyd teasingly. "Because if we do a trust circle or group massages, that would be p-r-e-t-t-y gross." He looked around at us—his audience—and bowed. "Am I right or am I right?"

Tommy started to respond but stopped himself. "We're just waiting for two more people and then we can begin."

I looked at Tommy, shocked. "One minute," I said, pulling him out of the den and into the hallway. "What are you talking about? Everyone we need is in the other room."

Tommy seemed anxious. "Don't get mad at me, but I invited two other people."

"I thought we were in this together, Tommy. *Partners.* Partners don't go behind each other's backs and invite people without their approval to secret meetings!"

"I know, I know," Tommy said. "But I knew that if I asked, you'd say no, and well, we *need* them."

There was a lot more yelling to be done at Tommy, but now wasn't the time. Not with people in the other room who were ready to leave at any second. "Fine," I said. "Who are they?"

I heard footsteps heading in our direction. My gaze shifted from Tommy—who looked as nervous as a thirteen-year-old at his bar mitzvah—to the guests who'd been invited to our undercover rendezvous without my knowledge.

I couldn't believe my eyes.

"Marni?" said a formal baritone.

"Jed?"

As you may have expected, there was an incredibly awkward silence, the kind you could slice with a knife and smear on a chunk of bread. Tommy cleared his throat. "So, uh, does everybody know each other?"

Yes. Everyone knew each other. It was such a motley crew, however, that I wouldn't have been surprised if this was the first time any of them had hung out together after school. Bennington was like that: small enough to feel incestuous, but large enough to hide behind self-constructed walls. I stared at Boyd with his pink tie, Monique with her mustache, and Turbo with his skater getup, wondering whether I would have even said hello to these people before I graduated if Jed had never dumped me and Clarissa had never exiled me from the Diamonds.

"You all want to know why you're here, I'm sure," I said, letting my eyes linger on Jed, who was sitting next to Darcy, seeming unsure of what to do with his hands. I understood why Tommy had wanted them to come—Jed had a lot of pull with the faculty and knew how to impress a crowd, while Darcy was basically Queen of the stoners, ballers, and after-school cigarette smokers—but the sight of them together made me sick to my stomach.

Not to mention that Jed had never even apologized for cheating on me. And dumping me. In public.

"I can't take back what I did when I was a Diamond," I continued. "I've certainly made some mistakes, but I'm ready to fix them. And I want to start with overthrowing the Diamonds. Tommy and I are going to expose them for who they truly are, and we can't do it without you."

"You want our help?" asked Monique, scooching as close to Anderson as possible. "What can *we* do?"

Tommy reached into his backpack, removed the book I'd given him, and held it up for everyone to see. "You all took American history, right?"

Turbo snorted. "That shit was *wack*."

"I did my final report in that class on the history of *Broadway*," said Boyd. "I don't suppose that's why I'm here?"

Tommy shook his head. "No. I'm talking about when this country was *founded*. Does the American Revolution ring a bell?"

Boyd thought for a moment. "I don't believe it does, Tommy."

"What *about* the American Revolution?" Jed asked. "What does it have to do with our current situation?"

Tommy relished his moment in the spotlight. "Great question, Jed. Now, as all of you know—or *should* know—the American Revolution marks the time in our country's history when the thirteen colonies stood up to the British Empire and declared their independence."

"Dude," said Turbo. "Colonies are so crunked."

"Uh, sure," Tommy replied. "What's happening now at Bennington is just like what happened to our country in the past. Why should the Diamonds have the power to judge us, to create laws that *affect* us, when we have no actual *say* in those laws?"

"They shouldn't," said Darcy. I noticed that her chin was trembling, and the top of her head was beginning to reveal her blond roots.

"The way I see it, we have two options," Tommy said. "Let this go on until we graduate, *or* take a stand and fight for what we believe in."

Boyd spoke up. "What *do* we believe in?"

Silence.

I took a deep breath. "We believe in fairness," I said, "and we believe that everyone at Bennington has the right to make their own choices. The Diamonds are only powerful because we *let* them be. Each of you was chosen for a reason. I know that if we put our heads together, we can think of something."

I wanted them to believe in me, in what I was saying, but mostly I wanted to believe it myself.

"So," I said. "Who's with me?"

Nothing happened at first. And then, like a rocket, Jed's arm shot into the air, taking his entire body with it until he was standing taller than I'd seen him stand in weeks. "I am," he said.

"Me too," said Darcy.

Three, four, five, six—almost everyone stood like reversed dominos until we were gathered in a make-shift circle.

"The French were *quite* involved with the revolution, you know," Monique said. "I feel a kindred spirit to my people. And you know what?"

"What?" I asked.

She smiled. "I kind of like eet."

I glanced around the room. There was a small gap between Darcy and Turbo waiting to be filled by the only person who had yet to respond: Jenny.

"You're the missing link, Jenny," I said. "We need you."

"You don't need me." There was a vulnerability in her voice that made me wonder just how much the

Diamonds had scarred her over the years. "You don't even like me."

I took a step forward. "That's not true, Jenny. You're the only person in the entire school Clarissa is afraid of. You're cunning, smart, and very stubborn," I said with a grin to show I wasn't trying to insult her. "Those are pretty necessary skills for a revolutionary. I don't expect you to forgive me in a single afternoon for what I did to you. I just want the chance to show you that I am truly sorry."

Slowly, Jenny unwrapped her arms until they were dangling at her sides. "We need a name," she said. "The colonists who fought for independence had a name. They called themselves patriots."

It was a good point—one I hadn't even thought of.

Then, unexpectedly, Boyd said, "What about the Stonecutters? You know, since we're fighting against the Diamonds, and diamonds are gemstones, and they're, like, one of the hardest substances known to mankind. Ever."

The Stonecutters. I loved it.

I looked at Boyd and smiled. Then I turned back to Jenny, who had inched her way into the circle. It was now complete.

"Kewl," said Turbo.

Afterward, when everyone was leaving, I felt a tap on my shoulder. It was Jed.

"Can we talk?"

Anderson was still in the den with Jenny, ever the

artiste, and Boyd was relaxing on the couch (by that, I mean lying down with his legs spread wide open). Darcy was nowhere to be found.

"Okay," I said, leading Jed up the narrow hallway and upstairs, into the only room in the house I knew I was allowed in. Anderson's bedroom.

♦ ♦ ♦

Jed was sitting at Anderson's desk, while I was on his bed with my back against the wall, feet dangling off the side. It was strange, being in my current boyfriend's room while talking—or *not* talking, as the case might be—to my ex-boyfriend.

Let me remind you that Jed was never much of a chatterbox. At least, not about anything that actually *mattered* (otherwise known as Feelings).

"What do you want?" I asked.

He supplied a constipated grimace. "We haven't had a chance to talk properly since, well, you know, and I simply thought—"

"Either say something or don't. But whatever you do say, *mean* it."

Jed ran his fingers through his hair and let loose the top button of his collar. He had changed. I could tell from the thinness of his cheeks and the ever-so-sparse stubble around his jaw.

"I never cheated on you with Darcy," he said. "Not in the way you think."

"What do you—"

Jed put up his hand. "Let me explain, okay? Then you can ask me whatever you want and I promise to tell you the absolute truth." He waited, then continued. "The last week in August, Clarissa stopped by my house. I was surprised, but I figured she wanted to chat with me about you. I was wrong." Jed looked at me sadly. "One night, over the summer, I ran into Darcy at the Burger Shack. It was a complete coincidence. You know she isn't the type of girl I would normally . . . *associate* with, but we wound up sitting together and she was actually quite nice.

"It got late, and I walked her to her car. I went to give her a friendly hug, and she kissed me. Out of nowhere. I stopped her and explained I was seeing someone, *you*, but even if I wasn't, I would *never* be as presumptuous as to kiss a girl without asking first. When we weren't even on a date. I told her she should be ashamed of herself, and I got in my car and left."

I wasn't sure where Jed was going with this story, but it rang true. We'd been dating for weeks before he'd "officially" asked me out. I couldn't imagine him kissing a girl he barely knew.

"I thought about telling you, but really it was nothing, and I knew it would upset you. So I never mentioned it. When Clarissa came to my door, however, everything changed. She must have been at the Shack that night; God only knows how she managed to take a picture of Darcy's and my embrace—it couldn't have lasted longer than a few seconds!—but she did, and she showed it to me. I was shocked. Everything about it screamed '*Secret Love Affair!*' and I knew that if you ever saw it, you would be heartbroken."

"So you dumped me on the morning announcements to spare my feelings? Great plan."

Jed sighed. "Clarissa told me that if I didn't 'dump' you in that particular manner, not only would she show you the picture, but she would make sure that no one voted for me in the student government election."

Whoa. I started to respond but felt the words tangle in my throat. Clarissa was behind this? *Clarissa* had orchestrated Jed's dumping me? Everything she'd done afterward—putting Jed on trial for his crimes, pretending to be a friend when really she was the worst of enemies—had been planned and plotted. One huge lie.

"You should've just *told* me," I managed to get out. "If nothing happened, I would have believed you. Why didn't you trust me?"

"I made a mistake, Marni. I knew how much you valued Clarissa's friendship. I'd rather you hated me than discover she was a fraud. Besides," he said, "it was my word against hers, and honestly, I thought you would believe her over me.

"Never in my wildest dreams did I expect Clarissa to put me on *trial*. And then, well, I was removed from office regardless. I was *still* going to tell you the truth. All of it. But then Anderson came into the picture, and despite everything, you seemed happy. So I kept my mouth shut," he said.

"But you and Darcy . . ."

214

"We're good friends," said Jed, swiveling in the chair. "Nothing more."

I didn't know how to respond. For all these weeks I'd thought *I* was an awful person, a liar and a sneak who'd stabbed my best friend, Clarissa, in the back. I'd thought Jed was a cold, heartless cheater who deserved all the misfortune he'd received and then some.

It had never occurred to me that I might be mistaken.

"Now that you know the entire story," Jed said, "do you have any idea why Clarissa would do that to you?"

I felt my stomach churn. "No," I said. "Not really."

"Listen, Marni. I want to help you and Tommy. I want to do what's right."

I couldn't help smiling. "You really *do* belong in politics, Jed."

Even though his explanation didn't *change* anything, it was comforting to know that, deep down, Jed was still the person I'd once thought he was.

And maybe that was closure. Maybe that was enough.

◆ 4 ◆

All students have the right to keep the inside of their lockers private unless they are suspected of being a suspicious character (as determined solely by the Diamond Court).
—*The Diamond Rules*

You can't simply cut a diamond. It won't slice open with a knife or break apart with a hammer. That would be too easy. There is a skill to diamond cutting. Some might go as far as to call it a science. I'd call it an art.

Fact: The only tool that can separate a rough diamond into smaller pieces is another diamond.

This truth held strong for the Stonecutters. I might have no longer associated with Clarissa & Co., but they had been my best friends for years. I knew their strengths and their weaknesses. I was the perfect source of information; though at one point I would have kept my silence out of sheer loyalty, I didn't owe those girls anything. Not anymore. So once the Stonecutters were united in their goal to destroy the Diamonds and reinvent the social hierarchy at Bennington, I knew exactly where to begin.

"The first thing we need is a plan," I said.

It was the Stonecutters' second official meeting. Tommy had picked up one of those oversized Post-it boards on the way to Anderson's and was drawing on it with a black Sharpie. Boyd had taken a bag of Doritos hostage and was inhaling chip after chip while Monique braided her hair and Turbo played some kind of game on his cell phone.

Anderson walked into the den with an open can of Sprite. "Hey, babe," he said before taking a sip. "What did you say about a plan?"

Tommy motioned to the board, where he began making bullet points. The two of us had brainstormed that morning in the technology room before school. "Principal Newman said there was nothing he could do without proof. So," he said, smirking, "I propose we get him some."

"What *kind* of proof?" asked Darcy.

Jenny cleared her throat. "Yeah, how do you prove someone's a bitch?"

"Good question," Tommy said. "Clarissa's crime is not that she's, you know, a bitch. She happens to be one, sure, but that's not what's going to get her in trouble. Priya or Lili, either. What we need is substantial evidence against them. We need to build a case that is so solid no one—not even someone as dense as Principal Newman—can deny the truth."

"Easier said than done," said Jed. "Where do you propose we begin?"

"That"—Tommy pointed at me—"can best be answered by Marni."

Tommy was right. If anyone knew the true evil of the Diamonds and the letter of the law, it was me.

"Everyone thinks that Clarissa, Priya, and Lili are bringing *justice* to the halls of Bennington," I said. "That they're following proper conduct and exercising the rights and regulations people would have in a real court of law. Now, we know that isn't true, but that's why Townsen has let them have so much control, and why Principal Newman and Dean Meyerson are allowing them to determine actual punishments."

I thought about how Clarissa had twisted all the privileges she'd been given, about what she'd done to Joy Darling and other jury members who hadn't voted her way, about how she'd concocted lies and attacked people like Sharon Wu for no other reason than personal gain.

"We have to prove the Diamonds are actually doing the opposite of what the administration *thinks* they're doing," I said. "That they've tampered with the jury through bribes and intimidation, and that no one has *ever* received a fair trial."

"How do we do that?" Anderson asked.

"I can help," Tommy said. "We need to use the same tactics I use as a journalist."

"Sifting through people's trash?" Jenny said jokingly.

Tommy looked at her seriously. "If we need to."

"Dude," Turbo said, "I'm *not* putting my hands in Clarissa von Dyke's garbage can. That's rank."

Then Darcy spoke up. "My dad is a police detective." I was surprised; I hadn't known that about her. "He keeps a lot of equipment and stuff at home. I can't take anything important, but I do know how to bug a phone."

Jed turned his head. "You do?"

"There aren't a whole lotta perks to being the daughter of a cop," Darcy said, "but there are a few. My dad has these tiny mics you can put in someone's bag and they'll pick up everything that person says and record it. I don't know if I can get any of those, though. He might notice."

"Try," Tommy said, writing *record conversations* on the board in perfect script. "If we can get a clip of one of the girls talking about influencing a jury member or something, we can go straight to Principal Newman.

"Next," he said, writing *surveillance*, "we need to stake out the Diamonds. Someone has to be watching their every move."

Monique raised her hand. "I could do that," she volunteered. "Eet would be my pleasure."

"Ditto," said Boyd. "I watch Clarissa all the time anyway. I may as well be doing it for a reason other than copying her strut."

"Most importantly," said Tommy, "we need to be working diligently to stir up anti-Diamond sentiment. We can't let anyone know about our group, but connecting with other students who have suffered at the hands of the Diamonds could prove useful in the future. They could be our greatest allies."

"So, once we get all of this information," Jenny said skeptically, "which is basically going to be, like, *impossible*, what are we going to do? Show it to Principal Newman? What if he doesn't care? What's the point of putting all of this time and energy into catching the Diamonds doing illegal stuff if we don't know what we're going to *do* with that evidence once we get it? We need a game plan."

Then it hit me. "Hold on a minute," I said, rummaging through my purse. I took out a crumpled piece of paper I'd nearly forgotten about, unfolded it, and passed it to Tommy.

He stared at the flyer for a moment, a smile inching across his face until he looked genuinely pleased. In thick lettering he wrote:

FASHION SHOW

Tommy paused for a moment, letting the words sink into our brains. Then, underneath, he wrote:

THIS IS WAR!

We were about to call it quits for the night when I realized one major element in our freedom crusade that had been forgotten.

"Wait," I said, standing up from the couch. Anderson, who had been squished next to me, ran his fingers along the outside seam of my jeans as I spoke. "You know what I think we're missing?"

"A wedge of Brie and a poor attitude toward foreigners?" asked Monique.

"Not exactly," I said. "Our own declaration of independence."

I ran over to the Post-it board and grabbed the marker. "We need to write down what we want and use it as a motivator. That way, when times are tough, we can always remember what we are fighting for.

"So what is it that we want?"

"Er, liberty!" cried Monique.

"Justice," Darcy bellowed.

"The right to wear jazz pants whenever we feel like it!" Boyd shouted.

"Yes!" I said, the ideas coming faster than I could record them. "What else?"

We were done in less than twenty minutes. Please keep in mind that a good portion of this was borrowed from the actual Declaration of Independence. Don't think of it as copying. Really. It's more of an homage.

THE (STONECUTTERS) DECLARATION OF INDEPENDENCE
In High School

The Unanimous Declaration of the Stonecutters,

When in the Course of high school events, it becomes necessary for one people to react against the indecencies forced upon them by another, and to stand up for themselves against adversity and nasty skanks, taking hold of their God-given rights, it is necessary that they declare the reasons why their foes, the Diamonds, have given them no choice other than to revolt.

We hold these truths to be self-evident, that all teens are created equal, even those with physical deformities and/or fugly faces and/or bad breath, that they are protected from pretty, mean girls who try to deny them their Rights, which include but are not limited to: freedom, justice, and tongue-kissing whomever they desire.

Those rights should be protected by their institution, the Bennington School, and not denied them by any student-run organizations acting as a Government, such as the mock trial team. In such a case, after insurmountable abuses and injustices, it is the Right of the Students to overthrow said Government, the Diamonds, replacing it with a new foundation based on the above principles to ensure Equality, Happiness, and Good Grades.

Such has happened at Bennington, and we, the Stonecutters, have united to speak on the Students' behalf. It is necessary to abolish the Diamond Court, as their history is one of repeated wrath and indignities, having established an absolute Tyranny over the social lives of the Students. To prove this, below are a few of many wrongs enacted by the Diamonds:

- *They have refused to create laws for the good of the whole—only a select elite.*

- They have not abided by the rules of a "fair trial" and instead have unfairly influenced rulings for personal gain.
- They have issued rulings outside of the courtroom (also referred to as the chorus room).
- They have placed one of their Representatives at the helm of the student government, therefore denying the opportunity for any checks and balances from other arenas on their actions.
- They have attacked innocent individuals for their own benefit and made it impossible for said individuals to walk the halls with pride.
- They have attacked the moral fiber and character of individuals whom they do not like, and have insulted them in front of the entire community.
- They have made nearly every Student at Bennington feel bad about him- or herself.
- They have forgone the Bill of Rights and instead have created their own document, the Diamond Rules, which was not approved by the Students and is being used to deny their rights instead of protect them.
- They are bad friends.
- They are not as hot as they think they are.
- They are evil byotches with no sense of compassion, totally unworthy to be in control of any Government and in need of severe punishment.

Therefore, we, the Stonecutters, the Representatives of the Bennington School's Student Body, do solemnly publish and declare that We are no longer under the rule of the Diamond Court and are absolved of our allegiance to them and, as

Independent individuals, declare the Right to wage War against the Diamonds. For the strength of this Declaration, we mutually pledge to one another our Passion and our Reputations, which, though not without fault, are all we have to Give.

THE STONECUTTERS

Marni Valentine	*Turbo Samuels*	*Darcy McKibbon*
Anderson St. James	*Boyd Longmeadow*	*Jed Brantley*
Tommy Payne	*Monique French*	*Jenny Murphy*

• EXHIBIT N •

＊　＊　＊

School was more tolerable after that. People were still complete assholes to me, but I had a secret mission. And, it seemed, that was enough. Even when random kids gave me nasty looks or muttered dirty words or made fun of me behind my back, it didn't matter anymore. The end was in sight.

Let them smirk, I thought as I hurried between classes or opened my locker or sat alone at lunch. (Anderson had off a different period.) If I was particularly depressed, all I had to do was pass Monique near the girls' bathroom or lock eyes with Turbo outside the main office—only for a second!—to feel suddenly invigorated, like a burst of caffeine or a bolt of lightning had surged through my entire body.

Things were about to begin.

And I was ready.

The following week, Tommy assigned us "covert oper-
ation" routes on which we had to follow the Diamonds
around town, recording their every move. Who they
spoke to. What they did after school. "It's called 'trailing the suspect,' " Darcy told us. "My dad does it all
the time."

Supposedly, if we got the Diamonds' routines down
pat, we would be able to notice anything out of the ordinary and (hopefully) catch them doing something
incriminating, like meeting with a member of the jury
outside school or making a voodoo doll of me and setting it on fire. You never know.

As someone who already knew the Diamonds' routine, a lot of this "trailing" seemed unnecessary, but
since the whole thing had been my idea to begin with,
I felt obligated to participate. And besides, I *was* sort
of curious about what my former best friends were up
to. Who wouldn't be?

Here's what I'll say about my initial experience:
trailing Clarissa home in Boyd's PT Cruiser was an ultimate low. (And not only because Boyd refused to
play anything except the original Broadway cast
recording of *Kiss of the Spider Woman*.)

A month or so earlier, I would have been *inside*
Clarissa's Audi. Right beside her. Now I was outside—
in another car entirely—and the distance between us
was overwhelming.

"Chita Rivera was mad fierce in this bullshit," Boyd

said, turning up the volume. Ahead, Clarissa was making a left onto her street. "Don't you think?"

I liked musicals as much as the next person, but I was *sure* I didn't like them as much as Boyd did. And I didn't feel like getting into any debates at the moment. "I guess."

"You *guess?*" Boyd looked at me like I had slapped him across the face. "What kind of theater freak are you?"

"I'm not a theater freak," I said.

"Oh, please," Boyd said, waving me off with one hand. "Everyone is a theater freak. Even if they don't know it." He looked me up and down. "How many bootleg recordings do you have of Broadway shows? Twenty? You can tell me."

"Zero."

"Well, what about *Wicked?* You must at *least* have a bootleg of that."

I rolled my eyes. "Can we talk about something else?"

Before I knew it, we were in front of Clarissa's house, across the street, parked underneath a tree. "Like what?" he asked. "Jazz dance? Marimba?"

"How about something completely unrelated to musicals or Broadway?"

Boyd tilted his head until it was almost parallel to the ground. "I don't understand the question."

"All you ever do is talk about, well, very stereotypically—"

"Gay things?"

Boyd studied me, apparently waiting to see how I would react. Sure, I'd assumed Boyd was gay, but I didn't *really* know. I certainly didn't want to offend him.

"That's not what I meant."

"Oh no?"

I bit my lip. What *had* I been trying to say?

"You know," Boyd said, leaning back in his seat, "for someone who doesn't have a whole lot of friends at the moment, you're pretty judgmental." He blinked. "It's not a good look for you."

I couldn't think of anything coherent to say. Boyd was right. I might have been trying to get back at the Diamonds, but I was still acting like one.

I saw Boyd the next day right before first period. He was wearing penny loafers and a tight pair of khakis. His hair, I thought, had been Japanese-straightened.

"Hey!" he said, leaning his elbow on the locker next to mine. "Whaddup?"

I looked at him confusedly. "Hi," I said. "Um, how are you?"

"Oh, *fine*," he said, tossing back his shoulders and sighing dramatically. "Someone threw a bagel at me in the parking lot. It hit me in the head, which totally hurt, but then I was like, *Nice, free bagel!*" I glanced down and saw a half-eaten cinnamon-raisin bagel in his hand. "We still on for this afternoon?"

I shut my locker, books piled in my arm, and

narrowed my eyes. We were supposed to follow Clarissa again that day, but I wasn't sure if he would want to anymore. "You're not mad at me?"

"For what?"

"Yesterday," I said. I had an apology all prepared. Anderson had already talked me through it on the phone the night before. I'd gone over it in my head the entire drive to school.

ME: I'm sorry for making assumptions about you and your lifestyle, Boyd, and for being insensitive. And uncaring. And for my lack of enthusiasm re: *Kiss of the Spider Woman* and musicals in general. I really do like them, actually. A lot. Please forgive me?

Boyd looked as if he were about to say something important: his lips were slightly parted, his eyes incredibly focused. But then he shimmied, cementing both hands to his hips. "I have no idea what you're talking about, Marni." He glanced at his watch. "See you after school. Don't be late."

I smiled to myself. It seemed as though I had already been forgiven.

School was uneventful that day. I had a lab in physics. A test in calculus. Ms. Ariana made me audition for a solo in chorus, and the Diamonds laughed the entire time I sang. (I'm not a good singer.) Anderson's psychology class was canceled, and we left campus and had lunch at Wendy's. I ate a salad and half his fries.

In Mr. Townsen's class, we were supposed to pair up and choose a U.S. Supreme Court case, writing a report either in support of the majority decision or against it. Everyone immediately claimed a partner as I sat alone at my desk. I felt like the fat kid in gym class, except I wasn't fat. And I wasn't in gym class.

Finally, a kid named Arjit took pity and sat down next to me. Well, that's not exactly true. Mr. Townsen approached him and pointed at me, and Arjit slunk toward me with a look of defeat on his face. (You know you're unpopular when the teacher has to *force* someone to be your partner.)

Arjit was small, maybe five foot five, and had a constellation of acne across his forehead. His eyebrows were thick and untamed, and his sideburns trailed all the way down to his jawline. He was the type of guy I never would have spoken to a few months earlier. But I was a different person now. Wasn't I? I thought about my interaction with Boyd and decided that being nice to Arjit was exactly the type of thing I *should* be doing. Turning over a new leaf. Becoming a kinder, more sincere person. Arjit was probably a great guy, and now I had the opportunity to know him better.

"So," I said in a light, sweet voice. "Which case do you want to work on?"

Arjit glared at me in a way that said, *Back off, bitch*. "Arjit?"

"Whatever," he said, looking away. I followed his eyes, which were locked on the Diamonds. They were staring right at us. "I don't care. Can you just, like, not talk so much? Your voice is really irritating."

I won't lie: getting told off by Arjit was a definite

229

blow, but I was used to it by now. Kind of. I turned over a new page in my binder and wrote my name at the top. This whole being-nice-to-people thing was going to be a lot harder than I'd imagined.

"I can*not* believe he said that," Boyd said, taking a sip of his coffee. We were back inside his car, listening to *Sunday in the Park with George*. "Who knew Arjit could be such a douche?"

"Apparently I bring out the worst in people," I said, staring at Clarissa's house, an old Victorian with a wraparound porch and a canary yellow door. How many times had I sat on that porch? Knocked on that door?

"You're just going through a rough spot," Boyd said knowingly. "It'll pass. All storms do."

"It certainly doesn't feel that way."

Boyd traced the steering wheel with one finger. "You're actually pretty lucky, Marni. You just can't see it right now."

I laughed. Me? Lucky? "I can't see it because it's not true," I said, "but it's nice of you to say so, Boyd."

"No, I'm serious," he said, turning to face me. "I mean, sure, your friends turned out to be total gorilla bitches, but you're, like, gorgeous, you're smart *and* funny, and you have, like, a *way* hot boyfriend."

I raised an eyebrow, and he blushed. I guess he'd answered my question after all. "I won't say anything, you know. About you . . . being . . . well . . . you know."

Boyd shrugged. "I'm not ashamed of who I am, but I'm not ready to tell my parents. Not yet. Maybe once I go away to college." He touched my shoulder. "Thanks, though."

"You're welcome," I said.

"I know you don't think I'm right about your being lucky," he continued, "but I am. And even if I wasn't, you have friends now. You just have to give us a chance."

Despite our belonging to a secret organization, I had yet to think of the Stonecutters as my friends. Sitting there with Boyd, though, I realized that was exactly what they were. Well, not yet. But that was what they had the potential to be.

If I let them.

Nothing happened at Clarissa's until the fifth time we followed her home. It was a Thursday, around six o'clock. Mock trial had been over for nearly an hour. The sky was dark, and I had to squint to see anything at all. Boyd was in the driver's seat, as usual, but this time Turbo was with us, sprawled along the backseat as though it were a couch. Every five minutes or so, I would glance at him in the rearview mirror.

"Dude," Turbo said, taking off his hat and scratching his head, "how long are we gonna stay here for?"

"Why?" Boyd asked. He was reading the latest *In Touch*. "Got somewhere better to be? Hot date?"

Turbo snorted. "I wanted to do some skateboarding."

I was always surprised when people who looked like skaters actually *skated*. I thought it was more of a fashion statement than anything else.

"Are you any good?" I asked, craning my neck toward the back of the car. "I don't mean that in a rude way, Turbo. I'm just wondering."

"Nah, it's cool. I'm all right. I used to be a lot better."

"What happened?" Boyd tore his eyes from the magazine. "Did you pop a wheelie?"

Turbo laughed. "Do you even know what that means?"

Boyd shook his head. "I've always wanted to say it, though."

"I guess." Turbo put his hat back on. There was a skull on it, and it was incredibly tattered. I think he thought it made him look tough. "Anyway, I just practice a lot less. Back when I went to Dover, a bunch of my friends skated, so we'd all hang out after school and shit. But I lost touch with them when I started at Bennington, so, ya know. It sucks."

"Wait a minute," I said. "You went to Dover?"

Fact: Dover (elementary, middle, and high schools) is the public school district I belonged to before starting at Bennington.

"Yup," Turbo said. "Up through freshman year."

"That's weird," I said. "I don't remember you. I went there for middle school."

The years I'd spent at Dover middle school were ones I rarely spoke of. Not because it was a bad school

232

or anything (although compared to Bennington, it was) but because I was no longer the same person I'd been when I'd gone there. I'd grown out of my awkward, gangly years, of having as many friends as I had pairs of shoes (very few), of simply *waiting* for my real life to begin.

Oddly enough, despite my metamorphosis from public school caterpillar to private school butterfly, I felt more like the girl I'd been at Dover *now* than when I went there.

Turbo rubbed his chin, which was spotted with blond stubble. "I remember you."

I was shocked. "You do?"

"OMG," Boyd said, bouncing up and down, "I want to know *everything*. All the details."

I wondered what, exactly, Turbo remembered about me. The too-big jeans and plain colored T-shirts I wore? My L.L. Bean backpack? The lonely circular table I sat at during lunch with Franny Shirlington, who had the face of a pug and the body of a Great Dane?

For the first time since I'd known him, Turbo looked, well, thoughtful. "Marni was . . . Marni was"— he glanced at me and smiled with all his teeth—"really cute."

"Cute?"

"Yeah," Turbo said. "I had a crazy-ass crush on you in seventh grade. I wanted to ask you to the Halloween dance but I never did because I thought you'd say no."

Seventh grade. Halloween dance. I hadn't even gone.

"You can't be serious," I said. The idea of someone having a crush on me back in middle school was incomprehensible. I couldn't wrap my head around it.

"Dude," said Turbo, rubbing the brim of his hat. "I am."

"Awww," Boyd said, clasping his hands. "You two could have been, like, *lovers*. I think I'm gonna cry. Or throw up in my mouth a little bit."

"Whatever," Turbo said, laughing. "It's all old news anyway."

It wasn't old news, though. Not to me. Before I could think about it any more, however, I was temporarily blinded by a pair of headlights.

"Ow," Boyd said, covering his eyes. "Brights are *totally* unnecessary in a residential area."

The car—a dark-colored BMW—pulled into Clarissa's driveway. Once the lights were off, I was able to make out the identity of the driver. A thick scarf was wrapped around her neck, covering nearly half her face, but it was definitely her: Emmy Montgomery. Juror no. 9. (We didn't actually refer to the jurors by number, but it's more dramatic this way.)

"Quick," Boyd said, poking me. "Get my camera out of the glove compartment."

I grabbed the tiny Nikon and tossed it to him. He immediately began clicking away. I was worried Emmy would notice the flash, but she seemed all-consumed, rushing up the steps and knocking on the door until it opened and she slipped inside.

Boyd turned off his camera and rested it on his leg. "That was thrilling!" he said. "I feel like a paparazzo or something."

Turbo, from the back, said, "Well, what do we do now?"

I wasn't sure. We had shots of Emmy outside Clarissa's house, but they didn't really *prove* anything. Was this what we'd been waiting for all these days? Some random pictures taken from a few feet away? Suddenly, our plan seemed, well, futile.

"I guess we should go home," I said. Boyd nodded in my direction, and Turbo exhaled something that sounded like "Finally."

I pulled out my cell phone. One text. Anderson.

WANNA MEET UP LTR . . . 10PM?

The digital clock on my phone read 6:59. What was I going to do for three hours? Homework? The idea made me cringe.

Boyd started his engine. We turned out of Clarissa's neighborhood and onto Willis Avenue, heading nowhere in particular. I would probably go home and take a nap. Or avoid my mother.

"So," Boyd said, "who am I dropping off first?" He looked at me, then at Turbo, but neither of us said anything. I guessed that—despite his whining—Turbo didn't really have anywhere to be, either.

Up ahead, on the right, was a Baskin-Robbins Clarissa and I had frequented whenever we'd needed a little pick-me-up. The neon lights seemed to be calling my name.

"Anybody want ice cream?" Boyd asked.

My stomach rumbled. "I'd have some."

"Me too," Turbo chirped.

"Okay, then," Boyd said, putting on his blinker. "Baskin-Robbins it is!"

As Boyd parked his car and I opened the door, Turbo rushing out ahead of me, I thought, *This is the sort of thing friends do*.

♦ 5 ♦

If a friend, enemy, or frenemy accuses you of
a heinous crime, you have the right to appear
before the Diamond Court. Wear diamonds.
—*The Diamond Rules*

Opening myself up to the Stonecutters did not happen
overnight. Tiny things at first, like getting ice cream,
allowed me to shed the layers that had accumulated
during my years as a Diamond and discover what lay
underneath.

"I'm so proud of you," Anderson told me one night
in front of my house. We were inside his Jeep. Making
out. Ryan Adams sang from the speakers.

"Why?" I remember asking.

"For hanging out with these kids and not being a
total bitch."

"What's that supposed to mean?"

"Whoa," he said, both hands in the air. "I just
mean, like, you're being really nice to everyone."

"I *am* really nice." Wasn't I?

Anderson smiled. "You're a lot of things, Marni,
but nice isn't exactly one of them." He leaned over

and kissed me. "What's so good about being *nice*, anyway? The important thing is that the Stonecutters like you, and I think they're really starting to."

I couldn't have disagreed more. I wanted to be nice. I wanted people to like me because of the person I was, not because of who they *thought* I was.

But this was Anderson. My boyfriend. And sometimes you have to pick your battles. So I chose to focus on his lips instead of the words coming out of them, and let him kiss me until I was tired.

That conversation with Anderson kick-started a desire to return to a time pre-Diamonds, before Clarissa; the only problem was I didn't know the first thing about getting there. I decided to reach out to the Stonecutters—not just Boyd—and actually *connect* with them, hopefully finding some answers (and friends?) in the process.

One afternoon, I went skateboarding with Turbo. Believe me, I know. When he asked me to go, my immediate reaction was *No*, but then I thought, *That's the old you; the new you would go skateboarding.*

That's the interesting thing about self-improvement: you have to *try*.

So I met up with Turbo outside his house for my first lesson in "boarding." That afternoon—it was a Thursday—I was *supposed* to be trailing Clarissa with Boyd, but Monique went in my place. "Don't worry," she told me, "eet is my pleasure. Boyd always smells so nice—like soap. And babies."

Turbo had one of his old skateboards for me to use. Let me just say it was a lot harder than it looked. I stepped onto it and fell immediately. Then I tried again and managed to keep my balance for about all of three seconds before—you guessed it—dropping to the ground. I think I fell about ten times in the first minute.

"No, no," Turbo said, putting his hands on my shoulders. He'd been standing a foot or so away, watching from the sidewalk, but apparently it was time for a demonstration. "You're doing it all wrong."

"Of *course* I'm doing it all wrong," I said, frustrated. The insides of my palms were red and throbbing. "It's impossible!"

Turbo smiled. "Nothing is impossible, Marni." He dropped his skateboard—which had been tucked underneath his arm—to the ground and jumped onto it. "Watch." He kicked up his leg and went gliding down the street, arms loose and weightless in the air. Everything was sturdy and smooth beneath his feet. When he turned and stopped right in front of me, I couldn't help clapping.

"You're really good," I said.

Turbo blushed and ran his fingers through his hair, which was matted to his forehead. He took off his jacket and threw it onto the pavement. "That was nothing. Now you try."

"I don't think so." I held up my palms as evidence. "I can't survive another fall."

"Sometimes you need to fall so you can get back up again." He held out his hand. "Here. I'll help you."

239

"Okay," I said. What the hell, right? I grabbed his hand, which was only slightly sweaty, and hopped onto my board. It wobbled, but Turbo steadied me. I closed my eyes. When I opened them, I was standing on the skateboard, unassisted.

"Now, take your left leg and touch it to the pavement. Then, bring it back to the board," Turbo instructed.

Slowly, I moved my leg and pressed down, scraping my sneaker against the street. I was off before I knew it. The road in front of Turbo's house had a downhill slant, and I was picking up speed. I stretched my arms as if they were wings, and yelled, "*Shit!*" about a thousand times. I had no idea how to stop. I was moving so quickly there was barely any time to think.

Houses blurred past me. All I saw were colors—red, yellow, blue—and I was pretty sure I was going to die. Or at least break something. Like my neck. Or my boobs. *Can you break your boobs?* Suddenly, though, I was completely still. A pair of arms were wrapped around me. As soon as I caught my breath, I realized that Turbo was, well, hugging me.

I broke the embrace and stepped off the skateboard, planting both feet on the pavement. I felt like a sailor finding solid ground after months at sea.

"Are you okay?" His eyes were wide open and insanely green. He looked worried.

"Yeah." I pressed my hand to my chest and felt my heart pounding. "You caught me."

"Did you think I was gonna let you fall?"

Yes. No. Maybe.

"No," I said finally. "I didn't."

"Good." Turbo reached down and picked up my skateboard. "Do you want something to drink?"

I nodded. My throat felt scratchy and dry.

"Let's go to my house," he said, leading the way.

"It's unsweetened," Turbo said, handing me a cold glass of iced tea. We were in his kitchen, which was bright and sunny, on a pair of wooden stools that faced each other. Pictures of nicer kitchens were cut out of magazines and taped to the walls. "We have sugar somewhere," he said, opening an overhead cabinet and looking around.

"That's okay," I said, taking a sip. It was good. "I'm fine."

Turbo sat back down and played with the rim of his glass. "I never thought I'd see the day Marni Valentine was sitting at my kitchen table."

"Yeah, right," I said, crossing my legs, noticing each new scratch on my skin.

"I'm serious," he said in a voice that made me think he actually was. "You're, like, high school royalty. Well, I mean, you *were*."

I laughed. The pain in my hands was subsiding; I pressed them to the glass, letting the ice work its magic. "Thanks?"

The clock on the wall—which was light blue, like a robin's egg—ticked softly as we drank. It was nearly five-thirty.

"Do you miss your friends?" Turbo asked finally. A few seconds passed. "Is it weird I just asked you that?"

"No, but I'm not sure they were ever really my friends."

"Don't say that. I mean, they're nasty, yeah, but you must have liked them at some point, right? They must have *some* redeeming qualities."

I thought about the Diamonds—the times I did my homework with Lili, or went to the mall with Priya, or ate dinner with Clarissa and her parents—and nodded. "There are a few things I miss," I admitted, "but there are a lot of things I don't. I'm trying to, like, redefine my happiness and be thankful for what I *do* have instead of being pissed about everything I lost. It's hard, though."

Turbo swished his drink around. "Tell me about it. When I left Dover, I thought my life was over. Things got better, though. Not like they did for you, but I manage." He looked like he was about to ask something serious, but then my phone rang.

It was Anderson.

I knew exactly why he was calling—in case I was having an awful time skateboarding and wanted him to pick me up—but I didn't feel like leaving just yet.

"Aren't you gonna get that?"

"It's just Anderson. I'll call him back."

Turbo raised his eyebrows. "Trouble in paradise?"

"No," I said playfully. "We're fine, thank you very much."

"It's just that I never see you guys apart. You're basically attached at the hip."

Were we? I certainly didn't feel that way. In fact, it seemed like ages since Anderson and I had spent quality time together *alone*, without the Stonecutters. "We're close," I said, leaving it at that.

"Dude," Turbo said, "that's the understatement of the century."

"Oh, whatever," I said, getting up and placing my glass in the sink. "I think that was the longest you've gone without saying 'dude' since I've known you."

"Yeah?"

"Yeah," I said, pausing to notice the way his hair curled over his ears. "Can I ask you something?"

"Sure."

"Why *do* you talk like that?"

Turbo cocked his head. "You mean like a skater?"

"Yeah."

"I dunno. I guess it's what people expect of me."

I thought about the way I acted around Clarissa, about how important to me it was—used to be—that people were intimidated by me, in awe of me. That I sparkled.

"Well," I said, "if there's one thing I've learned, it's that being what people expect you to be sort of, um—"

"Sucks?"

I smiled. "Besides, I like it when you talk like a normal person."

Turbo returned my smile. "Okay, well, maybe I'll try it more often. *If* you keep on skateboarding with me."

I looked at my hands, which were as red as tomatoes, and considered his offer. "Sure. Why not?"

"Cool," Turbo said, sliding off his stool and standing next to me. "One more question—how did it feel? When you were boarding?"

I didn't even have to think about my answer. "Like I was flying."

The Diamond-helmed fashion show had turned into a *huge* deal at Bennington; what had once been an ill-formed idea at my lunch table back in October was now an extravagant reality. It was set to take place the Friday before the announcement of the official Snow Court, the next weekend—the last weekend in December before winter break—being the Snow Ball itself.

Clarissa had made sure that the event garnered more than its share of press, too. All the major department stores and local boutiques were donating clothes to be displayed by Bennington's elite. The custodians had even constructed a catwalk running the length of one of the aisles in the auditorium. Every single flyer read *FOR HOMELESS TRANNIES EVERYWHERE*.

The fashion show was an *event*. Not a single Bennington student, *plus* however many parents and faculty members purchased tickets, would dare miss it.

The basic structure of the Stonecutters' plan was to embarrass the Diamonds before the entire student body and expose them for the evil hobgoblin snatches they were. Tommy had the (brilliant) idea to print anonymous slips of paper depicting Clarissa's wrongdoings and slip them into the fashion show programs, which, since we didn't have any *actual* proof, would at least be enough to get people talking. (Tommy seemed unconcerned about our lack of evidence against the Diamonds. "It's called building your case, Marni," he told me one morning before school. "You're not going to get everything overnight. You have to keep collecting pieces until the proof is overwhelming. Guilty beyond a reasonable doubt.")

So I decided not to worry that all we had were a few blurry pictures to support our accusations. Instead, I focused on the details of our plan to correct all the wrongs the Diamonds had perpetuated over the past few months.

Allow me to set the scene: the show is about to begin. Audience members are leafing through their programs, chatting idly. Music is playing in the background. Suddenly, it stops. Everyone is wondering what the deal is. Clarissa and the Diamonds try to rush the models into their clothes and continue as if nothing happened. No one realizes (until it's too late) that the models are stuffed into the *wrong* clothes. The duds donated by the local stores have vanished, replaced with extra-large T-shirts featuring defaced pictures of Clarissa, Priya, and Lili on the front. The models float down the runway, unaware at first of what is happening; then, suddenly, the entire audience is laughing. A woman calls attention to the program insertion in a loud and obnoxious way. Clarissa & Co. trample onstage to see everything they've worked for crumble before their very eyes. I am standing in the back of the auditorium with Anderson, and later that night, the Stonecutters toast our success.

The next day, Tommy prints my exposé in the paper and the tables turn on my former BFFs. The Diamond Court immediately becomes defunct; Jed reclaims his rightful place at the head of the student government; and other students no longer feel the need to abide by the Diamond Rules or *any* rules whatsoever. Soon after, there are no more social cliques at Bennington. Druggies mix with preps; preps mix with druggies; boys hold hands with other boys in the hallway (even though they're just buddies!); and girls kiss other girls on the cheek before class merely as a way to say I *value your friendship*. Anderson and I apply to the same college; on the day we receive our acceptance letters, we gaze overhead, and I sigh in his arms and cry, *Look! A rainbow*.

Too bad I can't actually predict the future.

The fashion show was eerily close, which meant the Stonecutters had their plates full and *then* some. Anderson's house had become a sort of refuge from the tragedy of school. Clarissa had continued full speed ahead with her plan to purge the hallways of her Ice Queen competitors. She wasn't attacking only the girls, either. Everyone was a potential victim.

The worst part? She was no longer even bothering to create fake-yet-realistic reasons to bring people in front of the court. She was attacking the quality of people's clothes, the style of their haircuts, their complexions, who they hung out with, where they went on the weekends—their *lives*.

Clarissa knew that the best way to secure her own position as a princess (and future queen) was to discredit her competitors to the greatest degree possible. As a result, the trials of the Diamond Court had become even more sinister. Mock trial meetings were now closed to the Bennington public. Rulings were printed in the school paper and posted on Facebook, the sudden mystery behind the Diamonds' actions propelling them even further into an unparalleled, celebrity-like status.

"We, as a country, get the government we deserve," Mr. Townsen told us during AP Gov. I knew he was talking about the United States, but his words seemed perfectly relevant to the situation at Bennington. Principal Newman refused to shut the Diamonds down without multiple complaints from the student body (which, since everyone was scared shitless of Clarissa, were nonexistent); even Townsen himself seemed all too happy to let the Diamonds rule supreme as long as the majority approved.

Which they did.

Most people loved the Diamonds more than ever. But did that mean Bennington *deserved* Clarissa's wrath? It hardly seemed fair, especially since the minority— the outcasts—were the ones who were truly suffering.

At this point, however, nothing involving my former BFFs fazed me. Which was why when I noticed something white and folded sticking out of my locker,

I expected the worst. I pulled and saw that it was not *one* piece of paper but several, stapled together in a thin packet. It said:

THE DIAMOND RULES—UPDATED

To the Bennington student body—

Below you will find a list of addendums to the Diamond Rules. Please take note and adjust accordingly.

Lili Chan-Mohego • STUDENT BODY PRESIDENT
Clarissa von Dyke • MOCK TRIAL PRESIDENT
Priya Ramnani • FASHIONISTA

1. *If the Diamond Court determines that you have cankles, or any other body imperfections, you will be given one (1) warning by the Court. If drastic measures are not taken to fix said imperfections, you will be tried by the Court for Public Indecency.*

2. *Anyone found guilty by the Diamond Court is no longer allowed to voice an opinion in public, whether in an extracurricular club/organization or by publishing articles in the Bennington Press.*

3. *If your thighs touch and/or your stomach has more rolls than a bakery, never speak out loud. To anyone.*

4. *Anyone overheard "dissing" the Diamond Court or any members of the jury or the mock trial team will be tried for Treason by the Court.*

5. Preexisting student groups must reapply for funding through the Diamond Court and present a current roster of all group members for the Court's approval.

6. No student group or extracurricular activity (with the exception of sports teams) may have more than twenty active members.

7. Anyone found guilty by the Diamond Court is no longer allowed to vote in any student government elections.

8. Hooking up with a fatty does not count for community service.

9. If you come to school looking a Hot Mess (as determined by the Diamond Court), turn right around. You're not welcome here.

10. Any punishment issued by the Diamond Court is binding; afterward, if the Court does not feel that the recipient has learned his or her lesson, the Court is hereby allowed to reissue punishment, determining the length and severity on a case-by-case basis.

•EXHIBIT O•

I couldn't believe my eyes. I quickly folded the packet and slipped it into my bag. That was when I noticed that every single locker in the senior-year wing had a packet wedged inside it, too. The hallway was filled with students devouring the reports.

Wrecking the fashion show was a good idea. I honestly thought so. But I suddenly wondered if it was enough. Unfortunately, there was only one person I could appeal to for help, and there was the definite possibility that he was untrustworthy. Sometimes, though, you have to take a risk in order to succeed. A leap of faith.

I took a deep breath, letting my lungs expand with air.

Then I jumped.

Mr. Townsen's office was exactly as I'd remembered it. Too-neat desk, picture frames filled with smiles, the window overlooking the courtyard freshly scrubbed and slightly open.

I hadn't spoken to Townsen since I'd left the mock trial team. He was still my teacher, of course, but we never chatted outside of class.

Townsen smiled as if he were expecting me. "Marni. I'm so glad you stopped by. You know, when Clarissa told me what happened, I was very concerned. But I wanted to give you some space. I knew you would find me when the time was right."

"I'm sorry, what did you say?"

"You would find me when the time was right," he repeated.

"Before that."

"I wanted to give you some space?"

"No, before that."

Townsen paused to think. "When Clarissa told me what happened?"

"Yes," I said. "What exactly did she tell you?"

"Have you spoken with Dr. Andrews?"

Fact: Dr. Andrews is the school psychologist. He has a black mustache and a gray beard, and he smells like a fish market.

I shook my head.

"Maybe you should, Marni," Townsen suggested. "I had a cousin once who suffered from a mental breakdown, and talking to someone really helped her. She's an entirely different person now. And not in a schizophrenic way. In a good way."

"Clarissa told you I had a mental breakdown?"

Mr. Townsen reached across his desk and gave my hand a quick pat. "It's nothing to be embarrassed about."

"Uh, thanks," I said, not even bothering to correct him. "But that isn't why I came to see you."

"No?"

I took the packet out of my bag. "Have you seen this?"

"What about it?"

"You *have* to know what's been going on around here," I said. "The way Clarissa took over the mock trial team and got Jed kicked out of student government, and then she started making these, well, these *laws*, and at first I thought it was harmless and I played along—okay, I *helped* her—but I didn't know what I was doing, and then she turned on me and now basically nobody likes me except for—well, that's not important, but still, Mr. Townsen, she's, like . . . a tyrant! It's like the Salem witch trials all over again, except

251

instead of killing people for being witches, she's killing them *socially* because she's worried she won't be elected Ice Queen, and she's throwing this fashion show and she doesn't even care about the trannies. You have to *do* something—"

"Marni." Mr. Townsen placed his hands firmly on his desk. "That's enough, okay?"

A whoosh of air left my mouth like helium from a balloon. "I know you think it's the students' responsibility to stand up to Clarissa, but you have no idea what she's like, Mr. Townsen. This time she's gone too far."

"I've already spoken with Clarissa," he said.

"You have?"

"She came to me as soon as she found one of these"—he motioned to the amendments—"*packets* in her locker. She was very upset and asserted that neither she, Lili, nor Priya had anything to do with their creation."

I sat back in my chair. What game was Clarissa trying to play?

"That's ridiculous," I said. "Their *names* are on it. She is *taking over the school* right under your nose!" I clenched the packet in my fist. "Most kids at this school will do *whatever* Clarissa says. She's ruining people's lives, Mr. Townsen, she's—"

"With all due respect, Marni," said Mr. Townsen, "it's just as plausible that *you* authored the packet, isn't it?"

"What do you mean?"

"Clarissa told me about how you reinterpreted the

Bill of Rights. Why should I believe that Clarissa wrote these rules when she told me that *you* wrote them to get her in trouble?"

"But I didn't!"

Townsen gave me a sly grin. "Do you have any evidence?"

Evidence. I hadn't been able to convince Principal Newman without any, and now Mr. Townsen was saying the same thing.

"No," I admitted. "I don't."

Townsen rested both hands on his desk. "Clarissa, Priya, and Lili have been doing a fantastic job with the mock trial team. There is less fighting and cheating than ever before at Bennington. Your role was pivotal in the team's gaining momentum."

How could I forget?

"You're a smart, talented girl, Marni, with a bright future. Don't mess it up over a fight with your friends. If you feel so strongly that the mock trial team is no longer providing justice to Bennington, then you should try to shut the court down."

"But that's why I'm here!"

"I can't do it *for* you, Marni," Mr. Townsen said. "I strongly believe in letting students correct their own mistakes. Maybe Clarissa is right and you're wrong. Maybe not. But if you *are* right, you'll need the support of the student body behind you. No one is going to swoop in and save you except for you. And maybe Superman, but I wouldn't count on it." He smiled. "Instead of complaining to me, or Principal Newman, take charge and *convince* the other students of your claims. Gain their trust. Deliver them the truth; that's how you'll emerge victorious."

How could I make Mr. Townsen believe that despite his best (deluded) intentions, he was allowing the Diamonds to get away with murder? (Or if not murder, something practically as horrific.)

The answer was: I couldn't. At least, not without proof. And the Stonecutters.

After I left Townsen's office, I did something I really shouldn't have done.

I broke into Clarissa's locker.

(Give me a break. You would have done it, too.)

The Stonecutters needed evidence, and I wasn't going to sit around in Boyd's car, listening to musicals and waiting for proof to fall into my lap, any longer. I was going to *take* it.

After checking that the hallway was clear, I made my move. The Diamonds were near the end of a trial (*Bennington v. Stephanie Jones*, who was accused of smelling like a Chinese buffet and stinking up the hallway); I had a narrow time frame.

Clarissa hadn't changed her combination. I twisted the lock and popped open the locker door. The inside was as neat as I'd remembered, binders stacked in a rectangular tower, spines facing out. A pink magnetic mirror and a picture of the Diamonds (I was cut out) stuck to one of the walls.

I ignored her binders and grabbed the black

Moleskine notebook resting on top, which Clarissa used to write down her homework assignments. I flipped through the pages, searching for something—anything—that would incriminate her.

Each page was filled with the loops and swirls of Clarissa's enviable handwriting, but nothing useful popped out. Disappointed, I placed it back inside the locker. It was then that I noticed a second, identical Moleskine tucked behind one of her textbooks.

I picked it up and opened to the first page. It was a date book. Nothing struck me as particularly out of the ordinary—salon appointments, celebrities' birthdays—but as I continued reading, I came across the names of a few kids at Bennington. Underneath each name were two or three lines scribbled about them. One in particular stuck out:

Steffie Young
Blond, pretty, slightly mannish jaw.
Green eyes. Treasurer of Key Club.
re: Sharon Wu

• EXHIBIT P •

To the untrained eye, there was nothing particularly odd about this entry. I, however, knew better—especially after my conversation with Sharon in the courtyard. This was a list of the people Clarissa had convinced to lie and/or vote in her favor on the jury.

The last page I saw was a list of the top twenty—the ten guys and ten girls eligible to be nominated for the Snow Court. All the boys were crossed out except Ryan, Duncan, and Tiger, who were circled in red; as for the girls, Clarissa had circled her name along with Priya's and Lili's. Mine was the very next one down, and it was scribbled over so heavily I could see where the pen had broken through the page. The names that followed mine were crossed out as well, ending with Sharon's. There were two left on the bottom: Ali Roberts and Jenny Murphy.

I had discovered Clarissa's Hit List. Her competition for the Ice Queen crown, who she was taking down one by one.

"Can I help you?"

Without thinking, I shoved the notebook into my back pocket, closing the door with a bang and pivoting toward the intruder.

It was only Tommy.

"Asshole," I said, exhaling. "You practically gave me a heart attack."

He grinned. "Doing a little snooping, eh?"

I nodded.

"Find anything good?"

"Come on," I said. There was just enough time to photocopy the notebook and return it to Clarissa's locker before she noticed that it was missing. "I'll show you."

♦ 6 ♦

If you appear before the Diamond Court, you should look fierce. You may use one of the mock trial team members as a lawyer, or you may provide your own counsel, but he or she can have no working knowledge of the law and must be a freshman. (It's only fair.)

—*The Diamond Rules*

The following afternoon at the Stonecutters' meeting, after sharing the juicy info I'd uncovered inside Clarissa's locker, I asked everyone for a progress update.

"Monique and I followed Priya home almost every day last week," Boyd said, "except for Tuesday, because we stopped to get frozen yogurt."

"Did she do anything incriminating?"

Monique shook her head. "No. But she is quite cruel to the squirrels in her neighborhood. Eet is disgusting."

"*And* she almost ran over a homeless person," Boyd said. "Talk about road rage."

"Well, keep at it," I said, turning to JeDarcy. "What about you two?"

"Nothing yet," said Jed.

"My dad keeps his office pretty well guarded," Darcy said while applying her eyeliner, "but he's going out of town next week. That's when I'll make my move."

"We don't have anything, either," Jenny said. "And Turbo even went through each one of Lili's garbage cans."

"Dude," said Turbo, frowning, "it was so gnarly."

I was incredibly frustrated. There wasn't a single piece of new information we could use. "Everyone needs to step up their game," I said, "and try even harder, okay? This isn't a joke. Boyd, why don't we start trailing Clarissa again? We had some pretty decent luck before. Turbo and Jenny, you guys stick to Priya, and Monique, why don't you—"

"Why don't Jenny and I follow Clarissa instead?" Tommy suggested from the corner, where he was taking notes on his MacBook. "And Marni and Anderson can stake out the Starbucks on Lafayette Street. See if any of the Diamonds drop by."

It was a good idea, actually—despite the fun I'd had with Boyd the last few times we'd trailed Clarissa together. I grabbed Anderson's hand and squeezed.

"See you guys tomorrow," Tommy said, closing his computer and standing up. "And don't slack off. I want a full report from everyone."

•   •   •

"You know what I just remembered?" Anderson said as I grabbed my coat from his bedroom. I slipped it on and closed the door.

"What?"

"I have this huge history project due tomorrow. It's gonna take me all night, and I have to go over to Mark Shebar's house." He frowned. "I'm sorry."

I took his arm. "You know this stakeout is really important, right?"

He nodded.

"I feel like your heart isn't in it for some reason."

Anderson was the one who had encouraged me to hang out with the Stonecutters and make friends. It was because of him I'd put my best foot forward and opened up, but he'd yet to do so himself. Why was that?

"Do you not want to be a Stonecutter?" I asked. "You can tell me."

Anderson pulled me close; even underneath all the layers of cotton, I could feel his chest against mine as he breathed. "Of course I do," he said. "I'm just really stressed. I'm sorry I haven't been as proactive as I should have been. I'm going to try harder. I promise."

I stared into the blue-green of his eyes. Was I mad at Anderson? Not really. Just disappointed. Now that our relationship was out in the open, we seemed to be spending less time together than ever before.

"Why don't you hold off on the stakeout tonight?" Anderson suggested. "Go home and relax. This weekend we'll do something just me and you."

"Okay," I said. It wasn't as though I was dying to sit alone in the Starbucks parking lot.

Anderson leaned in to kiss me quickly on the lips. "You're the best."

When I got to my car, Monique was spread across the hood like a lingerie model. "There you are," she said as if she'd been waiting all day. "Let us go, *oui?*"

"Aren't you supposed to follow Priya with Turbo?"

"There was too much testosterone in his car. Eet was disgusting. I need to spend the afternoon with a lady." She dropped her legs to the pavement. "You do not mind, do you?"

I unlocked the car. "I was actually gonna head home. Anderson just canceled on me, and I figured I'd catch up on some homework."

"Do not be silly," Monique said, falling into the passenger seat. "I will go with you. Eet will be fun."

I barely spent any time alone with Monique. Maybe with her the stakeout *would* be fun. Well, fun-ish.

"All right," I said, starting the engine and turning on the radio. "Let's do it."

We drove away from Anderson's house, down the service road to the highway.

"Do you have any harpsichord music?" Monique asked.

"No."

"Why not?"

"I don't know." Who listened to the harpsichord? "My taste isn't very eclectic, I guess."

Monique clucked her tongue and rubbed the silver hoops of her earrings. Her hair was pinned to her head every which way and stuck out in the back like a peacock's tail. She reminded me of a gypsy from the Disney version of *The Hunchback of Notre Dame* (1996).

"What a shame," she said. "Music is the voice of the heart. Especially that of a harpsichord."

I kept on driving, past houses and trees and Bennington, until we reached the Starbucks in a tiny cluster of stores on Lafayette; it was pretty much equidistant from Priya's, Lili's, and Clarissa's. Over the summer, the four of us had gotten free iced coffees from a cross-eyed barista named Sean who had a crush on Clarissa.

I hadn't gone back since the Closet Incident.

I found a spot near the far end of the parking lot. Mostly out of sight. I turned off the engine; Monique rolled down her window and the cool air slapped me in the face. (It felt kind of nice, actually.) Then she rolled the window back up and reclined in her seat as if she were getting ready for a continental plane ride. "How long do we wait?"

"I dunno. An hour or so." I glanced at the digital clock on the dashboard. 5:17 PM. "Maybe two."

"What shall we do to pass the time?"

"We could just, you know, talk." Boyd had been such a Chatty Cathy I'd never had to worry about

261

what to say, and with Turbo, well, skating wasn't exactly conducive to conversation. Tommy and I discussed the Stonecutters. Anderson felt my boobs. What on earth did I have to talk about with Monique?

"Divine," she said, touching her hand to her forehead. "Let us play truth or dare, *oui*?"

I laughed. I hadn't played that in years. "Sure," I said. "You go first."

"Truth."

"Okay. Umm, where was your favorite place to live?"

Fact: I am terrible at coming up with questions for Truth or Dare.

"Paris," she said quickly. "Now you—truth or dare?"

"Truth."

"Who is a better kisser: Anderson or Jed?"

I cocked my head at Monique. "You little sneak! You just want gossip."

"Eet is part of the game," she said, blushing. "You have to tell me."

"Anderson. Hands down."

"His mouth is so big," Monique said. "I feel like eet would swallow me whole!"

"You're crazy," I said, pushing the lever on the side of my seat and reclining alongside her. "Now you go. Truth or dare?"

"Truth."

"Are you a virgin?"

Monique was silent. Had I gone too far? "I have never had a boyfriend," she answered, gazing out the window.

"You don't need a boyfriend to have sex," I said, which I immediately regretted. It made me sound like a slut. "I mean, I understand why it's important to wait for someone you love."

"Eet is okay, you did not offend me," she said quietly. "I just wonder sometimes if I will ever find that."

"Find what?"

She played with her earrings again, letting them move back and forth against her neck. "Someone to love."

"Oh, Monique," I said, reaching over and taking her hand. "You will. Of course you will."

"Who would want to date me? I am not like the other girls here. I am a freak."

"You are *not* a freak," I said.

A few months earlier, I *had* thought she was a freak. Monique, who danced to the beat of her own drum, who dressed more like a homeless person than someone who'd traveled the world, who had the mustache of a twelve-year-old boy, who spoke with a heavy accent and listened to the harpsichord in her spare time.

But she wasn't a freak. She was her own person. Granted, I didn't exactly understand who that person was—not yet, anyway. But she deserved to be happy, just like everyone else. Just like me.

"Maybe eet would be better if I looked more like you," she said, letting her eyes sweep over me.

"You don't want to look like me," I said. "I'm a mess. You need to be yourself. Don't change for anyone. You will meet someone, I promise, and then you'll know he likes you for *you*—not because of someone you're pretending to be."

Monique smiled at me, the kind of smile that came from inside her, if that makes any sense. "You are so smart, Marni. Thank you."

"No problem." I let my eyes wander for a moment, and there—walking into Starbucks—was Clarissa. "Monique, quick," I said, tapping her shoulder, "grab my camera."

Monique reached into my purse and got out my camera. I pressed the power button and waited a few seconds. Then I took a picture. *Click.*

"I wonder who she is meeting," Monique said.

"Me too."

We watched for what must have been a minute or so before another figure emerged from the parking lot, opening the door to Starbucks and following Clarissa inside.

"*Sacrebleu!*" Monique whispered.

The camera dropped out of my hand and onto Monique's lap. She picked it up. *Click.* But I didn't need a picture to remember whose face I had just seen.

"What is he doing here?" I muttered underneath my breath.

"Eet is extremely peculiar," Monique agreed, peering out my window.

"He said he had to work on a history project with Mark Shebar. He said it was important."

"Maybe he is meeting his friend inside?"

"And Clarissa just happened to show up one minute before? I don't think so."

Monique shrugged. "Eet could happen. A coincidence, no?" *Calm down*, I told myself. *Think about this rationally.* Anderson wasn't meeting Clarissa at Starbucks behind my back. That was ridiculous. Obviously Mark was already inside, waiting to meet up for the project. It was the only plausible explanation. But why then had Anderson told me *not* to continue the stakeout without him? Was there a reason he hadn't wanted me at Starbucks?

"Go," I said to Monique, "and see if Mark is inside. Please?"

I gave Monique a basic description of Mark—tall, brown hair, skinny—and sent her on her way. It seemed like an eternity before she returned. When she opened the door and slid back inside, though, she was smiling.

"Tall, brown hair, skinny," she repeated. "Mark Shebar. That is who Anderson is with. They both have their computers. I did not even see Clarissa."

A wave of relief washed over me. Anderson hadn't lied. "Thank God," I said. I had already lost one boyfriend over cheating (well, sort of); I couldn't bear losing Anderson that way, too.

"I think," I said, starting the engine and pulling out of the driveway, "it's time to turn in. What a night."

"*Oui,*" Monique agreed. "What a night."

A major element of our plan was getting a mole into the fashion show. Despite Jenny's being one of Clarissa's targets for social demolition, she had a decent shot at getting picked; she was leggy, tan, and firm in all the right places, and she was the only Stonecutter who hadn't yet been blacklisted. (Neither had Tommy, but let's be real: he was as likely to model in a fashion show as my mother was to donate her old clothes to the poor.)

The day auditions finally arrived, I was a nervous wreck.

"Do you think she actually went?" Boyd asked. We were at Anderson's, waiting for Jenny. Boyd was filing his nails with his teeth. "Because I could *so* see her pulling an Invisible Woman on our sorry asses."

"Dude," said Turbo, sticking his hand into a glass bowl filled with mixed nuts and crunching down on a cashew. "These are good."

"I bet they are," Boyd smirked.

"She went," I said. "That's not the problem."

The real problem: there was no guarantee the Diamonds would pick Jenny for the fashion show. Clarissa hated her. But thanks to that list I'd found, I was hoping Clarissa would want Jenny around so that she could publicly ruin her in front of a packed audience. Jenny was surprisingly eager ("Just *let* her try to make a fool out of me!"); I prayed that the intrigue factor would get her chosen.

"Where is Tommy?" Monique asked.

After a few general suggestions on my part, Monique had started wearing more fitted clothes (which, after wearing a *muumuu*, pretty much meant anything) and showing off her figure. Now she was in a simple pair of black pants and a turnip-colored sweater.

"He had to stay after school for the paper," I said. It was easy to forget that people had things to do other than attend Stonecutter meetings. Without Tommy and Anderson (who had joined the basketball team now that football season was over and had made me a copy of his house keys), the group was definitely quieter. Jed and Darcy had both stayed for calculus help after school.

"Oh, Boyd," I said, reaching into my bag, "before I forget . . ." I withdrew three pictures—Glamour Shots the Diamonds had gotten at the mall freshman year— and handed them over. "For the shirts."

Boyd's father, a photographer, owned a shop on Leonard Avenue, where he did everything from portraits to reprints to framing. It was called PHOTOS! ("I told him to add the exclamation point," Boyd informed us. "It really makes it pop.") Boyd had assured me it wouldn't be a problem to get the pictures blown up and copied onto plain white T-shirts.

"How many do we need?" Boyd asked, staring longingly at the glossy photos.

"Maybe twenty?" I said, forking over a fifty-dollar bill.

"Don't be silly," said Boyd, refusing the money. "It's on me. *If* I can keep these pictures."

"What pictures?" said a voice new to the conversation. It was Jenny, and she looked *hot*. Model hot. Her hair was tucked behind her ears, rouge accented her naturally high cheekbones, and her lips were detailed in two different shades of pink. She was in the same outfit she'd worn to school—knee-high socks, a plaid reddish skirt, and a cream-colored blouse with pressed cuffs—but had donned a pair of dagger-sharp heels for the occasion. She looked like a photo in *Vogue* or *Glamour* come to life.

"*Très chic,*" said Monique.

"Whoa," said Turbo. "Man, Jenny. Dude."

Boyd squealed like a pig. "Aye aye aye! Here comes trouble!"

"*Stop,*" Jenny said, even though the tone of her voice led me to believe she wanted us to do the exact opposite.

"So?" I asked. "What's the verdict?"

Jenny sauntered down the steps and into the den. She leaned over and fished through the bowl of nuts until she found what she was looking for—a pistachio—and nibbled at it until Boyd was about to explode.

"Say hello to the Bennington School's newest fashion model, bitches!"

With Jenny an Official Mole, the rest of us got down to business. Most days it was just me, Turbo, Boyd, and Monique. Tommy, like I said, had the paper ("It's not going to write, edit, lay out, and print *itself*, you know!"), while Jed and Darcy attended our meetings as though they were rock stars: late and with no excuses. At least they were consistent about their tardiness.

On Wednesday, though, I called JeDarcy out when they showed up an hour after schedule with a pair of annoying smiles and matching cups of coffee.

"What's the deal, guys?" I was frustrated that the Stonecutters hadn't all been together in the same room for what seemed like an eternity. (It's *so* hard to schedule extracurricular super-secret committees.)

"You're always late, which sucks, but if you *are* going to be late, don't come with coffee. It's just rude."

"Point taken," said Jed. "But we can make it up to you."

"Oh? And how are you going to do that?"

Boyd, from the living room, yelled, "You can make it up to Marni by giving me a ball massage, Jed." He paused, then giggled. "I mean a *back* massage. Oops."

"Shut up, Boyd!" I yelled. Then I looked at Jed and Darcy again. Their lips were red and puffy; either they'd both been punched in the face or a serious make-out session had taken place just before their arrival. I hoped for the punching option.

Darcy handed over her iPod. "Here," she said. "Listen."

Clarissa: Ugh, Arlene, don't come so close. You smell like tuna.

ARLENE: That's because I had tuna fish for lunch.

PRIYA: Lesson One—don't ever eat tuna. That's, like, in the Bible.

LILI: I'm not sure it's in the Bible.

CLARISSA: Well, it should be. Ugh. Emmy Montgomery is *pissing* me off lately. She tried to be my partner in gym and I was like, "Hello? Does it *look* like I want to be seen with you?" I liked her enough at first but now I am *so* over that byotch.

PRIYA: Somebody needs to Taser the shit out of her. She is *so* game.

LILI: What does that mean?

PRIYA: Oh, I made it up. It's like gay and lame but I combined them. Game.

LILI: I like it.

CLARISSA: Ditto. I mean, of course I understand why Emmy wants to be a Diamond, but give me a break. She's not that pretty and she's not that fun. And she's a *sophomore*. Come on!

LILI: She did help us score a guilty vote for Mark Ryan *and* Trish Greendorf last week, though. Some of the other jurors are scared of her, I think, which is a good thing.

PRIYA: She reminds me of apple pie.

CLARISSA: Shut up, Priya. I guess Emmy is *fine*, but there are only so many people I can promise spots in the fashion show to. I can't have any crunked-out trolls walking down the runway. I mean, these are *designer* clothes.

LILI: At least she isn't as lame as Joy Darling. She was awful. She looked like a piece of pepperoni pizza.

270

(*Approximately one minute of giggling*)

CLARISSA: I know. She, like, actually thought her opinion mattered. Thank God we got rid of her. Arlene,
what are you doing? Only horses sleep standing up.

ARLENE: Sorry, Clarissa. It's just that with writing up all
the case reports for mock trial, plus my regular homework, I don't really get to bed . . . ever.

CLARISSA: God, Arlene, I didn't ask for your effing life
story. (*shuffling*) Here's five dollars. Go get a Red Bull
and snap out of it.

PRIYA: Get me one, too.

LILI: Oooh, and a Diet Coke.

ARLENE: Sure.

CLARISSA: Oh, and, Arlene?

ARLENE: Yes?

CLARISSA: I appreciate you.

(*click*)

• **EXHIBIT Q** •

"That's the end of that clip," Jed said, "but there's
tons more. And I mean *tons*."

I couldn't hide my excitement; I was practically doing jumping jacks. "So you were able to get one of your
dad's bugs after all?"

Darcy nodded. "Who knows what'll happen when
he finds out it's missing," she said, laughing. "But for
now it's okay. We planted it on Arlene last week and
we have over a dozen hours of them saying the most
incriminating shit *ever*."

"I'm going to edit the best parts into a five-minute

271

audio clip," Jed said. "Clarissa says all this stuff about how lame everyone at Bennington is, and how she's only using the court to become Ice Queen. It's priceless."

"People will go ka-*razy* when they hear it," said Darcy.

"Dude," said Turbo, slapping Jed on the back. "Nice job."

Jed squeezed Darcy's shoulder, and I noticed something electric pass between them. "I barely did anything," he said. "Darcy made it all happen."

Even though it pained me the slightest bit, I leaned forward and said, "Thank you, Darcy."

She smiled without showing her teeth. "I'm glad I could help. Now, let's get those girls!"

It was the first real conversation the two of us had ever shared. It felt nice.

That night, Anderson and I went to a movie. Just like he'd promised. I don't remember what it was called. Something corny and romantic, I'm sure.

Afterward, he parked his car in my driveway and we snuck into my backyard, making sure to avoid the motion sensors as we stumbled onto the cool grass, dropping to our knees and falling backward, gently, until we were side by side, arms touching, legs overlapping, my hand on his chest feeling everywhere, for a pulse, for a heartbeat.

It seemed like hours before either of us spoke.

"What are you thinking about?" I asked.

There were times, it seemed, when Anderson had everything to say and other times, like now, when he had practically nothing at all. The silence killed me. Did he ponder the mysteries of the universe? Worries I could barely begin to comprehend? Or was he thinking about what kind of snack he wanted when he got home or if he needed to cut his toenails? I never could tell.

"Nothing."

"Oh, come on." I moved closer, resting my head on his shoulder. "Right now. What are you thinking about?"

"Nothing. Really."

"Tell me," I said. "I want to know."

We hadn't talked about the night I saw him at Starbucks. There had been plenty of times I could've brought it up—don't get me wrong—but I decided not to. I didn't want to be a crazy girlfriend. I couldn't help thinking about whether he'd bumped into Clarissa, though (he probably had), and whether they'd spoken (they probably had).

I felt him sigh. "Do you ever, like, miss the way things were?"

"What do you mean?"

"I don't know, like, before all this? Having people at school want to be around you. Having a life less . . . complicated. The Stonecutters are fun and all, but it's not the same."

Anderson, I thought, was like an old jewelry box that you opened inch by inch because you didn't want it to fall apart in your hands. I wondered how long he'd been storing this inside and what, if anything, his question truly meant.

"Of course," I said, trying to comfort him. I ran my hand along his arm and up his neck, then caressed his cheek softly with my fingertips. "But being popular isn't everything. And besides, I have you now. I wouldn't trade that for anything in the world."

I waited for a response but all I could hear was the whistling sound the trees made as the wind rustled their leaves. I wiped the wet grass from my forehead and kissed him softly on the lips. "That was your cue, kiddo. You were supposed to tell me you feel the same way."

"I feel the same way."

But did he? Or was he just saying it because I asked him to? I hated being the one to admit my feelings first. I wanted him to tell me how he felt about me without prompting. "Anderson?"

"Mmm," he said. "What?"

"Do you want to . . . ?"

"Want to what?"

"You know."

I maneuvered my legs so that I was practically on top of him, our chests moving up and down in a tender competition. It was a perfect night, with a wide sky and encouraging stars watching over us.

"Mmm," he said, kissing me more deeply.

His body was hard against me and I melted into

him, our noses tip to tip. Why had he been so quiet before? Something about this moment suddenly seemed wrong. I couldn't rid Clarissa from my mind. Anderson was kissing me, that much was clear, but his mind seemed elsewhere. Was he thinking of her, too?

"Do you ever feel guilty," I whispered, so softly I could barely hear my own voice, "about what we did to Clarissa?"

There was a long pause before he answered. "Do you?"

"Yes," I said, kissing him again, and again, but then he pulled away. "What?"

"I think," he said, moving so that I rolled off him like a log, "I should go."

I felt heavy and disgusting. I never should have brought her up.

"I'm sorry," he said, staring at me, so beautiful. "I'll call you in the morning."

He got up to leave, but it was so dark I could barely see. "Anderson?"

No answer.

I thought maybe I would follow him, but the longer I waited, the longer he'd been gone, and the less sure I was of what to say when I found him. It was then, on the pillowy grass of my backyard, in the middle of the night, that I realized nothing is ever truly what you wish for it to be.

♦ 7 ♦

If money or makeup are involved in the dispute, you have the right to a fair trial. (All disputed funds go to the Diamonds for purposes to be determined.)

—*The Diamond Rules*

The night before the fashion show, in celebration of finally scoring enough evidence to destroy the Diamonds for good, the Stonecutters decided to have a sleepover. Correction: the Stonecutter *girls* decided to have a sleepover. I wasn't sure exactly what the guys were doing, although Boyd claimed they would be having "some serious effing male-bonding time."

Whatever that meant.

I volunteered my house, because I knew that my father would stay inside his study and my mother was going out that night with her friend Barbara. Jenny promised to meet up with us as soon as the dress rehearsal for the models was over, so I decided it would be fun if we all went to the Ghost House. The plan was to head over around nine, have some coffee, enjoy the live music, and get to bed early—well, early*ish*.

Monique was the first one to show up. "Here," she said, thrusting a bottle of wine into my hand. "Eet is for later. My favorite."

I looked at the label. It was all in French. I'd had wine only twice in my life—one time at my bat mitzvah, the other when Clarissa and I stole a bottle out of her parents' wine cellar and drank ourselves to sleep. I'd also had Manischewitz during Passover, but that didn't really count.

"Thanks," I said. "I'm sure it's delicious."

"Eet tastes like the bark of a tree," she said. "Where shall I be sleeping?"

"In my room," I said, pointing to the stairs.

"Divine," Monique said, draping herself across the banister. "I love American homes. So majestic. So satisfying."

I glanced around my living room. It was anything but majestic. Monique was unrolling her sleeping bag upstairs when the doorbell rang; I swerved into the foyer and swung open the screen door for Darcy, who stood on my porch looking incredibly uncomfortable.

"Hi," she said, waiting for me to invite her inside.

A few months before, the idea of inviting Darcy McKibbon into my home would have made me gag. Now I was actually sort of glad to see her.

"Come on in," I said.

◆ ◆ ◆

"Your room is really nice," Darcy said, tossing her sleeping bag onto my floor and placing her pillow on top of it.

"Thanks."

"Eet reminds me of my old room in Paris," Monique said longingly, running her fingers across my bulletin board and studying a few of my pictures. They were mostly of me and Anderson, but there were still a few of the Diamonds I had never taken down, and even one of Jed. I hoped Darcy didn't notice. "Before it burned down, of course," she added.

"I was thinking we could all go to the Ghost House," I said, gauging their reaction. I wasn't sure if either of them had ever been.

"Do you think we should?" Darcy asked.

"Why not?"

"It wouldn't be dangerous for us to, you know, be seen together?"

Up till now, the Stonecutters had been incredibly careful about keeping our distance from one another in public. Groups of two were okay, but the three of us—plus Jenny—could arouse suspicion.

"I doubt the Diamonds will be going out the night before the show," I said. Darcy's instincts were right, technically, but I *so* wanted for everyone to have a good time. We deserved it. "Besides, what could possibly go wrong?"

The Ghost House was packed. No surprise there. We found a table for four in the corner and sat down. Jenny texted me that she was on her way over. The atmosphere was loud and dark and everything smelled like chocolate. I wanted an Iced Blaze like nobody's business.

Monique took a cigarette from her purse and put it between her lips. I'd made her leave her beret at my house; her hair, brown and shiny, fell past her shoulders and looked great.

"I don't think you can smoke in here," Darcy said, pointing to a NO SMOKING sign on the wall.

"Oh, eet's not real," Monique said, snapping the cigarette in half. "Eet's candy." She popped one half into her mouth and gave the other half to me.

"Thanks," I said, following her lead.

A waiter I didn't recognize came and took our orders. A band I had seen before—the Tea Party—was setting up on the stage. I didn't recognize anyone from school, which was a good thing, and the three of us were having a fantastic time. When Jenny showed up, we gave her a candy cigarette and ordered two brownies to share.

"What do you think the boys are doing?" I asked before taking a bite of the brownie.

"Who knows?" said Darcy. "Probably talking about politics."

"Or listening to show tunes," Jenny said, removing some of her eye shadow with a wet napkin. "Boyd's probably choreographing a dance for all of them."

"I'd pay good money to see that," Darcy said, laughing. I had never heard her really laugh before, I realized.

"Maybe they are all on skateboards," Monique said. "Eet would be *grand* if they were, no?"

I tried to picture Jed on a skateboard. "I doubt it," I said.

"I hear you've gotten pretty good," Jenny said, taking a sip of my drink. "At least, that's what Turbo says."

I had been practicing with Turbo two or three times a week; I'd reached the point where I could get on a board without falling down immediately, but I would hardly say I was *good*.

"Turbo's a liar. You should see *him* skate. He's amazing. I look ridiculous."

"You have to start somewhere," Darcy said.

"True. Anyway"—I turned to Jenny—"how was rehearsal?"

Jenny relaxed into her chair. "Crazy. You should see some of the outfits I'm wearing." She shook her head. "I'm just glad it will all be over tomorrow night. Then I can get back to my former life."

You know how it is when someone says something you already know but hearing it out loud makes it suddenly (and overwhelmingly) real? That was how I felt when Jenny finished speaking. The next day, everything the Stonecutters had been working toward the past few weeks would be realized. The Diamonds would be exposed, and there would be no need for a secret revolutionary group.

What would happen to us when this was all over? Would we remain friends? Was that even really what we were?

"Well, well, well," a familiar voice said behind me. "Look who decided to show their busted dog-faces."

I didn't have to turn around to know who it was.

Clarissa.

I glanced over my shoulder. Slowly. There she was, in a light green sweater and a tight pair of jeans. Her hair was wild and fierce as shit. Priya and Lili stood behind her, trying their best to look menacing. Arlene cowered behind them.

"I didn't realize the Ghost House served butt-fugly whores who have no self-respect or fashion sense," Clarissa said. Her eyes swept across the table. "I'll have to speak with the manager. Let him know what kind of riffraff are tainting his establishment."

"It's such a shame, too," Lili said, staring directly at me. "This place used to be so . . . *classy*."

Ouch.

"Now it's just trashy," Priya said, reaching over and grabbing a chunk of brownie off my plate. "Are you going to eat this?"

The table had suddenly gotten extremely quiet. Monique stared at her hands while Darcy avoided making eye contact with anyone. Jenny sat uncomfortably still. It was up to me to say something; that much I knew.

"Why don't you just leave us alone? There's no reason for this night to get ugly."

"Oh, it's already ugly," Clarissa said. "I mean, how could it not be? The three of you are here." She then directed her attention to Jenny. "You really shouldn't be sitting with these losers. Come with us. We have a table in the back."

Jenny looked at me for instructions. I couldn't say

much of anything with the Diamonds present. I took a sip of my Iced Blaze and stirred it with my spoon. "Go if you want," I said casually. "I don't care."

"You *don't* need her permission," Priya said. "It's not like anything Marni says actually matters."

I wasn't surprised by the Diamonds' meanness. I expected it. But there was only so much I could take. "Go," I said to Jenny. "It's fine."

"No," Jenny said, shaking her head. She looked a tiny bit nervous, I thought, the light from the candle on our table causing shadows to flicker across her face. "I'm fine here, thanks."

A cough escaped from Lili's throat. "What did you just say?"

"I'm fine here," Jenny repeated. "So . . . thanks, but no thanks."

"Whatever," Clarissa said with a shake of her head. "You just made a really big mistake. Huge, actually. Let's go, ladies." She snapped her fingers and Arlene straightened her back, as if she were a marionette. Priya gave me the finger and Lili walked across the room to sit on a black couch with silver pillows.

"You should've gone with them," Darcy said once they were gone. "They're really pissed."

Jenny shrugged. "Who cares? You couldn't pay me to sit with them. Not in a million years."

"You are so brave," Monique said, fanning herself with a napkin. "Like Joan of Arc. But not such a dyke."

"I'm sorry about that," I said. Even though it wasn't my fault that Clarissa was such a bitch, I *did* feel responsible for getting Darcy, Monique, and Jenny involved in this whole mess. They didn't deserve the Diamonds' wrath; they hadn't done anything wrong.

"Do not apologize to us," Monique said. "Eet is completely unnecessary."

"Clarissa wouldn't have made fun of you like that if you weren't sitting with me," I said. "If you guys want to leave right now, I don't blame you. It was a bad idea to come here."

"Nobody is going anywhere," Darcy said, looking around the table. "Right? That's what friends are for."

Friends. Monique, Darcy, and Jenny. They couldn't have been more different from the Diamonds. But "different" didn't mean bad. It simply meant different.

"Right," Jenny said, taking my hand. "After the fashion show, everything will change. Now, let's order another brownie. Or two."

"Or four," Darcy said.

I smiled. "Okay."

Then I had an idea.

"Be right back," I said, getting up from the table and heading toward the bar. A guy in his twenties, with crazy brown hair and tattoos up and down his neck, was at the cash register.

"How can I help you?"

"See those girls"—I pointed at Clarissa, Lili, and Priya—"over there on the couch?"

They were impossible to miss. They were the most glamorous people in the entire place.

"What about them?"

"I'd like to order them drinks." I rattled off their standard coffee orders and placed a ten-dollar bill on the counter. "We're sort of in a fight and I want to make amends. Could you just say it's a peace offering?"

The guy nodded. "Yeah, sure. No problem."

"Thanks."

I walked back to my table and sat down, two additional brownies in hand.

"What was that all about?" Darcy asked.

"You'll see," I said between bites. "Are you guys almost ready to leave?"

"Eet seems like you are in a hurry," Monique said. She was about to say something else when the barista caught her attention; he walked past us with the Diamonds' drinks on a large brown tray. We all watched as he set them down, whispered something to Clarissa, and pointed at me. I gave a little wave.

They were obviously confused about why I would buy them drinks when they'd just been so nasty to me. I didn't blame them. I was too far away to hear their conversation, but when Arlene—who was perched on the edge of the couch—frowned, I knew that Clarissa was going to make her taste everything. Talk about paranoid.

"You didn't put anything in the drinks, did you?" Jenny asked. "I mean, I wouldn't care if you did. I'm just wondering."

"Give me a break. I'm not evil," I said. "But I may have forgotten to tell the barista to use soy milk. And I may have specifically asked him to use cream." I let the information sink in before continuing. Clarissa's lactose intolerance was as legendary as her shoe collection.

Darcy's eyes widened. "You *are* evil," she said, "and brilliant."

I shrugged. "All in a day's work. Now, don't stare." I watched as Arlene tasted all the drinks. I was counting on her *not* to notice the cream in Clarissa's coffee. It took what seemed like forever for her to sample each cup.

"Eet is the worst kind of sabotage," Monique said, giggling. "*Sacrebleu!*"

For whatever reason, Arlene failed to notice the dairy in Clarissa's drink (or maybe she *did* notice and kept quiet? I'll never know) and gave her approval. I watched as the Diamonds drank and gossiped, tossing glances my way every so often until they stopped caring.

"Okay," I said, turning to the Stonecutters and initiating our exit. I tossed some money onto the table and they each followed suit. "Let's get out of here before the shit hits the fan."

Darcy laughed. "Literally."

That night, underneath my covers, I thought about the prank I'd pulled on Clarissa and how she was probably cursing me at that very moment. Did I care? No. Yes. Maybe a little. I thought about the girls in my room and how incredibly random and wonderful they were. It was Darcy in her sleeping bag on my bedroom floor— not Priya. Monique curled into a ball near my door— not Lili. And Jenny Murphy was using one of my pillows. Not Clarissa. The next day, at the fashion show, the Diamonds would chip and break; they would be seen for who they truly were and for the awful things they had done.

I just hoped that after all this I would finally be happy.

The next morning, I met Tommy in our usual spot at school: the technology room. The girls were going to sleep in and miss first period; Darcy was driving them to school.

I brought coffee—Tommy liked his black—and sat down on a stool next to him. A bunch of notepads were spread out in front of him. There was a lot to go over before that night. His hair was sloppy and the circles underneath his eyes were darker than usual.

"How was last night?" he asked.

"Oh, it was fun," I said, tearing open the plastic lid on my coffee and taking a sip. "We ran into Clarissa."

"How was that?"

"Let's just say she probably had a rough morning."

Tommy chuckled. "Sounds more eventful than our night. Boyd swiped a few beers from his dad and we drank a little. He passed out before nine, though— total lightweight."

"How was Anderson?" I asked. Every girl wanted her boyfriend and her friends to get along, and I was no exception. "Did you two make nice?"

Tommy scratched his chin. "Sure, yeah. We had

fun. He left early, though. Said he wasn't feeling well. Is he sick?"

Was he? I had no idea. The last I'd spoken to him, aside from a few text messages, was the night I'd practically thrown myself at him and he'd left me alone, in my backyard, staring at the stars.

"I think so," I said. "He hasn't been acting like himself lately."

I didn't run into Anderson all day. He wasn't in art class, and by seventh period I was starting to get really worried. But then, on my way to calculus, someone grabbed my arm and I could tell from the gentleness of his grip that it was my boyfriend.

We were in the science wing by the stairs, which were more or less deserted. There was a tiny alcove big enough for two people to fit—maybe even two people and a very thin midget—and we tucked ourselves inside.

"Hi," he said.

"Are you okay? Tommy told me you were feeling really sick last night."

He frowned. "Yeah. I think I had, like, a twenty-four-hour stomach bug or something. I'm fine, though."

"Oh. Well, that's good." I wrapped my arms around him. "I'm sorry you didn't feel well." I leaned in to kiss him but he pulled away.

"You probably shouldn't kiss me," he said. "I may still be contagious."

I nodded. "So, to what do I owe this pleasure?" I

asked in a silly voice, running my fingers up and down the scruff of his almost-beard. "I've missed you. About the other night—"

"Don't worry about it, Marni. It was my fault." He looked me in the eyes and touched my forehead with his fingers. "Okay, so, I have to tell you something. But don't be mad."

"Why would I be mad?"

"I dunno," he said, adjusting the collar of his shirt. "Just don't be."

"What is it?"

"Clarissa called me this morning, and—"

"Excuse me?"

"Calm down, Marni," Anderson said, keeping his voice steady and even. "It's not a big deal."

"It's *totally* a big deal. I hope you hung up on her." No answer.

"You *did* hang up on her, right?"

Anderson shook his head.

"I can't believe this," I said, pushing past him, back into the hallway. "I can't believe you had a conversation with her after everything she's done to me. To *you*. It's unfathomable."

"Will you just calm down?" Anderson said, snaking his arms around me. "John Schneider's grandfather died and he has to go to Connecticut tonight. He can't be in the fashion show, and she needed a replacement."

"And?"

288

"I said no."

Even though it was the answer I wanted to hear, it didn't make me happy. That Clarissa had the nerve to call Anderson after she'd ruined his life, well, it didn't surprise me. It was a total von Dyke move.

"You should do it," I said to him after a few moments.

"I should?"

I would be the bigger person. I would *not* be a jealous girlfriend. "I don't like the fact that she called you, but we could use another Stonecutter behind enemy lines. You can help Jenny."

"If you say so." He kissed me again and winked. "Let's just hope Clarissa doesn't try to put the moves on me."

I knew it was supposed to be a joke, but really, it wasn't very funny.

♦ ♦ ♦

Fifteen minutes before *Passion 4 Fashion* was set to begin, I was in a bush, dressed in black, waiting behind the art wing until I could sneak into the auditorium and watch the Stonecutters' masterpiece unfold.

8:46 Stepped on a twig and scared myself.

8:49 Bored.

8:50 Started singing Kelly Clarkson's "Breakaway" to entertain myself.

8:54 Finished singing "Breakway."

8:54 Shivered.

8:55 Stepped on another twig and fell backward.

8:56 Repositioned myself in the bush and continued waiting.

8:58 Cried silently.

Just before I was about to head inside, I felt a tap on my shoulder.

It was Tommy.

"What are you doing here?" I whispered, dragging him over to the building and hiding behind the wall facing away from the student parking lot.

"Whoa," he said, out of breath. "You should, like, join the FBI or something. You're totally stealth."

"Thanks," I said. "So what *are* you doing here?"

"Keeping you company," Tommy said. "Anderson told me he was gonna be in the show."

"You talked to Anderson?"

"Yeah." It was so dark I could barely make out Tommy's features. I waited for him to tell me that sending Anderson into the fashion show was a good idea, but he didn't. "You shouldn't be alone when it all goes down. It's much more fulfilling when you can share the glory with someone else who wants it, too."

"I guess." It would have been nicer to share that moment with Anderson, but Tommy was a fine runner-up. Since he'd helped me form the Stonecutters, I had come to appreciate his friendship.

"Should we go?"

Tommy listened to the wind for a few seconds. "We're good."

Unexpectedly, he leaned over to give me a

good-luck kiss. (Only now have I come to realize that Tommy had no intention of planting a big wet one on my lips. It was merely the angle we were at, and the darkness, the awkward excitement of the night, that made me think otherwise.)

"What are you *doing?*" I whispered harshly, pushing him away.

"What?" he said. "I'm sorry. I meant to kiss you on the cheek. Don't be so touchy."

In another time and place, I would've gotten into this with him. But there was no time. The fashion show was about to begin.

So I said, "Whatever," and crawled around the side of the building. I heard Tommy's feet shuffle behind me, and then we were inside.

The Bennington School auditorium was the size of a small Broadway theater. Jed and Darcy were in the sound booth, which was at the back of the orchestra level. (One of Darcy's friends was on the AV squad and let them hook the Diamonds' tapped conversation up to the house speakers. It would play on cue instead of the music.) Tommy and I were at the very top of the mezzanine level, enveloped in the shadows.

I don't think there was a single empty seat. Chatter filled the air, and I noticed a few people flipping through the programs; I squinted to see if anyone was reading the Stonecutters' tell-all addendum. Why wasn't anyone reacting?

Then the house lights dimmed and the onstage

colors grew more and more intense, blanketing everything in a glossy sheen.

"Here we go," said Tommy.

This was it. The moment when I would *finally* get the Diamonds back for all the pain and heartache they'd put me through. And not only me. The Stonecutters. The entire student body.

When they entered from the wings, there was an immediate silence. Clarissa was in a dress that clung to every curve of her body, as if it were made just for her. (I wouldn't have been surprised if it was.) Her hair bounced with every step she took. Priya and Lili followed, completing the Terrible Trio: Priya in a white minidress that showed off her turbo-charged boobies, and Lili in something racy and blue that laced up the front and rested just above her knees. Just looking at their shoes made my feet hurt.

After their obviously choreographed prance, Clarissa stopped in the middle of the stage, Lili and Priya on either side of her. Arlene—in a plain black cocktail dress—poked her head out of the left wing and handed Clarissa a microphone.

"Testing," Clarissa said, pressing the microphone to her lips. "Applaud if you can hear me."

The applause was immediate and intense.

"You can stop now," Clarissa said, and the auditorium became silent again. "Thank you."

"*I love you, Clarissa!*" someone—a boy—shouted from the back of the orchestra.

"*You're so hot!*" another guy screamed.

292

Clarissa didn't change her demeanor whatsoever. I couldn't wait to see her when all the models flew down the runway in T-shirts with her face ironed onto them. It would be the best moment of my life. Well, one of the best. Informing the entire audience that the Diamonds had fixed the mock trial jury would be pretty great, too.

Priya leaned into the microphone. "I'm not wearing any underwear."

Clarissa smacked her. "Welcome, everyone, to the *Passion for Fashion* show!" The crowd broke into applause for the second time. A few people even whistled. "We have a very special evening planned for you. Our models will be presenting the most exquisite clothing in the tristate area for your enjoyment, all to benefit one of the most important causes of our time: the plight of the homeless trannies. Here to speak about these individuals is your student body president, Lili Chan-Mohego."

Clarissa transferred the microphone to Lili. "Thank you, Clarissa. For those of you who do not know, homeless trannies are discriminated against *double* the amount of regular homeless people and regular trannies." Someone gasped. "Which is why we are proud to donate the proceeds of *Passion for Fashion* to those in need."

There was, for the third time, applause, and Priya grabbed the microphone in what seemed like an unplanned coup. "Wear your fishnets loud and proud, trannies! May you all find homes!"

"Priya, you're freaking hot!" someone yelled.

Lili took back the microphone before Priya had a chance to respond. "Without further ado," she said, "the Diamonds bring you the first-ever Bennington School fashion extravaganza!"

The first clue that the Stonecutters' plan was not working came merely seconds later. Instead of music playing, there was supposed to be an awkward amount of silence during which, we'd imagined, Clarissa and the Diamonds would be running around backstage, clueless about where all the clothing was. Then, suddenly, Boyd—who was hiding, of course—would reveal the garment bags filled with the T-shirts we'd made. The models would slip them on without thinking as Clarissa pushed them onstage one by one, blinded by the backstage frenzy.

That is *not* what happened.

As soon as the Diamonds made their exit, Rihanna came blasting through the speakers, and the first pair of models walked down the runway in designer clothes.

I turned to Tommy. "What's going on?"

The theme was day wear, and model after model— please keep in mind that the "models" were Bennington students, girls Clarissa had bribed into servitude, which made the entire event doubly nauseating—covered the stage in overly expensive jeans and skimpy tops. Where were the T-shirts? Where was the voice-over of Clarissa admitting the Diamonds' crimes?

Soon I found myself watching Anderson glide

down the runway, looking impeccable and confident and irresistible. I expected people to boo him off the stage, quite honestly, but there was a surprising amount of applause. For the first time in a few weeks, he looked *happy*.

"Maybe they decided to wait," Tommy said. He must have sensed I was about to make a break for it. "You know, until the end. Make it the grand finale."

It was an entertaining idea, but I still couldn't understand why the plan had been changed without my knowledge. Or Tommy's.

"Give it a few more minutes," he said. "I'm sure everything will be fine."

Fifteen minutes later, I couldn't take it anymore. I'd had enough.

"Let me see that," I said, snatching a girl's program out of her hands. (I didn't recognize her and assumed she was a freshman.)

"What are you doing?" asked Tommy.

It was extremely difficult to open the program—my hands were shaking—but I made my way through each and every page. The slip of paper that was supposed to have been inserted by Turbo and Jed earlier that day, the one describing Clarissa and the Diamonds' crimes, the one that would *spawn* a *revolution*, was absent. Missing.

I wanted to scream.

Just then, the music changed from upbeat to romantic. Time for evening wear. Jenny was the first model, in a gown right out of *Cinderella* (Perrault, 1697)—pearly white, with iridescent beads and Swarovski crystals clinging to the satin. When she reached the tip of the runway and posed, something incredible happened: in less than a second, the entire dress flew off her body like a two-year-old down a playground slide. Suddenly, Jenny was naked (except for her underwear) in front of the entire auditorium. You could hear laughter, shock, and awe all at once, masked only by the beat of the soundtrack.

As quickly as she had appeared, Jenny ran out of the auditorium as if she were being chased, crying and leaving the fallen dress behind. (The girl behind her, Elizabeth Kelp, wound up dragging the gown like a too-heavy bag offstage.)

I looked at Tommy, and he looked at me.

We both mouthed one word: *Clarissa*.

There was no way that was an accident—not when we'd been trying to sabotage the Diamonds ourselves. It immediately made sense why they had cast Jenny in the first place—somehow, they had known *why* she was auditioning, and had every intention of embarrassing her during the show—and why nothing the entire evening had gone as planned.

The Diamonds had succeeded.

The Stonecutters had failed.

And somewhere in our midst was a traitor.

♦ 8 ♦

You have the right not to be spoken to like a
little byotch—unless you deserve it, in which
case the members of the Diamond Court will
treat you as they see fit.

—*The Diamond Rules*

The next morning, I slept in.

I went downstairs around noon to make myself a
cup of coffee. It was the only thing I could do without
pulling my hair out and crying. I didn't even check my
Stonecutters Gmail account; I was sure my in-box was
flooded with tons of What Went Wrongs, but I
couldn't deal with the repercussions of our stunt-gone-
bad. Not yet.

I was bustling around the kitchen—what does that
even mean? Who *bustles* anymore?—when I saw a familiar license plate roll into my driveway. For a minute
I was puzzled about where my own car was, but then I
remembered I had left it at school, which meant I
would have to get my dad to drop me off at some point
later that afternoon.

I closed my robe, tied the flannel strip around my

waist in a floppy bow, and opened the front door. "What are you doing here? I'm busy."

"Yeah, you look *really* busy," Tommy said. He was dressed casually that morning, his black hair tangled and loose; if I'd seen him randomly on the street I would've assumed he was twentysomething and bohemian—a musician, perhaps, or an artist. Not a neurotic, news-obsessed seventeen-year-old who carried two tape recorders and a notepad in his pocket at all times.

Tommy had one of those recycled-paper holders from Dunkin' Donuts in his hand, two cups of coffee resting diagonally. A paper bag was wedged between them. "Hungry?"

I looked back at my bowl of Cinnamon Toast Crunch. I hadn't put the milk in yet. "Sure," I said, letting him inside. He was wearing a pair of soft-looking khakis (brown) and a thin long-sleeved shirt (orange). "You look like a pumpkin."

"Thanks," he said. "That means a lot coming from you."

We sat on opposite ends of my kitchen table, staring at each other. Tommy passed me one of the coffees—skim milk, two Equals—and opened the bag. There were two bagels inside.

"Regular or vegetable?" he asked.

"Regular." He slid one across the table (don't worry, it was wrapped) and took a sip of his own coffee. Before I knew it, I was done with my bagel, and my coffee was only half full. "I know why you're here."

"Okay," he said, tucking his hair behind his ears. It was the kind of gesture that would make some guys seem effeminate but, for some reason, made Tommy seem pretty chill. "Let's go."

"Go?" I asked. "Where?"

"To get your car," he said. "Why else would I be here?"

Right. My car. "No reason," I said, even though I could think of ten or so right off the top of my head—specifically, the Fashion Show Fiasco. "Let me get dressed."

"So," Tommy said, pulling up next to my car and shifting into neutral once we arrived at Bennington. "What are you up to this afternoon?"

I shrugged. "I'll probably hang out with Anderson for a while."

"Yeah, about that . . . ," Tommy said. "Can I tell you something without you getting, like, crazy offended?"

"What is that supposed to mean?"

"I don't know. It's just that, well, I don't want you to take this the wrong way. But I think there's something you should know. About Anderson."

"What about him?"

Tommy looked at me skeptically. "Are you *sure* you're not gonna be offended?"

"You're really freaking me out."

He shifted in his seat so that we were facing each other. "I have some, uh, information about him, and, well, this is hard—"

"Just spit it out, Tommy."

"Anderson's a rat," Tommy said quickly, as if he were a contestant on a game show and his time was almost up. "He's been slipping Clarissa information about the Stonecutters."

I laughed. "You can't be serious."

"I *am* serious," he said. "He's the reason they knew about our plan for the fashion show."

"And what, exactly, makes you think so? *I* was the one who told him he should do it in the first place!"

Tommy's cheeks pinked. "I can't say. But it's true, Marni."

"So, you're expecting me to believe that my boyfriend, who absolutely hates Clarissa, has been going behind my back, sneaking information about the Stonecutters to the Diamonds—without my knowledge—and you have no proof?"

"I have proof," Tommy said nervously. "I just can't tell you what it is. But I have it."

"Whatever, dude," I said, opening the door. I was about to step outside when a realization hit me. I turned back to look at Tommy. "Is this about last night?"

"Yes," he said. "That's what I'm trying to tell you. *Anderson* is the one who sabotaged our plan."

"No," I said, "not that. You. Me. Outside the art wing. When you tried to kiss me."

Tommy rolled his eyes. "It was an accident, Marni."

"I don't know, Tommy. Last night you basically try to soul kiss me, and this morning you're bringing me

300

bagels and telling me that my boyfriend is double-crossing me. That's pretty messed up, even for you."

"What is that supposed to mean?"

"Oh, *sorry*," I said. "I meant, even for a *reporter*." I banged my fist on his dashboard. "You know what I think? I think *you're* the snitch. I think *you're* the one telling Clarissa everything just so you can have more information for whatever article you're in the middle of writing. You've never liked Anderson. You're just using this as an opportunity to pin the blame on him." I got out of the car and slammed the door behind me. "I never should have trusted you."

I fumbled for my keys and unlocked my own car door with a single click.

"You're wrong, Marni," Tommy said. "If you think about it, *really* think about it, you'll know I'm telling the truth."

"Leave me alone," I said, sliding into the driver's seat and closing the door. I could still hear him through the window.

"Think about it," he was saying.

But that was the last thing I wanted to do.

Four more cups of coffee, three phone calls, and two (pathetic) voice mails later, I decided to pay Anderson a visit.

Tommy's accusation had jarred me: without him or Anderson, I had nobody left. Sure, there were the rest of the Stonecutters, and we'd grown to be pretty great friends. If I'd felt like eating fondue (Monique) or skating in the park (Turbo) or sewing my own clothes while listening to Broadway cast recordings (Boyd), I would have given one of them a ring in a second. But just to *talk*, well . . .

It was one of the moments when I truly missed my girlfriends. Clarissa or Lili—even Priya!—would know exactly what to say. I realized I was at an all-time low when I considered going to my mother for advice, but she wasn't even home. So I did the only thing I could think of: took a shower, got dressed, and drove over to Anderson's house.

When I arrived, I knocked about a million times and rubbed my hands together to keep warm. I called Anderson's cell phone, then his landline. Then I knocked again. Just as I was about to give up and go home, the door opened.

"Hi!" I said enthusiastically.

Anderson looked sleepy-eyed and sweaty. A pair of sweatpants were tied loosely around his waist. No shirt.

"You didn't pick up your phone."

Anderson frowned. "Sorry. It's broken, I think."

"That sucks." I was still standing outside, mind you, and it was cold. The wind blew the back of my dress up, and I shivered, smoothing it down with my hands. "Um, Anderson?"

"Ya?"

"Can I come in? It's freezing."

"Oh," Anderson said, opening the door a little wider. "I was actually just about to hop in the shower.

Tough practice today. And then I have to get some work done."

"I could wait for you." Then, in my sexiest voice (which wasn't too different from my regular voice): "Or I could *join* you."

"You want to play basketball?" Anderson said, sounding confused.

"No, silly." I stepped toward him, resting my head on his shoulder. "The shower part."

He sniffed my hair. "But you already took one. You smell clean."

"I'm trying to be romantic. Give a girl a break."

Anderson sighed. "I'm just really tired and I have a lot to do. You understand, right? We can get together tomorrow." He kissed my forehead. "Maybe even later tonight if I get enough done."

What was there to say? I was getting the boot from my own boyfriend. Dejected, I turned to leave when the glimmer of something silver caught my eye.

An Audi.

Now, around where I lived, a lot of people drove Audis—Clarissa von Dyke being one of them. And it wasn't as though I had a eureka moment when I saw the license plate and realized that it was Clarissa's, and everything Tommy had told me clicked into place like the pieces of a bookshelf from IKEA.

What *did* happen was I saw a car I was pretty sure was an Audi almost entirely concealed by the arms of a weeping willow nearly two blocks away. And when I saw that car—which might or might not have belonged to my former best friend—I thought about what Tommy had said. Mostly, I thought about my relationship with Anderson, which, though exciting and passionate in the beginning, had remained somewhat stagnant since the Closet Incident.

I thought about how he had surreptitiously scored a spot in the fashion show and how, even though we were both technically outcasts at school, he'd somehow managed to maintain the thinnest strands of his former friendships while I had absolutely nothing left. I thought about our history together. His relationship with Clarissa. His relationship with me. I thought about other things, too, but those are private.

Propelled by the collection of all those musings and, of course, by Tommy's cryptic speech from earlier that afternoon, I said something I normally wouldn't have.

"That's okay. I should actually get home myself, because I'm writing this huge exposé about Clarissa and the Diamonds that Tommy is planning on printing in this week's paper. Even though the fashion show didn't go off as planned, I have enough evidence—what with all of the files I've saved from the trials and such—to really end this once and for all."

Anderson looked at me with fresh eyes. "Oh, wow."

"No one else knows about it," I said, "except Tommy, of course. I'm going to tell the Stonecutters tonight."

"Cool," Anderson said, rolling back his shoulders. The muscles underneath his skin danced with every movement. "Let me know if you need any help." He leaned over and gave me a peck on the lips. He tasted salty. "I'll call you later. Love ya."

I walked back to my car, trying to calm myself down. Anderson wasn't sneaking off to see Clarissa behind my back. He loved me. He was proud of me, and he wanted me to succeed. Sure, it was weird that all the lights were off, and *yes*, it was bizarre that he didn't invite me inside, but there was simply no way Tommy could be right.

I would find out soon enough, though. No one except Tommy and me (and now Anderson) knew about the exposé. I had no intention of telling the rest of the Stonecutters about it that evening. If Clarissa and the Diamonds found out, their only possible source was Anderson; it would mean he was a liar, a bastard, a sneak—everything Tommy had claimed. If not, Tommy was the liar, trying to get Anderson out of the way for some unknown purpose and exploit me for the benefit of his journalistic pursuits.

The exposé, I realized, was the key to everything. I would simply have to wait and see what happened next. And meanwhile, I'd have to write the damn thing.

◆ 9 ◆

Any rights not specifically discussed in the
Diamond Rules are applicable only to those
who score a four or higher on their AP exams
and/or compliment the Diamonds on their
hot faces/hair/bodies, etc.

—*The Diamond Rules*

The rest of the weekend passed as weekends do—
quickly and without warning—and on Monday it was
back to school.

In English, I couldn't help overhearing the twins'
gossip.

"And did you *see* her disgusting Jell-O legs during
the fashion show?"

"I know. But wasn't Clarissa's dress ah-freaking-
mazing?"

"We should totes get ones like that for prom. But
we don't want to look like we're copying, you know?"

"We should get them in, like . . . *a different color.*"

"You're so smart."

I had totally forgotten that the Snow Court—the
final five princes and princesses—was being announced

today. When the television flickered on for the morning announcements, I suddenly felt nervous.

Onscreen, Lili held two sealed envelopes. "The moment we've all been waiting for . . . ," she said.

Watching Lili, I felt both angry and sad. Hurt and enraged. It was the paradox of my entire life—wishing things were the way they used to be, but having enough perspective to understand that would never happen and that maybe, just maybe, it was for the better.

Lili ripped open the first envelope (boys) with her pinky and read the names. Ryan, Duncan, Tiger. Anderson. Jed.

My mouth was as open as a twenty-four-hour diner.

Then the girls: Clarissa, Priya, Lili. (Big shock.) Jenny Murphy.

Lili paused, staring at the bleached paper in her hands. "And, uh, that's it," she said into the camera.

"That's only four!" Dara exclaimed.

"There's one more!" Dana echoed. "Do you think it's us? Did they count us as one person?"

Mr. York, who supervised the announcements, walked onto the screen and whispered into Lili's ear. He pointed at the piece of paper, and then at her.

"Oh, fine," Lili said as he walked offscreen. "And Marni Valentine."

Everyone in class looked at me.

"No effing way," Dara said.

"Who voted for her?" asked Dana. "Everyone hates her."

"Yay, Marni!" Mrs. Bloom exclaimed, jumping up

and down. When she realized that no one else was clapping, she stopped.

"Finally," Lili said, drawing everyone's attention back to the screen, "as of this morning, the student government has decided that all newspaper articles, no matter their content, must be preapproved by the Diamond Court before printing. This is to protect the student body from defamatory and disparaging material of any kind." She nodded emphatically. "Thank you, Bennington, and have a nice day."

I knew two things immediately:

1. There was no way on earth that enough of the student body had voted for me to earn me a princess spot (or Jed a prince spot, for that matter). Someone else was behind this, and I had to find out who.

2. Anderson was the rat.

Anderson had been hiding something Saturday night; he was the only other person who knew about the exposé. There was no way the Diamonds came up with the idea of censoring the *Bennington Press* without prompting. After all, the newspaper was one of the ways they'd furthered their power in the first place. They wouldn't publicly insult Tommy unless they believed he was working against them. And the only way they would think that was if Anderson had spilled the beans.

I tried, really tried, to think of other excuses. Any excuses. Only I couldn't. The more I thought about it, the more I wanted to run and find Anderson, to pound my hands against his perfect chest and tell him I knew his secret.

I remembered the wondrous look on Anderson's face during the fashion show, when the student body had seemed to accept him like they had before the Closet Incident; I remembered the night we'd spent underneath the stars and the conversation we'd shared; I especially remembered the way Anderson had given me the boot over the weekend. Had Clarissa been inside with him that night? When had been the moment he'd decided that our relationship was no longer enough? Why hadn't he told me?

Then I flushed each and every one of those thoughts from my mind. If I'd learned anything from Chinese military strategist Sun Tzu (and my entire experience with Clarissa), it was this: keep your friends close and your enemies closer.

So that was exactly what I did.

When I saw Anderson in the hall, I gave him a kiss and said, "Congratulations!" Later, when I saw Tommy, I told him to contact the rest of the Stonecutters and call an emergency meeting for that afternoon.

There was work to be done. Crying would simply have to wait.

"It's really over?" Boyd asked. He had on a black top hat and white sunglasses. "Like, for good?"

I nodded. The Stonecutters were assembled in Anderson's den for our final meeting. "We've had a great run, but there's no way we'll ever accomplish what we set out to do. The Diamonds are just *too* good," I said, trying to conceal the inner monster gnawing at my stomach.

This was the only way.

"I agree," said Tommy, a somber expression on his face. "Now that the *Bennington Press* articles need to be approved before the printings, I have my work cut out for me."

"Dude," said Turbo softly.

"So that is eet?" Monique said. "We throw ourselves down and surrender?"

"This blows," Turbo said.

Jenny was typically silent, and Jed looked at me as if to say, "What's up your sleeve, Valentine?" His fingers were *just* touching Darcy's; they were almost holding hands.

Anderson, looking slightly uncomfortable, rubbed my back. It made me cringe. "I guess it's for the best," he said.

That was our cue to leave. Everyone stood up, looking confused, and gathered their belongings—backpacks, purses, notebooks, tap shoes (Boyd)—before filing down Anderson's narrow hallway. Someone—I think it was Turbo—said, "I can't believe Marni is a quitter. I never would have guessed."

Keeping my mouth shut was one of the most difficult things I've ever had to do. We left one by one, dispersing into the afternoon as if we had never met to begin with.

As if the Stonecutters had never existed.

I lingered in my car, fiddling with the knobs of the radio until nearly everyone was gone and only one other car remained in front of Anderson's house. I rolled down my window to catch Tommy's attention. He nodded once and sped off, toward his house.

I followed him.

Three days later—it was a Thursday night, seven o'clock—my mother grinned at me unabashedly during dinner. At first I thought she was merely excited (the casts for her carpal tunnel would be coming off the following week), but then I realized that she was all glittered and be-gayed (*Candide*, Bernstein, 1956) for another reason entirely.

She'd found out about Snow Court.

"When were you going to tell us?" Her lipstick, which I had applied that morning before school, was smudged and leaky.

"Tell us what?" Dad asked, looking up from the *Times*. "Did you win some kind of award?"

"No," I said. "It's really no big deal."

Mom, who was shaking in her seat, could no longer contain her hysteria. "*Marni* is going to be Ice Queen!" she squealed, waving her casts in front of her. "She's one of *five* princesses! Oh, honey, Rose told me, and *she* heard from Diana Aubingdale's mother! Why didn't you tell me? This is so *exciting*!"

I almost choked on a piece of chicken. "It's really not a big deal," I said, "and I'm not going to win, so, whatever."

Dad pursed his lips. "Ice Queen, eh?"

"Oh, but you *could* win, Marni," Mom said before taking a sip of the Jamba Juice I'd brought her for dinner (Pomegranate Paradise). "Clarissa's prettier, of course, Priya's more fun, and, well, Lili's smarter, I suppose"—she looked at me with pride—"but it's not *totally* hopeless." She sighed into her chair. "What are you going to wear? David, give Marni your credit card. Let her go buy something *fabulous* at the mall."

"I don't need a new dress," I said, dropping my fork onto my plate.

Perhaps it was because the dance was that weekend and the winter pep rally—where the Snow Court would be introduced and each member would have the opportunity to say a few final words on his or her own behalf—was the very next day. Perhaps it was because of Clarissa and Anderson and every other minor disaster that had snowballed into the catastrophe that was My Life over the past few weeks. Or perhaps it was simply because I was insulted that the only aspect of My Life my mother cared about was something I (A) didn't deserve and (B) didn't care about, but I threw my hands down on the table and stood up.

"The Snow Ball means nothing to me. If you ever listened to me, you would know that," I said. "Maybe if you stopped thinking about yourself for, like, five minutes, you would see that my entire year so far has been a disaster. Jed dumped me, and the Diamonds stopped being friends with me because I started dating Clarissa's ex-boyfriend, who I thought I was in love with but, as it turns out, screwed me over. Now I have nobody."

I turned to my father. "And while I'm at it, Dad, you know I love you, but I don't want to be a lawyer. I never have. I don't have a clue what I *actually* want to do, but it's not that."

I paused, catching my breath. "Oh, yeah. And I don't want to go to Georgetown."

It was such a relief to say everything that had been bottled up inside me. I felt free, like the weight I'd been carrying on my shoulders for the past however many years had suddenly—and completely—been lifted. I didn't even care what either of them had to say in response.

"Well," my father said after a few minutes. He removed his glasses and massaged his eyelids. "That's certainly a lot to take in."

"I'm sorry," I said, sitting back down. "But it's how I feel."

Dad reached over and grabbed my hand. "You don't have to apologize for your feelings, Marni. I wish you had told me earlier, of course, but what you do with the rest of your life is up to you."

"Thanks, Dad."

"You really don't want to go to Georgetown?" he asked. "Not even a little bit?"

"No, I don't."

I certainly didn't expect everything to be la-di-da after a confession of that magnitude. Dad, I knew, would be okay; it was my mother who I wanted to say something, *anything*.

She reached out her arm and rested it on the table. All that stuck out of her cast were her fingertips—which I'd painted red for her—and she wiggled them at me. Slowly. With my free hand, I touched her fingers with mine, and the three of us sat there, silent, holding hands until our arms grew tired.

It wasn't perfect, but for the first time in a long while, it felt like home.

◆ ◆ ◆

Which leads me to the point in my story, dear reader, when I am forced to make a confession: I've kept something from you. A big secret. I didn't tell you because I knew you would think less of me, and you would have the right to. I did a terrible, awful thing, the kind of thing you lose a friendship over.

And I did.

When I ran into Anderson outside my house at the end of September with Hot Dog, it wasn't the first conversation we'd had alone—without Clarissa. It was the second. The first was in the parking lot of Dunkin' Donuts over the summer, when I bumped into him buying a Coolatta and he walked me to my car, and we chatted about silly things, the weather and what my plans for the weekend were. Then, out of nowhere, he kissed me. His mouth tasted sweet and tangy, like his coffee. He wrapped one sinewy arm around my back and kissed me harder.

"My truck," he said, cocking his head toward his Jeep a few feet away. "The back folds down."

It was still bright outside, not even three o'clock. "What about Clarissa?" I asked.

"What about Jed?"

And there it was. Anderson wanted to hook up with me in the back of his truck. He had a girlfriend. I had a boyfriend.

I followed him and left half an hour later. *At least we didn't have sex*, I told myself, climbing into the driver's seat of my Taurus and starting the engine, my head swarming with pictures of what I had just done. No one would ever have to know.

If I could take it back, I would. I was a nervous wreck the rest of the summer, dying every time I saw Clarissa and Anderson together, every time she mentioned his name, every time I listened in confidence as she divulged their most intimate secrets. I wanted to tell her so many times, and so many times I almost did. But then the incident with Jed happened, and she was such an extraordinary friend to me (or so I thought); and then Anderson asked to be my partner for art class, and my feelings for him, the ones I had tried so hard to extinguish, came gushing forth like water from a fountain. By then the two of them had already stopped dating, and I already had one secret. What was the difference, really, if I had two?

You know the rest.

I'm not proud of what I did. Honestly, I'm not. It was

clear that Clarissa had found out somehow, the only plausible explanation for her blackmailing Jed into dumping me over the announcements. Revenge. The only thing I was unsure about was how long Anderson had been seeing Clarissa behind my back. Days? Weeks?

Once I pieced together the intricate plot, I told Tommy everything.

"That's intense," he said.

"You tried to tell me about Anderson and I wouldn't listen," I said over the phone. "I'm sorry."

"You don't have to apologize. I understand."

I thought about the afternoon when I'd witnessed Anderson and Clarissa at Starbucks, about the night when he'd left me alone, lying on the cold grass of my backyard, about his strange and sudden involvement in the fashion show. Surely these were signs. Why hadn't I seen them?

"Is that why you had me stop trailing Clarissa? Did you see them together?"

A minute or so passed before Tommy replied. "Yeah. A few times. I was pretty sure they were up to something. When Anderson left our sleepover early, I followed him. He went to Clarissa's. That's when I knew for sure. I didn't tell you because I knew you'd be upset. I was trying to protect you, Marni."

"I guess I got what I deserved, huh?"

"No. Nobody deserves that. Why don't you call Anderson and talk to him? Explain how you feel."

I couldn't, though. Not yet. Even though the idea

frightened me more than anything, there was someone I had to speak with first. "Listen, I've gotta hang up."

"Where are you going?"

"To see Clarissa."

"I figured," he said. "Let me know what happens."

Clarissa's house was just as I'd remembered it. Her mother let me in (either she didn't know we were fighting, or she was too sloshed to care) and I crept up the stairs to Clarissa's room, my feet silent on the black carpet.

I knocked twice on her door.

"What, Mom?" Clarissa said from inside. "I told you I was—"

The door opened, and she was obviously shocked to see me. I couldn't blame her. I wouldn't exactly like opening *my* bedroom door and finding Clarissa on the other side.

"Oh *God*," she said, one hand still on the door-knob, the other holding a cordless phone. "What on earth are *you* doing here?"

"I came to talk." I was wearing a fleece jacket, and I played awkwardly with the zipper.

"I'm on the phone," she said, "and besides, I don't want to speak to you. Ever. So you can go away now."

Clarissa started to close her door, but I pushed it open. "We *really* need to chat. It's important."

I knew that Clarissa's curiosity would get the best of her. "I have to go," she said into the receiver. "Call you back in five." Clarissa tossed the phone onto her bed and crossed her arms.

Once I had her attention, I wasn't sure where to start. "There's a lot we need to discuss."

Clarissa batted her eyes. "Like?"

Just say it, Marni. "Like Anderson."

"What about him?"

"Well, uh . . . I—"

"If you're here to tell me that you hooked up with him behind my back this summer, save your breath. I already know. Obviously."

I exhaled until my lungs felt completely empty. "I'm so sorry, Clarissa."

Her face was blank. Her eyes were flat. I had no idea what she was thinking.

"I really am. But that doesn't excuse—"

"That's enough," she said. "I'm not interested in having this conversation with you."

"What you're doing at school is *out* of *control*, Clarissa. I know I hurt your feelings and you have every right in the world to hate me for that, but it has nothing to do with anyone else." I searched her expression for something, anything familiar. "Haven't I been punished enough? Aren't you ready to end this?"

Clarissa looked at me with the most disgust anyone in my entire life has ever shown me. "No. You can go now."

But I wasn't finished. "You're not exactly innocent, Clarissa. You basically forced Jed to dump me in front of the entire school. You pretended you were *helping* me when it was all your fault to begin with!"

"My fault? It's not *my* fault he likes to hang out around trash," Clarissa said, rolling her eyes.

"Who even knows what sort of sick arrangement you have with Anderson," I said. "Has this all been one huge joke to you?"

"I'm not the one who hooked up with my best friend's boyfriend, Marni," Clarissa spat. "That title belongs to you. You've earned it." She blinked and for a moment looked on the verge of tears. "Do you have any idea how much you hurt me?"

Yes, I thought. *I do*.

"And to top it all off, I had to hear it from Anderson. Not you. I kept waiting and waiting for you to say something but you never did. That's what the whole Jed ordeal was about. I wanted you to know what it felt like to have someone you love betray you.

"I was even ready to forgive and forget after that. But when I caught you and Anderson at Ryan's party," Clarissa said, shaking her head, "that was it. I never wanted to see you again. Or Anderson. But then, just like he did before, Anderson came to me right before the fashion show and repented." She considered me carefully, like a difficult question on a multiple-choice exam. "He practically *begged* me to take him back, and told me all about your little . . . *club*. It was sort of pathetic, actually," she said, "but I did, as long as he kept up his charade with you. I mean, he's gorgeous."

"You're so quick to forgive Anderson when *he* made the same mistakes I did!"

"I *broke up* with him, Marni."

"But you didn't ruin his life," I said. "That punishment was reserved solely for me."

Clarissa laughed. "When I break up with a guy, it *does* ruin his life. You of all people should know that."

There was no point in continuing this back-and-forth. I wasn't sure the details even mattered anymore. "When I hooked up with Anderson over the summer, it was a mistake. I never meant to hurt you," I said. "But you crafted this, like, horrific *master plan* of cruelty against me, Clarissa. When is it going to end?" My throat felt incredibly dry. My tongue stuck to the insides of my cheeks and the roof of my mouth. "Do you really hate me that much?"

Clarissa ran her fingers through her hair and sighed. It was something I'd seen her do a million times before. For some reason, this time I was able to look past her glean and shine and see her for who she truly was—a Diamond. Translucent. Cold. Without feeling.

Something I would never, ever be.

I left her room without an answer that night, but deep down I knew what she would have said. Mostly I was relieved, but a little bit it broke my heart.

◆ 10 ◆

Any rights unmentioned in the Diamond
Rules, and not prohibited by the Bennington
School or the State of New York, must be
fought for with passion.

—*The Diamond Rules*

At most high schools, pep rallies are a big deal. At Bennington, they're monumental.

People went nuts. I'm talking paint-your-face, shout-at-the-top-of-your-lungs, don't-wear-any-underwear *insane*. It was tradition for the popular senior boys—the ones who weren't athletes—to sit at the very top of the bleachers, spell "Bennington" on their chests in blue and white, and flash the crowd whenever anyone said, well, "Bennington."

Very classy, I assure you.

This was my first year *participating* in the rally instead of watching it with Clarissa and the Diamonds from our usual spot (on the right, near the basketball hoop). Members of the Snow Court were seated in a semicircle facing the crowd of students on both sides of the gymnasium. There was a podium with a microphone where the

MC of the rally—usually one of the teachers—would call people, such as Principal Newman and Coach Brown, up to speak. This was also where the members of the Court would introduce themselves and say something nice about the school. The actual announcement of king and queen would be at the dance.

Now, I don't want to ruin the surprise by telling you prematurely what was about to go down, but it was pretty brilliant. And I'm not just saying that because it was 75 percent my idea.

Truth: the disbanding of the Stonecutters was a ruse to fool Anderson. Afterward, they were all contacted one by one, their help enlisted for the day's ultimate coup. I couldn't do it without them.

My speech would be different from anything anyone at Bennington had ever heard before. Whoever had rallied for me to get my spot on the Court—I still hadn't figured it out—would be sorely disappointed by my display of public *dis*affection.

◆ ◆ ◆

Unsurprisingly, our pep rally was being helmed by Mr. Townsen. As we stood, waiting to be ushered to our prime seats, he lectured us about proper conduct: things that were appropriate ("I love Bennington!") and *in*appropriate ("Bennington sucks my [insert private part here]!") to say. In some bizarre twist of fate, I would be the last one to speak, and my seat—which was unchangeable; I'd asked—was right next to Clarissa.

Priya, Lili, and Clarissa stood close together, as if

322

a plane had dropped them off in the middle of a leper colony and they were trying their best to avoid infection. Lili was dressed simply, hair down, very little makeup. Priya looked as if she were competing for Miss Teen USA, in a puffy red number that was corset-tight around her waist and billowed out like an upside-down parachute at the bottom.

Clarissa, of course, was perfection. She was wearing a champagne dress passed down from her sisters. It had become a sort of good-luck charm and had been sitting in a garment bag in Clarissa's closet for the past two years. Her hair was in a French braid, tiny roses (white) woven inside.

Arlene was crouched next to them in a corduroy skirt and a white sweater. "You look beautiful, Clarissa," she said, spritzing perfume on the soon-to-be Queen's neck.

"I know." Clarissa wafted her hands in the air. "That's enough, Arlene. Go get me a bottle of Evian."

"But they only have Poland Spring in the cafeteria."

Clarissa shot Arlene a look of death. "I don't care if you have to climb the French Alps *yourself*, Arlene. I want a bottle of Evian."

"O-okay, Clarissa," Arlene said, shaking. "Sure thing."

"I appreciate you."

"Well, that's about it," said Mr. Townsen, straightening his tie and checking his watch. All the boys except Jed were on the basketball team, so they would make their entrance separately. "Everyone ready?"

"Marni's *always* ready," Clarissa said.

Priya looked confused. "Because she's, like, a slut?"

Clarissa smiled venomously in my direction. "Exactly."

"Where's Jed?" asked Mr. Townsen. From our position in the corner of the gym, we could see everything: the bleachers were overflowing with bodies and backpacks, and there were enough painted faces to cast Blue Man Group twenty times over.

I locked eyes with Jenny.

"I think he went to the bathroom," Jenny said, smoothing her hair back. "He said to start without him if he wasn't back in time."

"Start with*out* him?" Townsen glanced down at his clipboard, then his watch. "Well, all right. Jed will just have to find his seat by himself."

Phase One: complete.

This year, Boyd had been chosen to perform "The Star-Spangled Banner." (Are you even the slightest bit surprised?) He sang in a sweet tenor with minimal riffs—which I appreciated—and when he hit the high note, everyone went wild. Even people who hated him applauded. (That's what I love about "The Star-Spangled Banner": it brings people together.)

Then, the spotlight, so to speak, was on us. The Snow Court walked across the back of the gym and took our assigned seats. I was pretty sure I heard a few distinct cries of "Marni sucks!"

When Mr. Townsen took the mic and started speaking, Jed's chair was still empty. "You guys know the drill," Mr. Townsen said in his way-too-chummy voice. "The Snow Court represents the brightest stars of the senior class, as chosen by the administration, faculty, and you—the students. This year was a particularly interesting process, as one prince and one princess were chosen directly by the faculty. The rest were chosen as a result of your votes."

Ah. Jed and I were obviously the faculty picks; there was no way anyone would've voted for us. Still, though, while I didn't think anyone really *hated* me (not even you, Mrs. Cooper), who could have advocated for me enough to be chosen over Sharon Wu, for example?

"Let's hear from our first prince, Anderson St. James."

Anderson strutted toward the podium, looking like the embodiment of the all-American teenage male. Even though he'd lied to me and betrayed my trust, I still wanted to leap from my seat like a gazelle and jump his bones. That's life, I guess.

"This speech is supposed to be about Bennington. Why I love going to school here. There are a lot of things I could say, for sure: my fellow students, the incomparable teachers, the beautiful grounds. But the *real* reason I love Bennington," Anderson said, "is because of how willing everyone is to forgive."

People stirred in their seats, waiting for him to continue.

"A month ago, the idea that I could stand in front of you all and make a speech without having something heavy thrown at my head"—a few chuckles escaped the bleachers—"was ridiculous. But here I am. Thank you to everyone who voted for me. Thank you for taking me back and making me proud to be a Cougar."

Naturally, a round of applause followed. I would be lying if I omitted that I was sick to my stomach. Anderson and I had connected on so many levels. We'd stayed up until one in the morning chatting softly about art and music and writing. We'd kissed until our lips were raw. My feelings for him had turned my world upside down. But in the end, he had chosen this—a roomful of people who barely knew him and appreciated him only for the genes he'd done nothing to inherit.

Before Anderson sat down, he looked at me, his eyes forever blue. I wondered how much he knew. If Clarissa had shared our talk in her bedroom or kept him in the dark. If he would ever have the guts to seek me out and apologize for betraying my trust and discarding me like something used up and completely unwanted. I felt an enormous sadness blossom inside me, and I chose to simply look away.

The rest of the boys' speeches were uneventful. When Jed's turn came, his seat was still empty.

Mr. Townsen stepped back to the podium and said, "I'm not sure exactly where Mr. Brantley is, but I know that he is very honored to be a part of this year's Snow Court, and—"

At that moment, Townsen stopped talking, because

the two televisions on the gym walls turned on. Jed was on the screen: he was in the studio where the announcements were done. (Turbo was behind the camera.)

"What's going on?" Mr. Townsen said into the microphone, turning toward Principal Newman as if he knew the answer.

"Hi, everyone," Jed said, more at ease on screen than ever before. "Most of you know me as the former student body president who was booted from the position. There are a few things I want to tell you. First, I was blackmailed by Clarissa von Dyke into breaking up with my girlfriend, Marni Valentine. Something I'm sure all of you remember.

"More importantly, Clarissa is not who you think she is. She is evil and manipulative. She has been controlling the mock trial team and bribing the jury in order to control social life here at Bennington."

Clarissa immediately stood up. "This is ridiculous! Somebody shut that thing off!"

"Those of you who have been on the receiving end of Clarissa's wrath know exactly what I mean," Jed said. "Those of you who've been spared, be thankful.

"Clarissa and the Diamonds have taken the principles of democracy, the very backbone of our country, and turned them inside out to get their way. To deny equality. To condemn innocent people without a fair trial. And all for what—scoring a spot on the Snow Court? Commanding power over the high school plebes?

327

"Their list of many offenses includes tampering with the mock trial jury—promising spots in the fashion show and instant popularity if people voted the way Clarissa wanted them to—and taking advantage of the system Principal Newman put in place to *better* our school, turning Bennington into a place of terror where students are attacked for no reason whatsoever at the whim of three snobby girls."

I should let you know that the audience was on the edge of their seats this entire time. (Someone actually fell out of the bleachers and onto the gym floor.) Clarissa, by this point, was begging Principal Newman to turn off the television screens. I watched as he ignored her, mopping his forehead with a handkerchief and waddling over toward Mr. Townsen.

"The Diamonds have reigned supreme long enough," Jed said. "It's time for them to be put in their place."

The last thing he said before disappearing off the screen was: "If you don't believe me, Bennington, here's proof."

The *proof*, which I'm sure you're wondering about, was the audio clip Jed put together from the bug he and Darcy had planted on Arlene, which played over the speakers in the gym. In it, the Diamonds admitted to influencing the jury (which, let's face it, wasn't such a shocker), but the *best* part was how much nasty shit Clarissa & Co. said about individual students, faculty members, and Bennington in general. Talk about airing your dirty laundry.

There was a stillness in the room I had never experienced before in such a large crowd. People were offended. Then someone—a guy whose face I couldn't see—yelled out, "The Diamonds suck!"

Another person said, "Yeah! They suck!"

Someone else said, "Dick!"

Before I knew it, one or two voices had turned into a shower of sound. People were clapping (for Jed, I think) and booing (for Clarissa, I think). Just when I thought the entire room was about to erupt in the kind of support that would banish the Diamonds forever, Clarissa stole the microphone from Mr. Townsen and screamed.

"*New Jersey!*" she screeched, her voice amplified and charged with ferocity. Immediately, people quieted down. "There," she said. "Now that I've said something *disgusting*, let's continue."

Clarissa marched in front of the Snow Court and planted herself in the center of the gym. "Not only are all of Jed's claims lies," she said, "but they aren't true. What can you expect, though, when he dated Marni for almost a year?" If I had been less shocked, I certainly would have been offended.

"You know that I have your best interests at heart, Bennington," Clarissa said. "That I've tried my best to bring the mock trial team to an entirely new level. To actually *help* people solve their problems. And I think

I've done a pretty good job." She looked at Priya and Lili, who nodded. "Actually, I think I've done a *great* job, and I'd like to *keep doing* a great job.

"Jed and Marni are only trying to disparage my reputation because they are unhappy with their own mistakes. That audio clip was completely doctored. I would *never* say such horrible things about a school I love so much." For a moment, I thought she was going to speak to me directly, but that didn't happen. "In fact, I wasn't going to say this, but it's only fair that you all know the truth.

"Marni Valentine used to be my dearest friend. Over the summer, however, she *seduced* my boyfriend and had her way with him. What kind of person would do that to her *very best friend?*"

I grasped my thighs. I would not let Clarissa get to me. I would not show anyone at Bennington that I was weak. Even if I had been wrong.

"Don't believe a word she says about me. Marni is the one who's a liar. Not me. Not Lili or Priya. *Marni.*"

By this time, Mr. Townsen was standing next to Clarissa. He tapped her on the shoulder and held out his hand, curling his fingers to indicate that he wanted the microphone back.

"Thank you," said Clarissa. "Oh, and vote for me!"

Clarissa sat down and crossed her legs. "Tired yet?" she said to me triumphantly. It irked me. Mostly because even though she was so very deluded about so many things, she was also right. About me. I *had* betrayed her trust and been with her boyfriend behind her back. I'd hurt her and kept what had happened a secret.

But she still needed to be stopped.

"This is certainly different," Mr. Townsen said. There was a low hum among the crowd, but for the most part, the whole of Bennington was still paying attention. Principal Newman was breathing into a paper bag; his secretary, Ms. Rose, was fanning him with a manila envelope.

"It seems like we should wrap things up and, uh, get back to class." Townsen looked over at the court. Of the princesses, Clarissa had been the only one to speak. "Do any of you ladies mind if we skip the formalities?"

Now was the moment I'd been waiting for. When I was supposed to take the microphone and list the millions of wrongs Clarissa had accrued over the past few weeks. To name names, reveal secrets, and be sure that every single person who had made my life a living hell since the Closet Incident would understand what was *really* going on. But suddenly that didn't seem like the best road to travel.

I finally had the attention of the entire school, and it was time to apologize.

"I have something to say, Mr. Townsen," I said, rising from my seat.

Clarissa coughed. "Hasn't she already done enough?"

"Everyone has the right to a fair trial. In America, we are innocent until we are proven guilty." Townsen handed me the microphone. Then, so that no one else could hear, he said, "Make it count."

My wrist wobbled as I lifted the mic to my face. I felt like a substitute teacher trying to get the attention of an unruly class.

"Hi, everyone," I said.

A second or two went by, and then a girl whose voice I recognized (either Dara or Dana Hoebermann) screamed, "I haaaaaaaaaaaate you!" Then an identical voice echoed, "I love your dress!"

People laughed, and the bleachers came alive. I couldn't tell if the students were for or against me. I could barely even see anything.

"I know what you all must think of me. But this isn't about me, Clarissa"—I turned to her—"and it's not about Anderson. It's about *you*.

"When I first started at Bennington, you were there for me. You were a friend when I needed one, and you made this school—which we all know can be extraordinarily difficult at times—enjoyable. Priya and Lili too. Being popular was more than I could have ever asked for. But it's not everything. It's not the most important thing. Actually, it's not really important at all. When I stopped being friends with you, I met a group of people I never would have gotten to know otherwise. People who are amazing and loyal and funny. And just because they aren't Diamonds or on the football team or the basketball team or *whatever* team doesn't mean they don't deserve the same kind of happiness."

332

I took a few steps forward, addressing the entire gym. "For the past few weeks, the Diamonds have been putting us on trial. For things we didn't do, for things we *did* do but are unimportant, for hanging out with the 'wrong crowd' or for any inane, ridiculous little reason. And we've all gone along with it. But this has to stop. Now."

I walked back to my chair, where my purse was sitting. I reached inside and pulled out a packet of white paper. "The Diamond Rules," I said, watching as people nodded in acknowledgment. "I'm sorry to say I was the one who first came up with these. I never intended for them to make anyone feel uncomfortable or unwelcome in their own school." I dropped the packet onto the floor. Then I stepped on it with the heel of my shoe, reached down, and ripped it in half. "No more," I said, turning toward Clarissa, Lili, and Priya, who were watching me with a mixture of curiosity, fear, and glitter lip gloss.

"I think it's time for one last trial," I said. Jed and Turbo had returned from the television studio and were standing in the corner with Monique. "We may not have fancy robes or a stenographer or a bailiff, but we do have one thing: the truth. And, this time, a *real* jury of our peers.

"Anyone who has ever felt violated by the Diamonds, who has had an unfair trial or been accused of a crime you didn't do, please raise your hand."

I didn't expect everyone in the gym to raise their hands. I didn't even expect half the students at

Bennington to participate, so when they did, I was overwhelmed. The gym was covered in arms and hands and fingers.

"Good," I said. "You can put your hands down. Now, raise your hand if you think that Lili should be removed as student body president, and that the Diamonds' membership on the mock trial team should be revoked on the charges of bribery, perverting a jury, slander, and purposely violating the principles of the United States Constitution. If you agree that, based on the evidence you've heard today, the Diamond Court should cease to exist—"

"Evidence?" Clarissa shrieked. She didn't even need a microphone. "What evidence? That recording was bogus, and you're a liar." She turned to Mr. Townsen for help. "This is ridiculous! You have no real proof!"

Then Tommy entered from the back of the gymnasium, through a door that had been closed off for the pep rally. With him were four freshmen, staff editors of the *Bennington Press*, each of them carrying a stack of newspapers on a rolling cart. "Actually, we do," he said. At the sound of his voice, two hundred or so heads changed direction.

Clarissa grabbed her hair and pulled. "*What* is going *on* here? Arlene? Arlene!" Priya was already calling someone (her father?) on her cell phone, and Lili, I think, was crying. It was hard to tell.

Despite the lights (and my exhaustion), I could see

Tommy smile at me from across the room. The freshmen started handing out the newspapers to each row of the bleachers. They were the thickest newspapers I had ever seen; they must have weighed ten pounds each.

"Here's the latest copy of the paper," he said for everyone to hear. "Everything you need to know is right here."

If you haven't already guessed what this particular edition of the *Bennington Press* was, then you haven't been paying close enough attention to my story. It was the exposé I had promised Tommy I would write detailing my journey with the Diamonds. It included transcriptions of their plans to handpick and bribe the jury, plus case files and pictures, and described Clarissa's "take no prisoners" quest for the Ice Queen crown, my secret relationship with Anderson, and my explosive confession about our past. It provided documentation of the students we'd wronged and the individual rights we'd violated and depicted my rise to and fall from grace, the mistakes made and lessons learned, and finally, my realization that I was better off without my so-called friends. Without the Diamonds.

It was longer than I'd expected, and way more personal, too, but I think it turned out pretty well. If you're wondering exactly what it said, don't worry.

You've just finished reading it.

Epilogue

We shall find peace. We shall hear angels, we
shall see the sky sparkling with diamonds.
—*Anton Chekhov*

In the end, Tommy got his article and the Diamonds got their due. After Mr. Townsen and Principal Newman read the exposé, Clarissa, Lili, and Priya were given a two-week suspension that went on their permanent records.[1]

The Diamonds were removed from the mock trial team, and Lili was impeached from student government. Jed was given back his old position in a unanimous vote by the executive board. As it turned out, Mr. Townsen was the faculty member who had nominated me for Snow Court. Apparently, our little afterschool chat *had* left an impression on him.

That night, at the dance, Jenny was elected queen and Anderson was elected king. (I later discovered that according to the actual votes, Clarissa should

---

[1] Lili was deferred from Yale, while Clarissa was admitted early decision to the University of Pennsylvania.

have won. There happened to be some pesky little rule about the Ice Queen having to *not* be suspended, however, and Jenny was the first runner-up.) When Jenny's name was called, she rejected the crown, saying that she would never want to share recognition with such a pig. Then she pointed at Anderson and laughed.

For better or for worse, Bennington went without an official Snow Queen. And much to everyone's surprise, no one died or anything.

A few days after the pep rally, Darcy and Jed were an official "couple." I was happy for them. Really.

Monique bleached her mustache and started dating a sophomore named Terry, who was really into computers. Turbo still went by Turbo and skated in the student parking lot after school, but now, whenever I saw him, I would stop to chat about pending college acceptances and wheelies. We still skate together at least once a week.

Boyd was cast as a lead in Bennington's spring musical, *West Side Story,* and I was thrilled for him.

Tommy continued as editor-in-chief of the *Bennington Press* but reverted to once-a-month issues, leaving him time to, you know, have a life. We eat lunch together every day.

As for me, well, there were best friends lost and gained, lessons about the Constitution learned, tyranny, betrayal, heartbreak, a student revolution, and last but not least, fleeting moments of true love.

◆　◆　◆

Just before vacation I got my art project back. I'd spent hours agonizing over the drawing and the (imperfect) way I had sketched Anderson's features. (Donaldson apparently realized I had no place in an AP Visual Art class and gave me a C+, which I totally deserved.)

I thought about ripping it into a million pieces or feeding it to my father's paper shredder, but ultimately I sat down, drawing in hand, and went back to work. Sometimes you simply need a little perspective to make things shine. And while the original portrait might have been incredibly mediocre, now, with the additions of my past few months at Bennington, of mock trial and the Diamonds and the Stonecutters, I've turned my assignment into a true work of art.

• EXHIBIT R •

I remember a conversation I had with Anderson just before Christmas. After the pep rally, we basically stopped talking. There was no huge fight. No big scene. One day we were together, and the next we were not.

I'd switched my seat in art class and perfected a routine of avoiding him at school, but one day over winter break—it was a Tuesday, and I was wearing a thick scarf and a leather jacket—we were alone together in the parking lot of Dunkin' Donuts. This was the second time such a moment had existed in the universe.

I had blindly parked my car next to his. As I went to open the door, keys and coffee in hand, he was suddenly only inches away.

"Hey," he said. Already his voice was foreign to me. "How are you?"

"Fine." The air nipped my cheeks, and my ears burned from the cold. I didn't return the question.

Anderson looked better than ever. I'd heard he was still with Clarissa, but I didn't know for sure. He'd also been accepted early decision to Wesleyan. Despite numerous attempts by the Stonecutters, he was never formally punished by the Bennington administration.

Anderson flipped up the sheepskin collar of his jacket. Behind him, twinkling holiday lights of red, green, and white were strewn across the storefronts. "You know, Marni, I'm really sorry about how things worked out. It probably doesn't seem that way, but I am."

I had envisioned this conversation a million different times in a thousand different ways, and suddenly,
now that we were having it, all I wanted was for it to
be over. What can you possibly say to the person who
opened your heart to feelings you never knew existed,
only to take them all away?

I still had no idea why Anderson had betrayed me
and gone back to Clarissa, why he'd betrayed the
Stonecutters and (potentially) ruined our chances for
success when he'd seemingly believed our cause was
just. Had it all been a game?

"Marni? Did you hear me? I said I was sorry."

"Yeah, well, I'm sorry, too."

"What are you talking about?"

"I don't know what I did wrong, Anderson, but obviously I was never good enough for you."

"That's not true."

"I thought we had something incredible," I said.

"We did."

"I thought we were meant for each other."

No response.

"Why couldn't you have just told me you were unhappy?"

Anderson's face was blank except for his eyes,
which were an icy blue. "I tried."

"When? When did you try?"

"That night. In your backyard. It wasn't you, Marni,
it was just . . . everything. That's when I started seeing
Clarissa again. I wanted my life to go back to the way
it was."

"But why did you have to lie?" I asked. "Why did you have to go behind my back?"

"I was scared, I guess. I never meant to hurt you."

I squeezed my eyes shut, trying not to cry. I had all my answers, so why didn't I feel any better? "You hurt me more than anyone in my entire life ever has."

He winced. "Do you think you'll ever forgive me?"

I wanted to punch him.

I wanted to kiss him.

I couldn't do either.

I lifted the tiny plastic lid on my coffee, steam rising from the cup like a phoenix. I took one last look at him. "Goodbye, Anderson."

Here's what I know: people enter your life for a reason. Sometimes they stay forever, I guess, but in my experience they come and go. Quickly. It's what they leave behind that counts, what stays with you once they're gone. Those are the important things.

I will never regret being friends with Clarissa and the Diamonds, because they taught me what to look for in *real* friends, like the Stonecutters; I will never regret dating Jed, because he led me to Anderson; and I will never regret my relationship with Anderson, because he showed me what it felt like to love, and be loved, and what it felt like—the raw intensity, the tears, the heartache—to be hurt. Those are things I will keep with me as I move forward to wherever it is I will go in life. Those are all treasures I will cherish and curse and ultimately, I believe, be thankful for.

This is how my story ends: Anderson left. My phone buzzed. I dug it out from my pocket. It was Tommy, wondering what was taking me so long. I smiled and clutched the phone in my hand as the noise from the parking lot sang all around me and it began to snow.

ACKNOWLEDGMENTS

Thank you

Nadia Cornier, for taking such good care of me; Stephanie Lane Elliott, for making me a better writer and loving musicals as much as I do; Beverly Horowitz, Vikki Sheatsley, Jennifer Black, and the entire team at Delacorte Press for making a dream come true.

Julia Alexander, Blair Bodine, Nic Cory, Alan Honigman, Dan Kessler, Jordy Lievers, Anna Posner, Brett Schrier, Michael Stearns, Amy Shebar, and Paul Wright for their encouragement and support.

Elly Daugherty, for believing in me, and the many fantastic educators I've had the privilege of learning from.

Kate Berthold, for bringing my characters to life and never letting me go hungry.

Peter Lerman, for giving Anderson a voice and for his friendship, which taught me many things. To hear Peter's music, please visit him at www.peterlerman.com.

Finally, my grandparents, Arnold and Eileen Honigman, and my entire family—especially my parents, without whom life would be meaningless.

ABOUT THE AUTHOR

Ted Michael was born in 1984 and grew up in Roslyn Heights, New York. He is a graduate of Columbia University and the Juilliard School and is a Presidential Scholar in the Arts. This is his first novel.